LONDON BOUND

LONDON BOUND

A HEART OF THE CITY NOVEL

C.J. DUGGAN

hachette
AUSTRALIA

hachette
AUSTRALIA

Published in Australia and New Zealand in 2017
by Hachette Australia
(an imprint of Hachette Australia Pty Limited)
Level 17, 207 Kent Street, Sydney NSW 2000
www.hachette.com.au

10 9 8 7 6 5 4 3 2 1

National Library of Australia
Cataloguing-in-Publication data:

Duggan, C. J., author.
London bound: a heart of the city novel/C.J. Duggan.

978 0 7336 3663 9 (pbk)

Series: Duggan, C. J. Heart of the city.

Romance fiction.
London (England) – Fiction.

A823.4

Cover design by Keary Taylor
Cover photographs courtesy of Shutterstock
Author photograph by Craig Peihopa
Text design by Bookhouse, Sydney
Typeset in 11/16 pt Minion Pro by Bookhouse, Sydney
Printed and bound in Great Britain by Clays Ltd, St Ives plc

For all those who were afraid . . .
but did it anyway.

Chapter One

I thought life would be one giant tea party.

Lawn croquet and cucumber sandwiches, men with monocles and ladies with lacy parasols. I thought the grass would be green and the sunshine eternal in the summer I came to London. Instead, I sat with crossed legs, indenting the puffy marshmallow cover of my bedspread, my long blonde hair tucked behind my ears as I scowled at my laptop. The blank screen scowled right back. I wearily rubbed the crease on my brow, wondering how my brain could be so devoid of inspiration, yet so full of despair. I looked out into the dull, grey light through the large window of my room. It was raining sideways again, icy splinters hitting the glass discordantly. I tried to convince myself that I was glad to be in here, away from the miserable weather.

Sure, keep telling yourself that, Kate.

'Katherine Elizabeth!'

Bang-bang.

I hated my name. Hated it with a burning passion. The very sound of it, though muffled by the space that divided my floor from the one below, and punctuated by the tapping of walking stick on floorboards, caused me to hide behind my screen and sink deeper into my mattress.

'Shut up, you old bag,' I mumbled.

'Katherine Elizabeth Brown!'

Bang-bang-bang.

Like the caller, that name, and that sound, were getting old – very, very old.

I sighed, slamming my laptop shut and chucking it aside.

'Coming!' I called out in the best upbeat, breezy voice I could manage, despite my dread at facing what lay on the other side of my door. Twisting the gold handle and stepping out into the hall meant two things: I was free from my prison, but about to enter another. The dreaded lower level.

Now don't be misled by all the beautiful old furniture, the impressive sweeping staircase or the sparkling chandelier that reflects off classic oil paintings from a bygone era. Nor by the impressive displays of silverware and china that would give any buck-toothed, tweed-covered *Antiques Roadshow* host heart palpitations. Make no mistake: beyond the impressive façade of this grand old terrace in South Kensington's Onslow Gardens lies a very tastefully decorated hell and, despite appearances, there's not a skerrick of Jane Austen-esque wit or drama to be found. I took a deep breath and squared my shoulders; my posture was under constant scrutiny these days.

Before the next series of thuds came, I twisted the handle, pushing open the final barrier between my world and hers with a silent prayer.

Plastering on a well-intentioned smile, my gaze moved from her usual spot by the fireplace to the overstuffed lounge near the picture window on the other side of the room.

She had moved? She must crave the sun . . . like a lizard.

Next to the window I saw the silhouette of a distinguished elderly lady, her stark white hair coiffed in an elegant high bun, her bony frame dressed in her usual Chanel and finished with antique double-strand pearls. She was the vision of grace, class and noble breeding. Her delicately arched brow kinked as she turned impossibly bright blue eyes on me, before they dimmed and her seemingly pleasant disposition fell away like the sun behind a cloud.

'Oh, Katherine, are you deliberately trying to look unattractive today?'

My shoulders slumped; my posture wasn't on the agenda today so I might as well rest them.

'No, Nana Joy, not deliberately.' I tried to keep my voice even, a little amazed that even after a month of enduring casual putdowns her comments still stung.

I also tried to stop myself from looking over my attire to see what exactly was wrong with what I was wearing.

How could a knee-length grey skirt and cream-coloured cardigan be so offensive? I wouldn't give her the satisfaction of seeing my self-inspection. I was sure she gained power from my paranoia like the emotional vampire she was.

'Tea, Nana?' I asked, placing the empty china back onto the tray I had carried in earlier, glancing at the mantel clock and wishing away the time until Vera, Nana Joy's carer called in for her daily duties.

Dear Saint Vera.

'No, I'll wait for Vera. Vera makes a nice cup of tea,' she said, waving me away.

My curious eyes roamed over the empty teacup and saucer, a little smirk lining my lips. She could say what she liked, when it came to making tea, I knew I rocked it.

'I'm hungry,' Nana Joy whined like a petulant child, which wasn't so far from the truth.

If I were a responsible human being I would have argued that a tray of shortbread (Nana's favourite) was not a good idea lest she spoil her appetite. But if it meant it kept her quiet, if not happy, then I would give it to her. In fact, I'd be willing to sacrifice a goat in her honour, if it kept her from calling me by my full birth name. I had tried in vain the first few days to insist she call me 'Kate' but there would be none of that. The irony of my nana's name being Joy was not lost on me either, because despite the cheery blue china and sugary afternoon snacks, Joy

Ellingham was a nightmare. And, for now, she was my nightmare.

I smiled brightly. 'I'll fix you something,' I said, manoeuvring the tray through the door and trying to avoid Joy's scoff, as she clasped her bony hands over her blanket and glared out the window at a poor passer-by. Come winter, if I had managed to survive that long, I planned to wheel her outside and put that glower to work: she could melt the snow from the pavement; sometimes evil can be useful.

I sighed, clinking my way down the hall to the kitchen, another cheery room flooded with natural light from the adjoining sunroom. Through the glass door, a beautiful rose garden lay in a private courtyard that was small but still a pleasant way to grab some sunshine if it decided to appear. I placed the tray on the sink and ran the hot water. Rinsing the delicate china always made me nervous and depressed.

So this was my life now. Cook and washerwoman to the devil.

The vivid memory of Mum warning me against my plans echoed through my mind again. What could I say? I had been blinded by the sparkling promise of travel, proximity to European fashion and, perhaps the greatest prize of all, free accommodation! And in, of all places, the very affluent South Kensington, where the streets were not paved with gold but as far as real estate went, they might as well have been. Known as 'Paris's 21st arrondissement',

I knew I'd be surrounded by culture and glamour; perfect inspiration for my blog.

My mum was never close to Nana Joy. I had put it down to her being more of a daddy's girl; she had adored Lionel Ellingham, and it was sad that I had no memory of the man so revered by my mother. The image Mum painted of Joy, however, was akin to a skull-and-cross-bone warning label. Highly corrosive – do not touch. But I hadn't listened. I may not have seen her since I was a small girl but how could I not love my own grandmother?

Landing on the doorstep of my nana's opulent home felt like the ancestral equivalent of discovering a treasure trove; such grandeur was unlike anything I'd seen back home in the 'burbs of Australia where your wealth was measured by how big your flatscreen TV was or whether or not you had an ensuite bathroom. I was on the cusp of a grand adventure. I had visions of bonding trips to Harrods for a spot of shopping, afternoon tea at the Ritz, strolls through Kensington Gardens, and that was just in the time we would spend together. Other days I would explore on my own: day trips to the countryside, York maybe, Stonehenge, further afield to Edinburgh. The world was my oyster . . . or so I had thought.

In the three-and-a-half weeks I had been in London I had seen nothing beyond Gloucester Road, the main strip a block away from our curved row of stark-white terraces. As I placed the fingers of shortbread on a dainty china dessert plate, I realised this was as close to high tea as it would get for me. There would be no bonding, no expeditions, no gallivanting of any kind.

A small degree of relief came in the sound of the front door opening.

Vera! Thank God.

I eagerly met her in the hall and helped her with her bags, bombarding her with big smiles and cheer. Vera was my daily dose of adult conversation; anyone would think she was *my* carer.

'Hello, Miss Kate, how are we today?' she puffed, handing me her cargo with red-faced appreciation.

'I'm so glad you're here, Vera.'

Vera smiled; her packet-dyed red hair was almost as bright as her sparkly blue eyes. She never asked why I was so happy to welcome her. We had a silent understanding about the creature that lurked beyond the parlour door.

She laughed. 'I'll take it from here, Kate.'

My eyes lit up; they were by far the most magical words I had ever heard.

'The rain has cleared out, why not enjoy the sun while it lasts? I won't tell.'

No, I was wrong – those were the most magical words I had ever heard. I went straight to my bag on the hallstand.

'Kettle's boiled and there's shortbread on the go in the kitchen for the three o'clock munchies,' I said, sneaking to unlatch the front door and wincing when it creaked. I really didn't want to be bombarded with a million questions about where I was going and how long I would be.

Going out for bread and milk was hard enough, let alone any 'me' time, which was seen as frivolous and selfish. But with Vera finally here I was allowed a small window of freedom, though I always rushed, making sure to return before Nana realised I had gone. It was exhausting, nothing like the free-spirited fun I had envisioned. Some days I swear it felt like I was in a sleeper hold, the lack of oxygen to my brain was no doubt going to cause me permanent damage; I was already concerned over my psychological state, and the sugar-laced cups of tea and shortbread were no doubt rotting my teeth while the lack of stimulation rotted my mind.

I winked at Vera and made my way out the heavy, black-glossed front door. It was these stolen moments that kept me sane, that gave me hope. Stepping outside, I closed my eyes and lifted my face to the sky, breathing in the alluring scent of rain in the air. The sky was a paler shade of grey now, things were definitely looking . . .

Oh no.

I always heard him before I saw him – the distant revs of his V8 could be heard from streets away. The sound made me instantly recoil behind the pillar of Nana's terrace as I looked down the road. A new sense of dread hit me in the pit of my stomach.

Why did this keep happening to me?

The sound of screeching tyres heralded the arrival of the rain-beaded, navy blue Aston Martin. The first few times I saw the car I held my breath, thinking there was no way he was going to pull up in time, no way he could slide into that narrow little parking space at such a speed. I have since had the misfortune of seeing the driver pull off the exact same stunt several times a week for the last three weeks.

The driver was our neighbour, a man I couldn't stand, a man who was sliding out of his car in front of me, all suave and swagger as he pulled his perfectly tailored jacket together, wearing ridiculously expensive sunglasses that protected him from the invisible English sun. His hair was thick and dark and a little unruly; I guessed that he was the kind of man who drove with the window down. He wanted to be seen, and he certainly moved to be watched. It was almost as if he walked in slow motion, like he was on the set of a *GQ* fashion shoot or something. Just because I didn't like him didn't mean I was completely ignorant of his pretty face and equally impressive physique, but it was offset by his infuriating arrogance. Yes, hating Jack Baker was oh so easy, I felt it whenever that high-wattage smile and those ridiculous dimples were in my presence. Like right now, his square-tipped leather shoes stepping along the pavement as he slowly peeled off his sunglasses, looking up at me on my doorstep. My arms were folded, my brows narrowed. My usual reaction whenever our paths crossed.

Jack stopped short of my steps, his gaze wandering over my attire as if intrigued, like he didn't often come across a creature who wasn't dressed in a brand name. Sure, I wasn't exactly Oxford Street fashionable, but I liked the finer things, I just couldn't afford them; my experience of high fashion was through the oft-thumbed pages of my treasured *Vogue* and *Harper's Bazaar* magazines.

I hated the way he looked at me; even standing above him I always felt so incredibly small and insignificant. My scowl deepened (usually I would just simply give him the middle finger, which always thrilled him no end, but I was trying to exercise restraint). He tucked his sunglasses inside his coat pocket, a little smirk pinching the corner of his mouth.

'Stop flirting with me, Kate,' he said, pressing the security button to his car without taking his eyes off me.

'Is that supposed to impress me?' I deadpanned, determined to stand strong on today's staring competition, a battle of the wills. I always seemed to win, mainly because Jack Baker rarely took anything seriously. His lazy one-shoulder shrug really ticked me off.

'Been waiting for me for long, have you?' he said, cocking his brow as he went to his door. I rolled my eyes, finally putting my feet into motion and leaving the safety of the terrace.

I blinked sweetly. 'All my life.'

Jack leant against his doorway, folding his arms. 'I sense . . . sarcasm.'

'Do you?'

'Little bit,' he said, measuring it with his thumb and forefinger.

I readjusted the strap of my bag, ready to leave this riveting exchange.

'You know I can't help but think we started off on the wrong foot,' he said.

I stopped wrestling with my handbag, walking back up to the edge of his wrought-iron gate, barely believing what I was hearing. 'Ah, ya think?'

Jack rubbed the edge of his jawline. 'Was it something that I said?'

Said? SAID? Was he joking?

I watched his genuinely blank expression, feeling my blood boil under the surface of my skin.

'YOU NEARLY FUCKING HIT ME WITH YOUR CAR!' I screamed.

Jack broke into a smile. 'Oh yeah, wow, that was when we first met.'

Oh, it was the first time we had met all right, a day I would have given anything to forget. I had been trying to escape from being Nana's human wool-holder while she knitted an ill-shaped tangerine scarf and scoffed about the 'myth' of global warming. My bid for freedom had been quickly derailed when Jack Baker appeared in his shiny blue death-mobile, slamming on his brakes. My scream had rung through the air as his car skidded along the rain-soaked street right before me, so close that the bumper touched my thighs and my hands anchored themselves to the bonnet. My eyes wild and wide, my heart thumping against my chest, I had looked through the windshield to an ashen face that mirrored my own: eyes big, brown and horrified. Jack had wrestled with his seatbelt before opening up the driver's side door with lightning speed to stand next to me.

'Bloody hell, are you all right?'

And my mortifying answer?

I had burst into tears. Yes, Jack Baker had seen me cry, and it was a something I would always regret. The fact he had forgotten the most traumatising event of my London experience (well, apart from living with Nana) made me even angrier.

'You are unbelievable,' I said.

He rolled his eyes, actually rolled his eyes.

'You didn't even say you were sorry.'

'Me, sorry?' Jack pointed to his chest.

'Yes, it's what usually happens when you nearly hit someone with your car.'

I glanced at the offending vehicle, a beautiful James Bond-esque piece of machinery. I mean, if you're going to be taken out, being hit by an Aston Martin on the streets of South Kensington would at least sound impressive in the papers. It still struck me as odd that Jack was the owner of such a car; he couldn't be much older than me. Looking over him again, in his beautifully tailored shirt, Rolex flashing from his wrist, I figured he was born into money. You could tell by the way he held himself. He wouldn't be the kind to dream over *Vogue*, he would simply have ordered from it.

'Are you quite done?'

My attention snapped back up to his face. Oh shit, had I been staring?

'Just stop driving like a lunatic,' I said, spinning on my heel, happy to have the last word.

'Well, I'll stop driving like one if you stop acting like one.'

I froze, slowly turning to face him. 'Excuse me?'

Jack laughed. 'You heard me.'

'What are you, five?'

Jack's response was broken by the distant knocking that had the both of us turning to see . . .

Oh God.

Nana Joy, tapping on the glass in annoyance, sitting in the window like something out of an Alfred Hitchcock movie.

'Are you being summoned?' he asked, so smug I could scream.

I wanted to die. Now I was the one who felt like a five-year-old. No doubt she had heard me screaming at Jack; oh God, had I dropped the F-bomb? This day was just going from bad to worse.

How I hated Jack Baker, hated him with such burning passion that even if I was returning to my stunningly decorated prison, at least I was getting away from him. Getting away from both Nana and Jack would be ideal, but that wasn't going to happen for me today.

'Night, Kate.'

I glared at him, his stupid smirk marking his face.

'Oh, piss off, Jack, why don't you go be a big hero and do some laps in Daddy's car.'

Jack laughed, so much so that I couldn't help but turn back to him.

'Daddy's car?' He shook his head. 'You know nothing about me.'

'And I don't want to,' I said indignantly, moving to push through the front door.

'Are you sure about that?' he called out.

I couldn't believe the gall of this man. There was only one possible answer to his question: I stepped inside and slammed the door behind me.

Chapter Two

'You could hear everything?'

Vera paused at the sink. 'Everything.'

I crunched on a biscuit, cringing at the thought. Now that the adrenaline had worn off I was regretting some of my churlish behaviour.

'Well, I hope you're happy,' came a voice from the doorway. Nana Joy shuffled into the kitchen with her walking stick, an air of superiority in her posture. Even when she was disgusted she carried herself with great dignity. 'God only knows what the neighbours must have thought,' she said, coming to stand near the kitchen table.

'I didn't think you much cared about the neighbours, Nana,' I quipped. I didn't have the patience for round two of the 'You stupid girl' routine, I had gotten enough of that the second I had come through the front door.

'And what have I told you about you walking the streets? If you were murdered, how on earth would I explain that to your mother?'

'Murdered. Jesus,' I said, rolling my eyes.

'Don't you roll your eyes at me, Katherine Elizabeth, the world is very different these days; there are sex fiends lurking in the bushes just waiting for a young woman such as yourself to walk down the street.'

I tried not to laugh because I knew it would be the death of me. 'I don't recall many bushes on Gloucester Road, Nana.'

Vera turned fully away, concentrating on scrubbing an old pot, but I could see the slight vibration of her shoulders as she muffled her laughing.

'Well, I don't want you leaving this house without a chaperone,' Nana Joy declared.

I straightened in my seat. 'A chaperone? It's not 1895.'

The men out there were going to be more Jack Baker than Jack the Ripper. I was seriously starting to wonder if Nana had a subscription to the Criminal Investigation channel or a copy of *London's Grizzliest Murders* on her nightstand. Maybe this was why my mother left home as soon as she was of age.

'I don't care, Katherine, as long as you live under my roof, you will do as I say. Vera, another pot of tea, please, I need to still my nerves,' she said, moving slowly back to the kitchen door and down the hall.

'I'm a prisoner,' I said, mainly to myself, but I could tell Vera's eyes were on me as she dried her hands on the tea towel.

'She just worries, is all.'

'Oh yeah, I could see how worried she was when I was nearly the victim of a hit-and-run; all she cares about is herself.'

'She'll ease up on the curfew as time goes by; there are going to be times when you'll need to go out.'

This did not reassure me in the slightest.

'There has to be more to life than milk-and-bread runs to the shop, Vera. I need to explore, be inspired, soak up the rich culture of my heritage. Have a pint at the local, pash an English boy in muted disco light: you know, the normal things we aspire to.'

'What, like the English boy next door?' Vera said teased.

I laughed. 'Oh don't. I can't bear to think about it,' I said, burying my head into my hands and desperately wishing I'd never met Jack Baker and his perfect bloody smile.

~

I stared, unblinking, at the flicking cursor on the page, the very blank page, which was even more depressing than the rain outside. It was a damning indictement of my lacklustre entrée into the blogging world. Don't get me wrong, the setup was amazing – flashy but classy, factual and interesting. Covering my three biggest loves – fashion, beauty, travel – my blog had been an absolute obsession of mine at home. Once upon a time I had been rather prolific with my daily musings about my destined travel. Blog entries of the latest, life-altering make-up haul I bought on sale, or the recent eBay package I had won, a pre-loved Burberry scarf that had cleaned out my bank account, forcing me to take on extra shifts so I could pay my phone bill; you know, the usual. The past three weeks, however, my muse had fled and I struggled to update my site; I had zero inspiration and my mood was utterly black. It hadn't happened instantly; I had afforded myself the luxury of exploring my surrounds and, as far as digs went, I couldn't exactly complain. I wasn't shoved into a base-ment, or a windowless attic with no heating. I occupied the whole second floor, which consisted of an apartment-sized room with bed, lounge and terrace. More than enough for Kate Brown Blogging HQ, should inspiration choose to strike again . . . ever. I was even more cranky when I was prevented from stepping out onto my terrace to enjoy the scarce sunshine. And after today's disastrous discovery, Nana Joy was going to be more diligent about me being a prisoner than ever before, including brief sojourns on the balcony.

Even before the Jack Baker incident, Nana had been vocal on the dangers that lurked beyond our front door. 'The neighbourhood isn't what it used to be, Katherine.' Her beady blue eyes focused across the road as she spoke about the increasingly multicultural neighbourhood, her borderline racism adding to the charming little package that was Joy Ellingham.

Mary and Tomas Peersahib were the cheery lower-level occupants of the terrace next door. They had an adorable little boy, Spencer, who would merrily thunder up and down the street on his bike, with his grandmother Esther in tow. Sitting in the back garden, my eyes would often stray to the long, colourful line of their clothesline that peeked over the top level of our courtyard, and the delicious spicy smells from their kitchen always made my stomach rumble. On the level above the infuriating Jack Baker lived a Belgian couple, and a German family occupied one of the split-levels. Aside from Jack, I enjoyed the interactions I had with the neighbours on the street; Lord knows I felt sorry for them having to live next to Joy. When I explained what had brought me to London and where I was living, their raised brows and nods of sympathy were enough to tell me that Nana Joy's reputation preceded her, and I couldn't help but feel embarrassed, wondering how on earth she had come to be so hateful. My mum was nothing like her: she was open, warm, friendly. It was no wonder she immigrated to Australia in her twenties; she had picked the furthest place she could think of.

Dismayed, I closed my laptop with a sigh, just as I had done every day for the past three weeks. I had such grand plans: blog about my London adventures; grow my subscriber list; become one of the internet 'It' girls and be offered a regular column in *Vogue*. I'd even changed the theme on my blog.

'Kate on the Thames': black-and-white tones with pops of red. The very first picture I had taken was of me standing in a red telephone box answering a call with mock surprise, which I posted with a short piece about my (now futile) plans in Ol' Blighty. But since then I'd written nothing, and in the fast-moving world of the interwebs I knew that a lack of new content meant certain death. I had to get my shit together, I had to find a way to balance being an attentive punching bag for Nana, and being able to get out and about. But any time I thought about leaving Nana's fortress, a certain man's smile would flash in my mind.

Seriously, Kate?

I flung myself back on my mattress, dragging the cushion from my side and muffling my scream into it.

What am I doing with my life?

Chapter Three

Sunday afternoon I finally had my chance.

It wasn't anything that I had concocted with Vera exactly; she was too much of a goody two-shoes to openly discuss plans of deceit. But her carefully phrased yet seemingly innocent words weren't lost on me as she took great care in putting Nana's coat on, slotting in her walking stick and helping her into her wheelchair, the preferred method of transportation for their daily outings: preferred by Vera, that is; it was one way to strap her in and take control.

'Now, we will probably be gone most of the afternoon, Kate, we're going to go visit Joy's friend Cybil.'

'Oh, okay, that will be nice,' I said, lurking on the staircase as they got organised in the foyer.

'Yes, well, Cybil's not long been out of hospital so she could probably do with some cheering up.' Nana sighed, as if the very thought of it was an imposition.

I cocked my brow. Nana Joy was making a house call to 'cheer up' her friend?

Poor bloody Cybil.

'Yes, we have a few goodies packed for the afternoon, and we should be back by four.' This time when Vera spoke, her eyes locked with mine and her eyes widened as she stood behind Nana, mouthing the word 'four' once more.

I recognised the opportunity she had presented me with, quickly calculating in my head.

Five hours of freedom!

I tried to keep my face neutral, even bored, as I nodded. 'Well, have fun!' I said.

'Don't go touching the gas stove, Katherine.' Nana gave me a pointed look.

'Oh no, with water and crackers in the cupboard, I should be just fine.' I smiled sweetly.

Nana simply looked at me. 'Sarcasm is very unattractive on you, Katherine.'

Normally I would have been annoyed by her parting words, but nothing could wipe the smile from my face as I waved them off. I stood for one full minute until I felt the black cloud of darkness lift from the house then I turned and bounded up the stairs, squealing all the way.

It was a race against the clock, every minute was of the essence. Peeling off my T-shirt and trackies, I pulled apart my drawers and wardrobe, flinging clothes over my shoulder to land on the bed behind, agonising over what to wear on my first trip out. This was my chance to explore my corner of the world, take some photos for my blog and sample the local delights. I could feel the blood pumping through my veins at all that the afternoon would bring.

If there was one thing I was passionate about, it was clothes, fashion, make-up – okay, that was three things, but they were my three things. They're what made me feel alive, and feminine, and confident. I wasn't merely boring Kate Brown from Oz or the disappointing granddaughter Katherine Elizabeth. Nope. I could be anyone I wanted to be.

I arranged the perfect outfit on the bed. A black-and-white textured tweed bow jacket with three-quarter pants and ankle boots. And my hot red, pebbled leather handbag with a cross-body strap, all the better to move quickly with. It was always my preference to wear bold pops of colour. Studying my reflection in the mirror, I was somewhat underwhelmed with my long, straight blonde hair and medium brown eyes. Still, height was on my side; I was the tallest in my family at five-eight, so that was something.

Resisting the urge to slide down the banister, I rushed down the stairs and to the door, ripping it open so fast my hair whooshed back over my shoulders and I stepped out to—

'You've got to be kidding me.'

A sky heavy with clouds and the beginning of rain which *could* be put down to a simple summer shower, but unlikely. I doubled back into the house for the brolly that I should have thought to pack. But seeing as leaving the house wasn't exactly a common affair for any of us, there was nothing more than a hat, scarf and coat on the rack behind the door.

'Oh, come on, Joy!' I sighed. Sure every British home contained at least three umbrellas? I couldn't recall if Vera had taken anything on her way out. I had been too excited about my imminent escape. The rain was more of a consistent drizzle now and I argued with myself about what to do. Walking in the rain may seem a romantic notion, but in the movies they never seem to be left with frizzy hair and panda eyes. Then what would I end up blogging about tonight? Waterproofing your leather accessories? Riveting.

Every minute I delayed, my amazing mood dimmed, no more so than when I found myself headed back up the stairs. There had to be something here that could shelter me from the elements: a poncho? Mexican sombrero? I searched through the hall cupboards, under the bed, in drawers, until I came to the door at the end of the landing, the room that I had been forbidden to go into. I hadn't asked any questions, I assumed that it was Grandad's study, or maybe a place where Nana mixed her potions and kept her broomsticks. And like a toddler told not to touch a shiny red button, I found myself drawn to the door, stilling before the ornate wooden barrier and biting my lip. I really shouldn't, but then again, everything on this floor was pretty much mine. Nana had been living on the ground level for nearly a decade as the stairs had become too much for her. I took a small degree of comfort from knowing she was unlikely to burst into my room. Surely she'd never know? The longer I held onto the handle, the less guilty I felt. I wasn't snooping; I was just looking for an umbrella, that's all.

'In and out.' I nodded with a sense of finality as I twisted the handle and pushed open the door revealing . . .

'Oh. My. God.'

Chapter Four

I died the moment I opened the door to the forbidden room. Surely I was standing in heaven, in the presence of all that was sacred and holy?

This wasn't Grandad's study, or a torture chamber, and certainly not an umbrella storage room. It was so much more exciting than those things, and so incredibly unexpected. And it had been sitting here all this time, mere feet away from my own door.

Why hadn't I ventured in sooner?

Before me was a giant room lined with powder-blue moulded cabinetry that hosted a mass of shelves and drawers with gold handles, lit by an ornate chandelier. Floor-to-ceiling shelves were filled with vintage designer handbags on the right and, to the left, shoes of every colour. The space was divided by a gold filigree full-length mirror that reflected my wide eyes and gaping mouth. Without blinking, without breathing, I stepped forward, anchoring myself to the gorgeous island bench in the centre of the room, under the chandelier. The top of the island was made entirely of glass, protecting an array of impressive earrings, bracelets, accessories of the most spectacular fashion, from dust. I shook my head, moving to the back of the room, running my hands over the opulent fabrics that hung along the wall.

Chanel, Burberry, Vuitton, Saint Laurent. Why wasn't this room protected by laser security? Why wasn't it temperature controlled with an eye retina scanner for access? My heart thundered in my chest. A lifetime's worth of the most beautiful designer brands, whose value I couldn't bear to think about, shut away on the second floor and forgotten. I felt like I had won a golden ticket into the chocolate factory. I wanted to spin around and sing, and I just might have if I hadn't been so terrified of knocking into something. Double doors in the middle of the wall caught my attention; would it lead to more clothes? My heart couldn't take much more. I grabbed both handles, surprised when they turned easily. It wasn't even locked! How could this woman be so wary about the dangers of the world and yet have such valuable treasures unguarded? Drawing in a deep, steadying breath, I pushed my way through.

'Wow!'

The doors led to a bedroom, large and chic with a beautiful dressing table lined with perfumes and powders, lipsticks and a gorgeous silver hand-held mirror and brush set.

This must have been Joy's room before she moved downstairs. The room was white and bright even though I hadn't turned on the light. The carpet was thick and plush underfoot, and there wasn't a thing out of place; it felt like a kind of time capsule, and for a moment I felt a sense of appreciation for my nana and her glamorous past life. So this was where I had inherited my love of beautiful things from. Mum and Dad were not in the least bit materialistic and had always frowned upon my appetite for the finer things in life; well, now it all made sense. I was the descendant of Joy Ellingham, and for the first time in my life I was excited about it.

~

After combing every square inch of Nana's collection, I found not one but five umbrellas. I had told myself to make good use of my time, seeing as it would be the one and only time I would come in here. But I had lost two full hours in the throes of euphoria, so my exploration time was now limited.

'Shit.'

I had to be back long before Vera and Joy to escape suspicion, which left barely two hours for my trip out. Besides, I had an idea, one I felt rather giddy about and one that I would sit down and draw up as soon as I was free from confinement.

I headed down Gloucester Road and straight into the path of the Stanhope Arms hotel, which was bustling with men lingering out front, downing a swift pint with mates. I took down my bright yellow umbrella as I brushed past the group to an even more crowded space inside. I was ready to go back out the door when I was pounced on by a cheery waitress.

'Lunch?'

I wasn't going to deny that my main draw to the pub was the blackboard out front, which promised the best traditional fish 'n' chips in town. I smiled, taking the menu from her, and quickly located the very thing that had my tummy grumbling in reply.

The nation's favourite dish! Chunky, hand-battered cod fillet, served with the traditional British accompaniments of chips, choice of mushy or garden peas, Haywards™ pickled onions, bread and butter, curry sauce and tartare sauce. SOLD!

'Yes, please,' I said, clutching on to the menu for dear life.

'How many?'

'Oh, ah, just one.'

If the waitress thought me tragic then she didn't show it; instead, she perused the cramped space for a spare table for a lone, sad diner. Just as I was ready to hand the menu back she stood on her toes to look over the crowd before spinning back so fast her ponytail nearly blinded me.

'Yes, there's one down the end, follow me,' she said, grabbing some cutlery and coasters for our weaving, awkward journey to a tiny table in the corner of the room near the toilets.

'Here we are, you just have to order at the bar when you've decided what you want. '

'Thanks, but I'm ready to order. Fish 'n' chips with mushy peas,' I said, sounding far too excited, but the waitress laughed.

'Good choice,' she said, taking the menu from me and wedging it between the salt and pepper shakers.

I'll say, especially washed down with a cold cider. My mouth watered at the thought as I headed for the bar, squeezing past locals, and despite the small confines of the crowded scene, I had never felt more free.

Paying for my meal, I stole some extra beer coasters from the bar, taking great care in weaving my way back to my little table in the corner. Dark, noisy and overcrowded it may be, but I was gloriously happy to be sitting in a true English pub, sipping on cider and waiting for my traditional pub meal. There was no time to delay: I took my seat and flipped over the coasters, foraging around inside my handbag for a pen before hooking my bag over the side of the chair.

Now, for total world domination.

Having discovered Nana's secret closet, I felt immediately inspired – I had finally found an angle for 'Kate on the Thames'. I could use the secret room as a stunning backdrop for my weekly blog posts; I mean, I wasn't doing anything overly wrong. It wouldn't be like I would be touching anything; well, not really. My mind flashed back to a gorgeous pair of gold Chanel earrings under the glass top of the island. Their classic, interlinking Cs were absolutely striking, completely classic. I may or may not have slid the glass aside and held them up against my ears to see what they would look like, but I was ever so careful with them. If there was one thing I was passionate about it was respecting Chanel.

I dot-pointed some ideas on the small pieces of cardboard with joyous abandon until the swinging toilet door flew open at speed and hit the back of my chair mid-sip of my cider.

'Shit!' I said, flicking my hands and grabbing for some napkins to wipe up the mess.

'No chance of anyone stealing this table,' I mumbled, and glared at the back of the man who walked without so much as a backward glance, annoyed that my coasters of amazing, life-changing ideas had suffered the full brunt of the spillage. Shifting from side to side in my seat, I tried to catch the eye of the friendly waitress to ask for a cloth when my eyes landed on the pub entrance. Or, rather, the person standing in it. Blinking once, then twice, I craned my neck to look again, my blood running cold, and then thought that maybe I was seeing things as the crowd shifted and I breathed once more.

Phew.

Kate, calm down, take another sip of cider and enjoy what's left of your freedom.

I glanced at my watch and lifted the pint up to my mouth again, just as a loud voice called over the murmuring of the patrons.

'Blimey. Jack bloody Baker, how the hell are you?'

I spat my drink out and coughed, lifting my watery gaze to the barman across the room, who was vigorously shaking the hand of the very real Jack Baker, the Jack Baker who had nearly killed me. The Jack Baker who was looking. Right. This. Way.

Chapter Five

So far I had knocked over the salt and pepper shakers in my desperation to barricade myself behind a laminated menu, but then my chair was hit with the toilet door once again.

'Seriously!' I yelled, receiving a confused glance from a man walking back to his group of mates.

I sighed, fixing my angry stare on the menu, thinking maybe Jack would just disappear, or would think that he was mistaken and hadn't really seen me.

Of all the pubs in all the world he had to walk into mine.

But as minutes passed, and I resisted the urge to adjust my menu for a peek, I became more confident that he wouldn't approach, that he hadn't seen me after all. I was safe; in the dark corner of my tiny table I had avoided discovery. I sighed, thanking the universe for small mercies.

'One ultimate fish 'n' chips for Kate!' called out a deep Cockney voice.

Oh my God.

I peeled the menu from my face to see a man with a grubby white apron circling the room with a plate of food. Why didn't they just have a flickering neon sign pointing in my direction? Seriously, didn't they believe in table numbers? I watched helplessly as the man worked his way closer to me.

'Order for Ka—'

'HERE!' I said, far too loudly, holding up my hand and wincing – beyond the man's shoulder I could see Jack, who was hiding his smile behind his pint and looking my way while chatting to the publican.

'Oh, here we go, one fish 'n' chips for Kate!' the kitchenhand yelled above the crowd, dumping the plate on my table. Any other time my eyes would have lit up with the massive feed that sat before me, but all I wanted now was to get the hell out of here.

'Ah, I don't suppose I could get this to go, could I? In a doggy bag?'

He looked at my plate then back up at me as if I were mad. 'No, sorry, we don't do doggy bags. Health regulations.'

'Oh, okay, no worries. I don't suppose there's a back way out of here, is there?'

'Only through the kitchen, but only staff are permitted there so . . .'

'Right, okay, no problem.' *Thanks for nothing.*

There was no escape. And as I picked at my plate, flaking the delicious morsels of battered fish into my mouth, loath to leave such a feast behind, it dawned on me.

He wasn't coming.

He wasn't going to approach me, or annoy me; he was going to let me be. I stole the odd glance between mouthfuls of food. Jack sat propped up at the bar, in deep conversation with the barman and no longer looking my way. For some completely irrational reason this annoyed me. All that time at Nana's really had sent me mad.

Was he ignoring me? Really?

I wasn't sure what the correct greeting ritual was when bumping into the girl one had nearly run into with one's car, but surely at least an awkward wave was required? Pfft, whatever; now I could finally eat in peace—

The toilet door slammed into the back of my chair again, this time with such force that the entire table skidded along the floorboards, sending my mushy peas sliding off my fork. I sighed, spiking the fork into the fish and grabbing for my bag. I had gone from wanting to hide to not caring if he saw me, and I strode up to the bar with my chin lifted. I placed my empty glass on the bar and waited for the barman to drag himself away from his conversation with Jack, who was four bodies down the bar, not that I was counting. I looked straight ahead, feeling his eyes on me as I ordered another drink, and grabbed a fistful of serviettes for any future spillages.

I can't believe he's not going to say anything.

He had certainly had plenty to say before. But let's face it, I knew men like Jack; okay, perhaps not firsthand exactly, but I had heard about men like Jack in the gossipy bathroom stalls on a Friday night. The kind who would make girls swoon, walk you to your door, kiss you goodnight, only to never call you . . . ever. I snuck a glance and saw him talking to a man to his left, who was dressed in a similar fashion: elegant tailored suit, glinting cufflinks, crisp white shirt and expertly knotted tie. I could only assume they were colleagues, or they had both rocked up to the pub embarrassingly overdressed; still, it had me thinking how well the white-collar professional look suited Jack, with his square shoulders and tall, lean frame. His dark hair had once again resisted all attempts to tame it. My attention returned to the drink that landed in front of me and as I reached for my purse the barman held up his hand.

'No need, lass, it's all taken care of,' he said with a smile. My eyes followed his down the bar to Jack, who was still involved in a discussion with his well-dressed mate.

Well, this is awkward. Is he extending an olive branch? Do I thank him? Try to make eye contact across the crowded bar?

I delayed taking the cider. 'Look, tell him thanks, but I've got this,' I said, placing the money on the bar and leaving before receiving my minuscule change. I just wanted to skull the drink in a dark corner then get the hell out of there. Heck, yes, that's what I would do. I wouldn't even sit back down; instead, I would just stand right here next to the table and – the men's toilet door flung open one last time, knocking the pint all over me and a little over the suited man before me.

'Bloody hell!' he screamed, wiping the tiny splashback from his cuff as I stood frozen, drenched down my front, gasping in shock.

'Watch where you're going, ya dozy cow,' he shouted, checking his pants and his shoes. I went to say sorry, then thought better of it.

What had I to be sorry for?

'Maybe you should watch where you're going!' I said.

Great comeback, Kate, total badass.

The man scoffed, looking me up and down like I was something that was stuck to the bottom of his shoe. I never thought a look had the power to make me feel so small, so pathetic; but then again, being soaked in cider wasn't exactly helping the situation. My day of freedom had become a complete disaster; it seemed that whenever I ventured outside my confines I was destined for bad things. I wanted to say something smart and cutting, something to dress him down in front of the pub patrons, all of whom seemed to be watching the saga unfold with great interest. Lord knows, I'd stored up plenty of Nana's icy remarks, so surely I had some retort to wound him with. As I tried trawled my brain for the right words, I felt something brush against my arm.

'All right?' said Jack, looking directly at the suit and towering a good foot above him, causing the suit's eyes to trail up to his face.

'All right, mate,' he replied, but the way his Adam's apple bobbed in his throat and his brows rose showed he was anything but.

Jack smiled, wolfish and seemingly pleased by how nervous the man was. 'I'm not your mate,' he said, taking the time to look him over. Now the suit was the one who felt small. Jack turned his attention to me.

'Kate, you seem to have met with an accident.'

I could have played it down, defused the situation, but as I glanced back at the now-pale face of the suit, I couldn't help myself.

I shrugged. 'I guess I'm just a dozy cow.'

Jack folded his arms across his broad chest. 'Now why would you think that?' he asked, amusement lining his face.

I went to reply when the suit started to delve into the inside of his jacket pocket. 'Listen, let me make it up to you,' he said, frantically thumbing through his wallet, shelling out layers of money onto my table. 'Let me buy you a drink – here. And dry cleaning, yeah, let me fix you up.'

'And her meal.' Jack nodded to the table.

The man glanced down at my partly eaten meal, confused, before looking back at Jack.

'It's gone cold, ruined.'

'Oh, right, yes, of course.' He pulled out another bill onto the pile and I almost snorted in disbelief. Jack simply watched, amused, like a cat toying with a mouse.

'So no hard feelings, yeah?'

Jack turned his dark brown eyes to me in question. I turned to the suit and shrugged casually.

Jack breathed out a laugh. 'Well, who said money can't buy happiness?'

Against my better judgement I laughed, thinking how bizarre my lunch had become and how this really was the worst seat in the house. The nervous laughter of the suit brought Jack's attention back to him and he reached past me to scoop the cash off the table. 'You can go now,' he said abruptly, while counting the notes.

The suit nodded. 'Right, yes,' he stammered, excusing himself for a quick exit.

Jack held the money out to me, and my eyes flicked to the neat little parcel he had created with the rolled-up notes. When I didn't take the cash, he grabbed my hand and shoved it into my palm. 'Spend it wisely, Miss Brown.' He smiled and I was aware of his skin on mine, burning like a brand. It almost distracted me from the devious glint in his eyes.

'Back in a minute,' he said, then walked to the gents', opened the door carefully, and disappeared. I stood near my table, confused, then looked at the wad of cash in my hand.

'What just happened?' I said to myself.

'Gotta hand it to Jack, he knows how to handle a crisis.' The kitchenhand who had delivered my meal appeared next to me, clearing the table and wiping up the spilt cider. 'You finished?' His eyes flicked to the half-eaten lunch.

'Oh, yes, sorry, I am.' I grimaced, feeling bad about the waste, and wondering what would happen when Jack returned. I wasn't in the mood for small talk, I didn't want to get to know him, and I really didn't want him to get to know me. What could I say? 'Oh, I'm just living on the second floor of my nana's terrace, looking for excuses to sneak out even though I'm twenty-five years old.' Even in my mind it sounded hideous. I had to get out of here, and fast.

'Excuse me.'

The kitchenhand stilled with his hands full.

'Do you do bar tabs? Credit?'

'Yeah, we do.' He nodded.

'Oh, great. Listen, I have to go but would I be able to set up a tab for Jack? He'll be back in a minute, but I just want to, well . . .' I held out the money.

He grinned broadly. 'I defy any man to say no to that,' he said, before nodding toward the bar. 'Hand it over to Leo, he'll fix it up for you.'

'Thanks,' I said, wasting no time and heading straight for the bar. I was keen to get away from the Stanhope Arms and put this whole event down as yet another awkward memory I would choose to forget.

As I quickly made my way back down Gloucester Road, I glanced at my watch and sighed with relief; I would make it home in plenty of time.

At least you got one thing right today.

And that's when I heard my name.

'Kate, stop!'

Chapter Six

I t was one thing to see a very attractive man running toward me. But to see said man running with a red leather handbag slung over his shoulder? That was something else. The sight of my bag made me skid to a rather abrupt halt.

Oh shit.

'Forget something?' he said, unhooking the bag and handing it out to me.

'Thanks,' I said, taking it from him. For the first time (without concussion, anyway) I took in the sight of Jack Baker close up. I had to lift my eyes to look at his very handsome face. Not literary-classic handsome, mind you; he didn't have the curly hair and broody stare of Mr Darcy, the kind of man I had dreamt of finding on my British expeditions. He was tall and built in all the right places, with olive skin. His dark hair was cropped and he had the slightest dusting of stubble along his strong jawline. His brilliantly white, slightly imperfect teeth were revealed by a cheeky smile, a smile which lit those warm brown eyes that were framed by dark lashes. *Lovely.*

'You headed home?'

I blinked out of my trance.

'Yes,' I said, instantly regretting the admission.

'I'll walk you,' he said, moving ahead with his hands in his pockets as he looked back at me expectantly.

'Look, you don't have to do that, I am perfectly—'

'It's okay, I'm headed that way anyway,' he said.

I started walking, three of my steps equal to his one. I thought it better to keep up, seeing as his offer was apparently non-negotiable.

'So, Kate Brown, do you always cause trouble wherever you go?'

'Excuse me?' I pulled my bag over my head and across my body so I could concentrate on keeping up.

'Always running into the path of men.' He stopped briefly at the corner, looking each way for oncoming traffic before tilting his head to follow. I double-checked for myself before moving.

'He ran into me! In fact, you ran into me, too!'

'A rather disastrous start to your London adventures, to say the least,' he said, glancing at me with a smile. 'Well, I'll be sure to get you home in one piece.'

I rolled my eyes. It's not that I wasn't grateful for his help at the Stanhope Arms, but I wasn't completely hopeless. I could look after myself. Just as the thought ran through my mind, I tripped on an uneven bit of path, grabbing Jack's arm to steady myself. I quickly whipped my hand away, trying not to look at what no doubt would be a cocky smirk, or to dwell on how his arm felt like granite under my touch. Jesus! Was the universe deliberately trying to humiliate me in front of this man?

'Are you all ri—'

'I'm fine!' I snapped, readjusting my bag and pushing my hair over my shoulder, trying to maintain some semblance of dignity. This time I walked on, taking the lead, until Jack caught up.

'So what is it that you do, Kate Brown?'

I sighed, wishing he would just call me by my first name; why was it that everyone wanted to call me anything but just Kate? Katherine, Katy, Miss Brown; I was sick of it.

I thought for a moment, mulling over the dreaded question. How do you best describe the fact that you really don't do much at all? Back home I had been the jaded manager of a hideous clothing chain store in the Bourke Street Mall for a painful five years, selling size six tank tops with slogans like *Bootylicious* scrawled in glitter across them. It was a nightmare for my fluctuating size twelve dress size; I could barely fit my wrist inside the sleeve let alone actually wear anything from the store. It may have seemed the height of fashion when I was a teenager, but the ten percent staff discount was not enough to make me stay. There had to be more to life, and I was going to find it, I just didn't expect it would come to this. Here I was, stranded in Kensington with my evil nana, with no job, no future. Only my savings to stop me from becoming a true tragedy, and as soon as they ran out, I would head home having accomplished nothing more than an emptying my bank account. But as I listened to the clicking of my boots on the pavement, I realised that, while I may be the damsel-in-distress, apparently hopeless, Kate Brown to him, I had the potential to be anyone I wanted to be. To be the Kate Brown of my dreams. Hadn't this whole trip been about reinvention?

'I'm a writer.'

Of a small blog.

'I run my own business.'

A small blog.

'Travel, beauty, health.'

On a small blog.

Leaving out certain details made it sound like a legitimate endeavour and, seeing as it was my life goal, it wasn't completely unfounded.

'Wow,' Jack said, raising his eyebrows, impressed. 'Quite the entrepreneur.'

'Oh, it's just about following your passion.' I tried to play it down as we turned into our street, walking along the strip of identical terraces that curved slightly. I ran my hand along the black wrought-iron fencing, feeling like a whimsical child.

There was a part of me that felt like a giant fraud, but there was another part of me that secretly delighted in Jack being impressed by me, and that wanted desperately for the fib I told to be true. That part won.

We came to a stop outside Nana's terrace. 'Well, here we are,' I said, instantly hating how lame I sounded. Still, there was nothing to be nervous about. This wasn't a date, it was broad daylight and Nana Joy was not inside. Before today's act of chivalry, I'd actively avoided Jack Baker, so surely I couldn't be having feelings for him. This was a good thing: adult conversation with someone other than Vera.

'Well, thanks for the escort.' I held my hand out to him so forcibly that Jack flinched back with a laugh.

'Ah, any time,' he said, taking my hand and firmly squeezing.

I felt sure that there wouldn't be an 'any time', so, as Jack's grasp engulfed mine and lingered, I committed the feel of his touch and the sight of his coffee-coloured eyes smiling down at me to memory. It was then I noticed the faint half-moon-shaped scar at the corner of his left eye, a childhood accident, maybe a drunken night out, or perhaps he'd forgotten to looked both ways crossing the road at some point. Regardless of the cause, I would never have thought a scar could be so . . . sexy. It then occurred to me that I knew nothing about him, this man I couldn't stop running into. I was tempted to ask about his background, but thought better of it.

'Well, thanks again,' I said, getting my keys from my bag and heading to the door. I glanced back with a forced smile and a wave as he headed down the steps, hands in his pockets.

I worked quickly to slot the key into the front door, twisting and pushing my shoulder against it, nearly knocking the wind out of my lungs when it refused to give. Confused, I jiggled the key more desperately but there was no budging, no magical click that sounded to let me in.

'Oh no, no, no, no, come on!' I twisted the handle and kicked the door for good measure. 'This cannot be happening, this cannot be.' And just as I glanced at my watch, my breath catching at the lack of time before Vera and Nana's return, a new panic set in.

My heart thumping madly in my chest, I looked up at the imposing terrace, trying to assess if there was any way to scale the building, to break in somehow. All I could see was certain disaster as my eyes took in the black spikes of the front fence.

Ah, yeah, I don't think so.

'Jack!' I called out, gaining his attention just as he reached his own door. 'I'm locked out!' I winced, jangling my keys, feeling even more unsure about my choice when a smile slowly lined his face and he started making his way back to me. He was rubbing his stubbly jawline as if he were trying to hide his amusement at my predicament. It only embarrassed me more; maybe I should have taken my chances at goring myself on the fence. I swear, if he said one word about my attraction to disaster I would tell him where to go. But as he stood before me, still trying to look serious, he remained silent.

'I don't know why it won't budge,' I said.

'Have you had this problem before?'

I went to answer but then I realised that I had never had to unlock the door before. Any time I had ventured out, Vera had always let me in. If there was some secret little trick to the lock, there was no way I would know about it.

'Um, I'm not aware of there being a problem,' I said, dancing around the answer.

Jack took the key and slotted it back in, twisting and jiggling and achieving much more brute force from his broad shoulder than I had with my narrow one. A part of me hoped he wouldn't open the door first try, I would never live it down, but as I looked at my watch I began to panic. Vera and Nana would be here any minute.

'Sure is stubborn,' he said, crouching down to get a better vantage point as he worked on the lock.

Come on, come on.

I stepped from side to side, too nervous to stay still.

'Listen if you can't do it . . .'

'It's all right, this isn't my first time,' he said, flashing a knowing grin my way.

I paused. 'Okay, so you're either a locksmith or a criminal.'

Jack stood, his head cocked to listen as he twisted the handle. Then I heard it: the magical click of the latch unlocking. Jack pushed the door open with a huge, cocky grin.

'I'm not a locksmith.'

Chapter Seven

I had no time to question the meaning of his words as I saw, there in the distance, a vision that iced my blood: Vera wheeling Nana along the footpath.

'Oh, Jesus.'

Jack's smirk slipped from his face. 'What?'

'Get inside!'

His brows rose into his hairline. 'Sorry?'

'Now!' I said, pushing at him and edging him through the door quickly. It was like moving a mountain, a very confused mountain. I slammed the door and locked it behind us, stepping left, then right, then left again. I danced this way several times, unsure where to go next.

'Listen, Kate, I—'

'Shh.' I held up my hand, hearing the distant sound of voices.

'Upstairs, now!' I grabbed his arm and lead him to the staircase, skipping every second step. 'Hurry, this way.' I burst through the door of my room, slamming it closed and pressing my back to it, breathless but relieved that I was home safe. I blinked, my eyes focusing on the man standing in front of me, looking somewhat taken aback.

'Wow, listen, if you wanted me in your bedroom, all you had to do was ask . . .'

Oh God, what must he think of me? I probably looked like a desperate lunatic, but the way his eyes sparkled and the corner of his mouth lifted, I doubted he was worried.

'It's not like that,' I said, wishing now that I'd been sprung with him on the front doorstep. A lifetime of Nana Joy's acid-tongued lectures about trust and betrayal would have been better than holding a stranger hostage in my bedroom.

'I'm sure it's not.' He laughed; he was loving this, watching me squirm.

'Listen, I—'

There was a series of thuds that vibrated against my back, causing me to jump out of my skin.

'Kate, can I come in?' Vera's muffled voice called through the door.

I looked at the six-foot-three wall of man standing in front of me, and wondered how the hell I was going to hide him. There would be no shoving him under my bed, or behind a curtain. I was so screwed.

'Just a minute,' I called back, a little too high-pitched.

Jack must have read the desperation in my expression as he joined the hunt for an escape route. I dived across to the cupboard to check the space inside but was stilled by Jack, who grabbed my arm and pointed to the terrace. We rushed to the window, pulled the curtain aside and opened the door so Jack could slide outside. I held my finger to my lips, then closed the door and drew the curtains, plunging the room into unnatural darkness. I ran to my bed, ripping the covers back before taking off my boots, stripping off my jacket and ruffling up my hair as if I had just woken up.

I opened the door, holding the back of my hand to my mouth as I yawned, while Vera stood there looking concerned.

'Everything all right?' she asked, her eyes darting over me.

'Hmm? Oh yeah, sorry, I was just taking a nap. What time is it?'

'It's just after four. Sorry, I didn't mean to wake you. I didn't know if you would be in yet.'

'Oh, yeah, very dull day, I'm afraid,' I lied.

Vera nodded. 'Right,' she said. Her eyes strayed to my top; I followed her eye line to see the cider stain that covered the front of me.

'Better hope that washes out,' Vera said, her mouth twitching a little.

'Oh, what is that?' I feigned surprise, pulling at my top.

'I'm not entirely sure, but you might want to change your clothes before you come down. You smell like a brewery.' Vera chuckled, turning from the door. I closed my eyes, willing lightning to strike me down.

I was a walking disaster. I should never go out; I was a danger to myself and everyone else around me. I face-planted onto my bed, my moans muffled by the mattress. I rolled onto my back and stared at the decorative rose cornice of the light fitting like I did every morning. I lay there for a minute until I sat bolt upright.

'Jack!'

I scurried to the terrace doors, whipping back the curtains and diving out to the balcony to find—

He was gone.

I leant over the edge, relieved that there was no body impaled on the iron pickets but with no idea where he had gone. Something moved in the corner of my eye and there he was, reclining on the opposite balcony. His feet rested on the ledge, crossed at the ankles, and his hands were linked behind his head, a huge smile on his face. I did a double-take – he could only have accessed the terrace by climbing across a perilously narrow ledge.

'What are you doing?' I whispered angrily, trying not to alert anyone down below.

'What does it look like I'm doing?' he asked.

'But how?'

Jack smiled broadly, assessing my apparent concern. 'Magic.'

Jack drew back his feet and stood up, stretching his arms above his head as if he hadn't a care in the world.

'Well, don't go making a habit of that,' I said, peering over the edge to the drop below. As much as Jack annoyed me, I didn't exactly want him impaled on a railing.

'Okay, I won't – if you agree to tell me what you're hiding from.'

'What?'

'Well, I assume your intention wasn't to drag me into your bedroom to ravish me.'

'No!' I said, clearly panicked, which only seemed to amuse him more.

'More's the pity, so what then?'

I stared at him for a long moment, distracted by the need to get him away from the ledge he was now sitting on. How could I tell him that the person I was running from was an elderly woman in a wheelchair? It sounded ridiculous, preposterous, that I would allow myself to be so controlled by a geriatric for the chance to explore, to experience, to discover myself in new, exciting ways – and to blog about all of it. And while I hadn't yet done any of those things, there was a new surge of excitement in me, now that I had discovered the secret room on the first floor. My muse was back and I hoped that, if I was smart and played my cards right, I could make a go of it here, maybe even establish myself as a legitimate fashion blogger, and the only way to do it would be by living here with my nana, rent free. And now, it was all on the verge of falling apart, because, rather than keeping to the plan, I'd got carried away talking to my suave, but ultimately idiotic, neighbour. Well, I would not be sharing another shred of information with this man. I folded my own arms, mirroring his posture, and shrugged.

'I'm not running from anything.'

Humour slipped from Jack's face and his arms slowly fell to his side. 'Riiiight,' he said. 'Like that is it, then?' And before I could change my mind, Jack moved to the balcony, climbing over the barrier.

'Better make some room.'

Chapter Eight

'Stop it, Jack, just stop.'

'Stop what?' He looked genuinely perplexed.

'Please, just stay where you are and I will tell you anything you want to know.' I couldn't believe what I was saying; I could hear the words coming out of my mouth but I couldn't stop myself. At this point I would have done anything to get him to go back over.

'Anything?' he repeated.

'Well, within reason.'

He placed a foot over and stepped onto the narrow ledge.

I closed my eyes and willed for strength. 'All right, anything.'

Jack moved his foot back, his eyes ablaze. He went to speak but was interrupted by a knocking sound. And to my relief it wasn't coming from my side, it was coming from Jack's.

We looked at each other as a door slammed and footsteps could be heard pounding the stairs.

'What the hell?' A hand peeled back the curtain, and a man stepped out onto the balcony. The man's hands were on his hips, a wry smile on his face as he looked over at Jack sitting on the terrace ledge. 'What are you doing? You never sit out here.'

The penny finally dropped: the man standing next to Jack was the same one he had been talking to in the pub – short dark hair and navy blue, three-piece suit; his workmate. Jack's mate turned to where I stood, then smiled as he glanced back at Jack.

'Oh, I see why you're out here.' He grinned.

Jack smirked. 'It's not a bad view.'

Only then did it occur to me that the balcony Jack stood on, the one directly opposite mine, wasn't his neighbours', but his. My mouth gaped in horror at our proximity.

'Kate, this is George; George, this is Kate.' He gestured, introducing us as if we were at a barbecue.

George waved with a pained smile, as though he wanted to be anywhere else than in the middle of whatever this was. Then recognition flashed in his eyes as he repeated my name to himself.

'Hey, are you the girl? The car girl, the crying girl?'

'Excuse me?' I asked, glowering at Jack, who closed his eyes as if telepathically willing his friend to shut up.

George caught on quickly, his eyes flicking between the two of us.

'Oh hey, I didn't mean anything by it.'

'No that's fine, George. Nothing wrong with a harmless nickname, we all have them.'

Jack's interest piqued, looking at me side on. 'Do I have one?'

I laughed, making my way back to my balcony door and opening it with a deep sigh.

'Oh Jack, believe me, you don't want to know.'

Chapter Nine

rying girl, pfft.

I violently peeled the potatoes at the kitchen sink. The day had started out so promisingly. And then I would remember that smile, that cocky, infuriating smile.

If I never saw Jack Baker again it would be too soon.

'I'm off now!' Vera called from the kitchen door. It was the time of day I hated the most, knowing that I was going to be left alone with Nana Joy.

'Joy's all settled for the night; she's had a big day so you should be left in relative peace.'

I had visions of Vera playing fetch in the park to tire Nana out and I couldn't help but smile.

'Now, that's more like it. You've had the sourest look on your face all afternoon.'

'Have I?' I asked, innocently.

'Yes, did the stain not come out then?'

'Oh, I don't know, I have to check.' I placed the spud in the pot and washed my hands. Wiping them on my apron,

I made my way out to the small yard where the washing line was strung along the fence. Unpegging my top and holding it up, I brought it back to the kitchen light where Vera was washing the pot of spuds and putting them onto the stove for me.

'It's come out!' I said, a mite more cheerily.

'Oh, very good, then.'

'Vera, go home, I can do that.'

'I haven't done much.'

'You've cooked everything for the shepherd's pie, all I have to do is mash the potatoes.'

'Yes, I'm sorry I didn't get to that, the visiting sort of put a spanner in the works.'

'Vera, it's not your job to feed me, or look after me. I'm fine,' I assured her.

I read something in Vera's face as she bit her lip and dried her hands, not looking at me.

'What is it?' I pressed.

'Oh, I don't know. I don't mind cooking for you – lets me know that you're looking after yourself.'

I smiled. 'I'm looking after myself.'

'It's just . . .' She stopped.

'What?'

She looked up at me, her eyes sad. 'You seem so lonely.'

And there it was. It was one thing to reflect upon my situation, knowing how things were, but when someone else voiced it, it seemed truly depressing. Vera must have read as much in my face as she touched my upper arm.

'So if there is any way I can make things a little easier, I will.'

Her words were the closest she had ever come to an admission, or was ever likely to, that living here with Nana was difficult. In the first week, I'd felt anxious whenever I heard my name and I had cried at her casual cruelty. As time went on something worse had happened: I became jaded. My primary emotion was self-pity, and was so obvious that Vera, who was the conversational equivalent of Switzerland in her opinions, was now trying to comfort me. It was nice to have her support; I wasn't able to turn to my mum as she took great pleasure in saying, 'I told you so.' And if nothing else, apart from all the things I was searching for, I wanted to prove to everyone back home that they were wrong, that I was more than some failed retail manager looking to find herself abroad. I had already stayed weeks longer than they thought I would. I had to remember that.

'Thanks, Vera, I don't know what I'd do without you.'

Vera smiled and her chest puffed out a little; her face was always red, but she seemed pink with happinesss. She looked behind her, down the hall, before she turned to me, lowering her voice.

'We've a doctor's appointment tomorrow at 2 p.m. and we might do a spot of shopping afterward,' she said pointedly. Again, there were no obvious signs of collusion, but a notification of a window of opportunity. I was ever so grateful.

'How long?'

'Two, three hours?'

I nodded; I wanted to say thank you but it would probably just make things feel weird.

'Well, you better go,' I said, breaking the silence.

'Yes. I'll see you tomorrow.'

'I'll be here.' I laughed, adjusting the stove and popping a lid on the potatoes.

I wasn't going anywhere. Well, not yet.

~

I sat on my bed. Legs crossed, back straight. My hair was twisted in a thick white towel on the top of my head. My face was cleansed, toned and moisturised. I cracked my knuckles and set my fingers on the keyboard.

Nothing.

I had nothing.

Don't panic, Kate, just give yourself a minute.

But as I stared at the still empty document, all I wanted to do was scream. I'd had a million ideas running through my mind today, where had they all gone? Maybe I needed to revisit the source of my inspiration. I yanked the towel from my hair, letting the damp tendrils fall over my shoulders as I padded to the bedroom door, listening at it, as I always did, before opening it. As I crept along the hall to the opposite door, I hoped that Nana had taken her hearing aid out before she fell asleep. Reaching the barrier in relative safety, I once again stilled, holding my breath and craning my neck to listen for any sound down below.

Nothing.

I bit my lip as I twisted the handle. I half-expected to find a broom cupboard behind the door, that the room I had found earlier in the day had all been a dream. But as I turned on the light and the darkened space twinkled in the crystal sparkle of the chandelier, my heart soared once more. I was overwhelmed by the sheer volume of Nana's collection, and the impressive, organised layout – it was a fashion blogger's dream, and I had direct access to it. I couldn't shake the feeling that me being here was wrong; I knew if I wanted to use this as a backdrop for my vlogs and talking point for my blog I would have to ask Nana. But I knew the answer would be a resounding no, and that I could very well be kicked out for snooping in the first place. I had come in here hoping for some form of inspiration, but all it had managed to do was make me feel guilty, and more depressed than ever. I switched off the light and closed the door.

Morality was so bloody overrated.

I was all but ready to shut my computer down and curl up into bed, officially writing today off when my gaze landed on my handbag slung over the edge of the chair.

The beer coasters!

The slightly cider-soaked repository of today's amazing ideas – surely I could gain something from them?

Whipping open the red leather flap, I delved inside, rummaging past the TicTacs, lip gloss and phone charger. Bingo! I found one of them, though the ink had run and my notes were barely legible.

'Shit.' I sat down at the little desk near the window and upended my bag, its contents spilling out all over the surface. I instantly located the other two coasters, and even a lone earring I had been searching for for weeks, then saw something else within the detritus.

'Surely not,' I said, reaching over and picking up what appeared to be a rolled-up stash of money. I unravelled the notes, counting what I suspected would be the exact sum of money I had received from the rude idiot at the Stanhope Arms, the very same money I had put on Jack's tab.

My memory called up the image of him chasing after me to return my handbag. I shook my head.

'Unbelievable.'

~

It was strange thinking well of Jack Baker. It was easier to imagine him a typical lad. Sure, he had looked out for me on my disastrous day trip, but I couldn't shake the need to be wary of him; there was something unnerving about that dimpled grin. Realising how close his terrace was to mine put me on edge as I stood on my balcony sipping tea the following morning, my eyes flicking to his balcony doors, torn between hoping he would appear and hoping he wouldn't. Yesterday I had sworn off the terrace, locking the doors and vowing I would never set foot onto it again. I stood there, money fisted in my hand, ready to return it. I didn't need the money . . . even if I did have my eye on a gorgeous Angel Jackson snakeskin clutch. I didn't want to owe anyone anything and, though it had been gratifying to watch Jack bully the money from the smarmy suit, I didn't want to be seen as the kind of person who would take it.

His curtains were drawn and there was no sign of life. Guessing he was probably at work, I relaxed, taking a seat and finishing the rest of my tea. Then I froze.

It was far too peaceful.

It was past 8 a.m. and there hadn't been so much as a sound; no thuds from Nana Joy's walking stick, no shrieks of 'Katherine Elizabeth', nothing. Nana Joy was always awake before the sun was up, and her demands started the minute her eyes opened, with tea and breakfast, as if she'd never been fed before. I worried at the eerie silence, cursing myself at how distracted I had become. I launched out of my seat, my tea spilling as I dumped it on the small table next to me.

'Nan?' I called out, bounding down the stairs and swinging into the front parlour where she always chose to have her breakfast.

But the room was empty.

'Nana, where are you?' I called out, hurrying to her bedroom. The door was open, the blankets ruffled, the bed empty. Oh God. I ran down to the kitchen, out to the back garden, praying that I would find her grumpy, hateful self, desperately wanting to be abused and see her eyes roll at me. But she was nowhere to be found, and my breathing was laboured as panic set in. My fear escalated as I ran various terrifying scenarios through my mind and I turned slowly from the back garden, walking a determined line through the kitchen and stilling in the hall.

'Oh God, please, no.' I stared at the front door, visions of her going on a solo journey and being skittled by a car, or abducted by someone out there in the big, bad world. Surely she hadn't gone out, she was too frail to do so. That's why she had Vera, that's why she had me to do the things that were beyond her now. Great job I was doing at that, I thought, as hot tears pooled in my eyes and I ran toward the front door.

'Nana Joy? Nana, where are you?'

And just as I unlocked and ripped the door open, ready to search the streets of London for her, I heard a faint, pained sound from back in the house.

'Kate, help!'

Chapter Ten

At first I thought I had imagined it, that my stressed mind was playing tricks on me. Nana never called me Kate. But when I heard the distant groan down the hall I knew I had heard right.

'Nana?' I yelled back, letting the front door slam closed. I ran back up the hall, narrowing in on the cries, until I saw Nana's walking stick wedged against the doorframe of the downstairs bathroom. I instantly cursed myself for not having seen it earlier.

'Katherine?'

'I'm coming, Na—' My words were knocked from my lungs as I twisted the handle and pushed, but the door would not open, even as I put my shoulder into it.

'Nana, open the door!' I called, pushing against the solid barrier.

'Katherine, is that you?' Her voice was weak, and she sounded confused.

'Yes, Nana, it's me, can you open the door?' I placed my palms against the glossed wood, silently willing her to open it. After a long pause, Nana replied.

'I fell.' Her voice cracked.

I tried to remain calm. 'It's going to be okay, I'll get some help.'

The cries from beyond broke my heart, despite their aggression.

'No, no, you stupid girl, don't you dare . . .' She yelled out in pain.

'Nana, don't move! Just stay still, help is on the way.'

Adrenaline pushed me to the kitchen so fast I slid sideways and overshot the home phone. I jumped back, frantically scanning the list of emergency numbers.

I called Vera, my panic ratcheting up when I heard her voicemail message.

No, no, no, no, no . . .

'Vera, it's me, Kate, please call back as soon as you—'

The message bank's beep cut me off.

'Shit, shit, shit!'

With nothing else to be done and the sound of Nana's cries haunting me, I dialled 999.

I tried to remain calm but my brain was foggy as I muddled through the questions that were coming at me.

'What's your location, including the area or postcode?'

'Exactly what has happened?'

'What is the patient's age, gender and medical history?'

'Is your nan awake, conscious, breathing and is there any serious bleeding or chest pain? How did the fall happen?'

The only piece of information I retained was that emergency services were on their way, and I clung to it.

'Nana, it's going to be all right – help is coming,' I said for the hundredth time, thinking it was helping me more than it was her.

'Get me out of here!' she cried. I went to look out the window, then came back to kneel by the door, affixing my eye to the keyhole. I could see only two feet where she lay on the floor and my chin trembled at the sight.

'It's going to be okay, everything is going to be okay.'

Hold it together, Kate, just like you always do. Remember Joy can hear fear in your voice, she's usually the one who put it there. Except this time was different, this time I was genuinely frightened, and feeling guilty that maybe she had called me and I hadn't heard, maybe she had gone to the bathroom unaided because I had neglected her. How was I ever going to explain to my mum that I had failed, that this was all my fault? How would I look Vera in the eye knowing that my own selfishness had hurt Nana? I wiped a tear from my cheek.

'Nan? You okay in there?'

I waited for the acidic retort of abuse but there was nothing. Only silence.

'Nan?' I called through the keyhole. 'Nan, answer me.' My voice broke as my fist pounded on the door.

'NAN!'

And just as I was readying myself to break down the door by any means necessary, I heard knocking at the front door.

I scurried to stand, my tear-stained cheeks flushed as I ran to the front door, unlocking it and ripping it open.

'Please, help, she's . . .' My words fell away; all the air was sucked out of my lungs as I saw Jack standing there.

'Jack?'

'Kate, listen, I just want to – what's wrong?'

I swallowed, breathless. 'My nan, she's fallen and I can't get to her—'

'Where's your nan?' Jack's voice was calm as he stepped into the foyer, filling the space with his towering body.

'She's locked in the bathroom,' I said, falling into step down the hall. 'She's stopped responding to me, I don't know whether she's conscious or—'

'She is a cat's mother!' called Nana Joy in a clipped tone.

Jack smiled, his concerned façade broken by hearing Nana's voice. 'Well, conscious enough to correct your grammar,' he said, moving to the door. 'What's your nan's name?'

'Joy.'

'Joy, my name is Jack Baker.'

'Who?' Nana's voice was panicked once more.

'Have you called 999?' Jack asked me, his voice low.

I nodded. 'Emergency services are on their way.'

Jack squeezed my shoulder reassuringly. 'You might want to step back.'

'Are you the police?' called Nana.

'No, not at all, just here with the brawn. I'm going to work on getting this door open so the medics can get to you, okay? You've had a bit of a nasty fall then?'

'It's my ankle, I-I think it's broken.'

'She never told me that,' I whispered to Jack, who simply winked at me.

'Well, Joy, there's nothing wrong with my ankle so I'm going to put it to good use, all right, darling? You anywhere near the door?'

'Ah, no – I'm near the bath.'

'Okay, well, don't stress. I'm going to give the door a good kick, all right?'

Jack examined the door with the palms of his hands, testing the handle and looking at the structure.

'Just hang tight, Joy, almost there.' And with one swift kick, the bathroom door flew open, and there Nana Joy lay, her eyes wide, a trail of blood trickling down her cheek from where she had hit her head on the bath. I pushed past Jack, moving to her side.

'Nana, I'm so sorry, are you all right?'

'Of course not – look at me! I'm mortified!' she said, straightening her negligee and peering up to see the towering figure of Jack. Her eyes followed him as he knelt before her.

'Taken a bit of a tumble, young lady?'

Something sparked in Nana's eyes, something I had never seen before: a kind of warmth.

'No thanks to this one.' Her eyes darted to me briefly.

'Now, Joy, if it wasn't for this one we may never have met, so you be easy on Kate, eh?'

Jack had a way of putting Nana back in her place that sounded almost charmingly flirtatious, which was probably why she didn't bite back; rather, a small smile pinched her wrinkly, thin lips.

'Jack lives next door to us, Nana, how funny's that?' I blurted out. I so desperately wanted her to smile at me just once to know that she wasn't mad at me, or no more so than usual. But she looked at me quizzically, as if to see if I was telling lies.

'So, Joy, if you ever need any sugar, let me know, but for now we're going to clear a path so the medics can get a proper look at you, okay?'

'You're leaving?' Joy went to move, anxious again.

'Easy now, we'll be right here, but we have to let the medics look at you. Can you do this for me, please, Joy?'

Joy looked up into Jack's face as he held her hand; she was in some kind of romantic trance and I couldn't help but feel mortified by how she was behaving. She would do anything he told her to – and no one told Joy Ellingham what to do – and she settled back down like a good patient.

Jack nodded, squeezing her hand. 'Good girl,' he said, turning to a man and a woman who stood at the doorway, waiting to come in.

'All yours,' he said, motioning for me to step out into the hall with him. As I watched them carry in their bags, I felt numb, like all that was surrounding me was white noise. I couldn't stand watching Nana wince in pain as they examined her ankle, so I walked to the back of the hall, my arms wrapped around myself as if to protect me from a chill. And I was cold, cold to the bone, thinking about what had happened, and what could have happened, and try as I might, I couldn't fight the tears as I let reality hit me. But what caused the tears to flow with even more force was the relief that she was okay, or would be soon.

Jack's tall frame came to stand beside me.

'She'll be all right, Kate.' Jack's voice was smooth, reassuring but, rather than stem the tide, I wept even harder.

I really was the crying girl.

Chapter Eleven

turned away from him, burying my face in my palms and wanting nothing more than for him to leave me alone. But that wasn't going to happen. His hand gripped my arm as he turned me to him and, without saying a word, brought me to his chest and put his arms around me. It was the strangest thing. He was a relative stranger and yet I was instantly calmed. Engulfed in his warmth and so close I could feel his heart beat against my temple, I was soothed as he gently rubbed between my shoulder blades. I wondered if he was trained in this kind of comfort, because he was most excellent at it. I tried not to think about the way he smelt, or the fact that the solid foundation of chest I was pressed up against belonged to Jack. Yeah, this was inappropriate. I moved back, working to put a little space between us as I wiped at my face and looked into his ever-watchful eyes. He let his arms fall away from me.

'You're very good at what you do,' I said, my voice croaky. I felt my cheeks flame, cringing at what I had said.

'Breaking down doors or hugs?'

Both, I thought. But I really didn't want to admit to either, and I was grateful when someone behind us cleared their throat. I stepped further away from Jack and turned to the young male paramedic.

'It's only a sprain, but we're going to take her in for observation because she's hit her head.'

'Oh God.' The guilt was back; a mere moment in the presence of this man had allowed me to forget. He was a serious distraction.

'Thanks, we're coming in.'

'Ah, and another woman has just arrived . . . short red hair?'

'Vera,' I said, rushing inside but pulling up at the sight of the stretcher that Nana Joy was strapped to. At the other end of the hall stood an equally concerned Vera, who, with great effort, slid sideways down the hall to reach me.

'Oh, you poor girl, I came as soon as I got your message. What happened?'

'I fell!' Nana interrupted. 'Lying there for hours, I was.'

'Nana, I'm so sorry.'

She ignored me, looking directly at Vera with fear in her eyes. 'It was so cold on the tiles, Vera. So cold.'

I felt so incredibly small; with Jack behind me, listening to the horror story Nana told, I was all but ready to book my ticket back home. At least Nana would have a better chance of survival with someone else looking after her.

'Ah, what do you want us to do with these? We found them wedged next to the bath; they look vintage, probably want to put them somewhere safe,' said the female paramedic as she placed a pair of silver high-heeled shoes on Nana's stretcher, waiting for her to respond.

I looked at the shoes, then to Vera, then Nana, who turned away, as though, if she didn't acknowledge their existence, then maybe no one else would.

Vera sighed heavily, her lips pursed together as she took the shoes from her. 'What have I told you, Joy? You can't go swanning about in heels anymore.'

'What?' I asked, still confused.

Vera took the shoes and handed them to me. 'She would have been playing dress-ups. It's not the first fall; I've had to hide all the heels. Seems like I didn't do a good enough job.'

I clutched the intricately detailed shoes, silver and silken, expensive, delicate. 'Nana, what were you doing at that hour trying on shoes?' I laughed, thinking it funny more than anything, but I realised my mistake when I looked at her. Her eyes were so wild with rage and hurt that I thought the flesh would melt from my face.

'Oh, it's all right for you, isn't it, prancing around without a care in the world, bounding up steps and wearing silly skirts. Well, let me tell you something. Just you wait until your beauty fades and your body aches and your independence is gone, when the biggest thrill of your day is wearing something that makes you feel young and beautiful in the privacy of your own home, then see how it feels to be humiliated and reminded of how old and silly you are.'

'Nana, I never said—'

'No, but you were thinking it, you all were. What a stupid old woman, dreaming of her lost youth.' Her angry eyes shifted past me to where Jack stood, and her eyes changed.

'Except you, you don't look at me like that.' Tears welled in her clear blue eyes and I felt for her.

'All right, Mrs Ellingham, we're going to take you in for observation. Is there someone who you wanted to—'

'I'll go,' I said, eagerly passing the shoes to Vera, but Nana had other ideas.

'I want Vera to come,' she said, turning her head away from us.

Vera's expression was sad as she handed back the shoes. 'Sorry, Kate.'

I smiled weakly; it shouldn't have been a huge shock, but I still felt unnecessary and unwanted as they wheeled Nana down the hall.

'Here we go, let's get you on the road to recovery,' said the man, carefully manoeuvring her to the front door.

Vera hugged me. 'I'll give you a call from the hospital.'

I nodded, clutching the shoes to my chest as I followed them out.

'Ow! Watch it, you stupid fool,' she snapped at the paramedics as they tried to gently take her down the terrace steps. I sighed. Despite all of my empathy for Nana's situation and remorse at my possible hand in it, I was relieved it wasn't just me; that Nana hated the whole world these days and everyone in it. Then I felt Jack's presence at my side, watching as I turned to look at his profile.

Well, almost everyone.

Vera climbed in to sit by Nana's side and the back doors closed.

'It's just a formality because of her age, and the head injury. It's a sprain, which is good, just means she'll be less mobile while she rests but her mind is as sharp as a tack, so I suspect she'll be home in no time.'

I studied the side of Jack's face, my attention only diverted as the ambulance pulled away from the kerb. His reassurance was exactly what I had needed to hear. His calm in a crisis, his bedside manner and the way he had made Nana putty in his hands. The way he soothed me at my most distraught, just by holding me; he seemed to know exactly what was needed. What I needed.

'Thank you,' I said, and unlike all the other words that slipped out of my mouth in the last few days, I really meant it.

Jack looked down at me with interest. 'I'm getting quite accustomed to saving you, Miss Brown. What will tomorrow bring?'

'Nothing,' I said. And I could feel lightness inside of me, watching as he cocked one eyebrow.

'You sure about that?'

'Yes.' I half-laughed, staring up at him in challenge.

Jack lingered between steps as he edged his way down, the cogs in his head turning. As he stood on the lower step, buttoning up his jacket, he looked back up at me with a boyish grin.

'What?'

He shook his head. 'Nothing.' And just as he was about to leave, I remembered something.

'Jack, wait!'

Jack looked up at me expectantly.

'Before, when you knocked on my door, was there something you wanted?'

Jack shrugged his shoulder in that cool, casual way he did. 'Um, not that I can recall.'

I shook my head; something told me Jack was lying.

'Fine, but before you go.' I ran back into the house and up to my room, grabbing the rolled-up money from my desk, before bounding back down to Jack. He hadn't moved from where he stood and took in my breathless state with a curious smile.

I reached out to shake his hand. 'Here.'

Ever so slowly, he took my hand, as if I might electrocute him. Only when he felt something in my palm did his brows raise with interest. Before he could try to return the money, I dived inside.

'Bye!' I said, slamming the door behind me and pressing my back against it with a huge grin, impressed with my effort.

Kate – 1

Jack – 0

As I was revelling in my victory I heard the sound of a squeaky hinge, and I watched in horror as a roll of money slipped through the letterbox and onto the floor.

'Sorry, love, I don't take tips,' he called through the door.

I swept up the money and pulled the door open just as Jack was sliding into his car.

'This isn't the last you've heard of me, Jack Baker,' I called.

He laughed, resting his elbow on the open window. 'Of that, Kate Brown, I have no bloody doubt.'

Chapter Twelve

'I'm sorry, Kate, but she doesn't want you here.' Vera's voice was apologetic over the phone line.

'But they're keeping her in overnight.'

'Only as a precaution. I'm going to swing by yours to pick up a few things.'

'Well, I could bring them to you.'

Vera laughed. 'Kate, it's fine, this is what I get paid to do.'

'Yeah, well, you're earning some serious overtime.'

There was silence on the other end, and I hoped that I hadn't offended her in some way. 'I should have answered your call. I should have been more diligent about keeping her shoes out of the way.'

It occurred to me that I wasn't the only one playing the blame game, that Vera too was feeling guilty over something that really wasn't anyone's fault.

'Vera, it was an accident. God only knows what Nana gets up to when we're not around; it's a part of that independent spirit of hers that can't be tamed. Not by you, or me.'

'Yes, well, maybe certain a hunky next-door neighbour could; she hasn't stopped gushing about him since he left here.'

'Left?'

'Oh, he dropped in to the hospital to check on her, which was really nice of him.'

I felt tightness in my chest but quickly blinked back to my senses. 'Yes, that was nice.'

'It was kind of funny though, well, not really, but Joy was at her grumpy worst, bossing people around, being nasty to the nurses, and Jack put her back in her place, in the most clever way I have ever seen. He was telling her off, but did it so that it didn't seem like it . . . does that makes sense?'

I laughed, having seen firsthand exactly what she meant. 'Maybe we could take lessons from him,' I said.

'I doubt it would work, we aren't blessed with those dimples.' Vera sounded far away, like she too was suffering from the Jack Baker Effect.

'So how did he tame the wild beast?'

'He just told her that people have a job to do, and that when people treat him like that in his workplace, it's not a nice feeling.'

What workplace could he be talking about? What was Jack's job? I really didn't know anything about him, and it was beginning to annoy me.

'And what did she say to that?'

'She actually thought about it, like you could see it rolling around in her mind, and she seemed a mite shameful. But she didn't actually say anything, just changed the subject.'

I couldn't help but laugh, so clearly able to picture the scene. 'Well, I doubt it will cure her in any way, but I hope she will be a little more careful in the future, if not a little nicer.'

'Yes, well, don't get your hopes up, Kate.'

It was the first time I had heard Vera let down her barrier; I liked it.

'Promise me something, Vera. Promise me you won't feel guilty about what happened. It wasn't your fault or my fault, not even Nana's. It was just one of those things and we can't carry it around with us, okay?'

'Okay, well, I'll promise you that if you promise me something.'

Somehow I didn't feel so assured with the tables turned.

'What's that?'

'Go out tonight! Have some fun, enjoy yourself. Don't waste your youth.'

'You mean swan around in silly skirts?' I quoted Nana's heated words.

Vera laughed. 'Exactly.'

'Well, after this morning's fiasco I really don't think I can—'

'Kate.' Vera said my name like a warning, and I knew she was right.

'All right, I'll go out and have the time of my life.'

'Good girl.'

'Even if I have no friends.'

'Go and make friends.'

'Riiight,' I said, thinking about how accustomed I had become to living like a hermit, the lonely blogger locked in her tower. 'I think I've forgotten how to interact with others.'

'Which is precisely why you need to do this.'

I knew she was right, that everything she was saying made complete sense. The Kate of yesterday would have jumped at the chance of a minute's freedom, let alone a night all to herself. What was holding me back?

Vera's voice brought me out of my musings. 'I'd better go, Kate, but I'll see you later?'

'You will.'

'You can show me what you're going to wear out on the town.'

I winced even thinking about it. 'Yay!' I said, rather unconvincingly. As I hung up the phone I realised I wanted nothing more than to hang out on my terrace for the night, but I really didn't want to think about why.

~

I did as I was told and went out to reclaim my youth and enjoy my independence. As much as I loved what I was wearing – classy boots, fawn sleeveless wraparound dress

with a corded black leather belt to match my black clutch
– I had never felt like such an imposter. I excused myself
through the crowd of the Stanhope Arms, the only place
I felt comfortable going due to its proximity to home and
familiarity. Yep, I was such a loser. I skimmed over the
crowd, thinking I might see Jack, but he was nowhere to
be found. I shouldn't have been surprised, I didn't know
enough about him to know if this was even his local
watering hole. Maybe it was just chance that had led
him here. But as I waited at the bar, I noticed the same
bartender was serving as yesterday, the one who appeared
to know Jack. The barman finally stood before me and
I wondered if he recognised me, but there was nothing,
just an expectant stare as his eyes dipped to the tenner
in my hand.

'Oh, right, hello,' I said nervously. 'Could I please
have . . .'

'A cider?'

He did remember me!

'Um, not tonight, I might just go for a house white,
thanks.'

He nodded, sliding the tenner from the bar and moving
to the fridge. I quickly tried to think of conversation topics
that would lead to Jack, and then I realised how creepy that
would be, and what a massive stalker I was. He was back
with my drink all too soon.

'Jack!' I blurted out, as he put the change on the bar
in front of me.

Kate, what the hell are you doing? Just shut up!

'Have you seen Jack? Jack Baker?'

It was like an out-of-body experience: I could hear myself saying things and I was powerless to stop it.

The barman shook his head. 'Not tonight.'

That was the pearl of wisdom he left me with and, alarmingly, I felt disappointed. There was only one thing to be done. I grabbed my wine and skulled it.

Chapter Thirteen

made friends! Lots of friends.

Lotty, Dave, Micky and Lou were my party mates for the night as the band played Rolling Stones covers, which would have made my dad happy. I downed shots with my new friends and danced until my feet hurt and the room spun.

'Come on, Kate, we're heading to Knightsbridge.'

I didn't know where that was but it sounded good to me, so I grabbed my clutch as Lotty took my hand and led me out through the crowd.

'Knightsbridge, baby!' I waved my hands in the air, feeling more alive than ever.

'Kate?'

I spun around, trying to see who had called my name, then my eyes landed on a familiar face.

'It's me, George. We met on Jack's terrace.'

Something fluttered in my chest as I heard the name of the man I had been drinking to forget.

'George, hi!'

'Hey, Kate, come on, let's go!' I turned to see Micky hanging out of a cab, laughing and trying his best not to fall out.

'Oh, sorry, I'm keeping you,' he said.

'NO!' I said a bit too aggressively. 'It's fine, I don't even know them.' I shrugged, laughing and swaying.

'Oh, you don't?'

'Never met them before in my life,' I admitted.

'Kate, come on, babe, he's not for you, I'm for you.' Dave peeled his shirt down and tried to lick his nipple, causing a mass of cackles from the group.

Even in my rather tipsy state, I recoiled from the view. 'Ew.'

I spun around to see George's expression mirroring my own.

'You can't go with them.'

'I can't?'

'Not tonight. Not any night, stay here.'

'But it's Knightsbridge.' I said it in a way that I hoped was self-explanatory.

'Do you want a snapshot of the decision you're about to make?'

I blinked at him, confused, trying to block out the catcalls from behind me.

'Go with them and you'll have a laugh until your drink is spiked or you end up in emergency, confused and holding the hand of a stranger who has just been glassed because he cracked on to the girlfriend of some bloke who just happens to be freshly out of jail for aggravated assault. All the while, you're being questioned by police and crying because the buzz from the alcohol is wearing off and you can't confirm your identity because one of your "friends'" mates has stolen your purse so you have no money and no means to get home. Oh, and you will also be missing a shoe, have a grazed knee and be about to lose the contents of your stomach in a very public and demeaning way that will stain your pretty dress, which you won't be able to get dry cleaned because not only have you no cash but you're not long off from checking your Visa statement where you will see the obscene amounts of money you spent on shouting your new "friends" drinks all night. Does that sound appealing to you?'

I stared at George, his rather vivid portrayal of my potential future turning over in my mind. I glanced toward the taxi where the group were shouting at me and the scene suddenly looked completely different; like someone had switched a light on and I could see all the dingy details in sharp focus.

I turned back to George, lifting my chin with as much dignity as I could muster while smoothing over my dress. 'I guess this is as good a place as any.'

He laughed, stepping aside and waving me in. 'After you.'

~

'Is it too late to head to Knightsbridge?' I said, staring hopelessly at the glass of water that sat in front of me. 'When you offered to buy me a drink I kind of imagined it coming out of a bottle and not a tap.'

'I can get you bottled water, if you want?'

'Geez, you're too kind. Clearly you don't have to worry about checking your Visa statement after a night out.'

'You'll thank me for it in the morning,' George said, lifting his pint of beer to his lips.

I tilted my head and looked closely at him. His hair was dark, matched by his dark eyes and olive skin. He was dressed in casual clothes, not a suit, hence why I hadn't recognised him right away. 'Is it in all Englishman's DNA to protect helpless Australian women?'

George laughed. 'Not at all,' he said, placing his drink down.

I took a sip of my water, thinking what a poor substitute it was for wine, but how much I needed it.

'So is this your local then?' I asked.

'Nah, not really, only when I'm crashing at Jack's place.'

My water went down the wrong way at the mention of his name, bringing on a coughing fit.

'Someone can't handle their water,' he joked.

I shook my head, trying to catch my breath. 'Sorry, went down the wrong way.'

George watched me with interest, as if trying to decide whether to tell me something.

'So, you're crashing there tonight, then?'

'Yeah, Jack was going to come out but he had a thing after work so . . .'

A thing.

Why don't people use proper words? What was this thing? Date night with the girlfriend maybe? I really didn't want to think about that.

'Oh, so he's not meeting up with you later, then?' I asked, spinning my drink around on the coaster in my best attempt to look uninterested.

'Nah, I'll just catch him later at home,' he said, and that was the extent of it.

Why don't men gossip more? Maybe he needed to loosen up a little and have a few more drinks, maybe then he'd dish the info. But then, why did I care so much?

I shouldn't be wasting my energy on the likes of Jack Baker – whose sudden allure I put down to being a symptom of my complete and utter isolation and boredom. Sure, he was easy on the eye and he made things interesting whenever he was around, so it was only natural that I was gravitating toward him. Having justified my momentary attraction, I felt at ease.

Enough was enough. I may not be piling into a car with a group of strangers to go to Knightsbridge, but I would become more proactive from this moment on. I would fight against the boredom, thus alleviating my interest in Jack Baker, and I would get on with my life. And just as I was determined to do that very thing and took a big ol' swig of H_2O, George's mobile phone lit up and started to vibrate across the table.

He swooped it up, smirking as he read the screen and answered.

'Hello, Jacky Boy!'

Chapter Fourteen

'Guess who I'm with.' George winked at me, his smile cheesy as he reclined in his chair. I wanted to mime 'don't say anything', but I was too busy hanging on the edge of my seat.

'Your lovely neighbour, Kate Brown.'

He'll think I'm some kind of stalker; I'll be having afternoon tea with his parents next and loitering outside his work.

I was dying to know what Jack said, and what he thought about me hanging out with his mate, and was answered when I saw the smile drop from George's face and his eyes shift quickly to me before affixing them to his drink.

'Right, I see.'

What was he telling him?

'No, look, I get it.'

Was he saying I was a bunny boiler? That I locked my nana in a room and sent her to the hospital and now I was after him?

'No, look, I'll crash someplace else, no problem.'

My stomach dropped. Jack had someone at his place – it all made sense now. I guess I should have been relieved that his no-show was nothing personal, but there was something that twisted my insides when I thought about it, and that, in turn, just made me feel stupid. I shouldn't care what Jack was doing or who he was with, it was none of my business. I was grateful that George made me stay so that I could finally put Jack out of my silly little head.

'Yeah, mate, right-o.' He hung up the phone.

'Not coming out then,' I said, breezy as you like.

George looked annoyed, his eyes far away, before his attention finally snapped to me. 'Hmm, oh no, no, he won't be coming out, and I have to find an alternative couch to crash on.'

An awkward silence settled between us that had me worrying about what Jack had said to him.

Careful, George, she's trouble.

George's puppy-dog brown eyes lifted up to me with interest; it was the kind of look that said, How about your place?

Oh, hell, no.

'Listen, I'm going to go, I'm starting to sober up now and that's just tragic.' I stood so quickly my chair flung backward, saved only by George's quick reflexes.

I thought George might say something witty, but his smile was sad and he didn't argue.

'See ya, Kate, be safe, yeah?' he said, but he was too busy texting on his phone to look up at me.

I grabbed my clutch from the table. 'Don't worry, I won't be hopping into any taxis with random partiers,' I said, but it seemed any attempt at humour was lost on George as he looked up at me, clueless.

'Night, George,' I said, and dodged through the crowd.

~

Though I hadn't done much exploring beyond my front gate, one thing was becoming quite clear: I loved my neighbourhood. Even at night there was a buzz surrounding the cafés, pubs and shops. I still felt like a tourist, though, as I stumbled my way across awkward intersections that had no give way rules, or none that I could see.

The Stanhope Arms was a mere five-minute walk from Onslow Gardens, where Nan's terrace was situated. On nights like this it didn't seem long enough, and I thought of how I had squandered my precious free time. I had intended to at least lose myself in the throes of alcohol, but even that had failed. Turning into my street, I took solace in the fact I didn't have to worry about waking up Nana, who would no doubt return with her wrinkled death stares and ready to blame me for her near-death experience for the rest of her days. But I would take it; let her use me as a punching bag if it made her feel better. Any time I thought of her struggling to try on those ridiculous shoes made me sad; age may have wearied her bones but it had not altered her mind or her will. As much as I complained about her limitations on freedom, it suddenly occurred to me that maybe her restrictions stemmed from resentment. I didn't know exactly what to do with that, but as far as her homecoming was concerned, I would try to mend the bridge with Nana. And the secret room? I wouldn't dare go there.

Surprisingly, thinking about my situation in a different light brought a degree of comfort, and kept me from dwelling on Jack Baker, especially knowing I had to pass his terrace to get to my own; to see his bright red door and try not to think about who he might be entertaining on his terrace –

Kate, stop it! Quick – think about your nana who hates you and cheer up!

I delved into my purse for my house keys, willing myself to think of something, anything else, when I heard the screech of expensive tyres. Jack's tyres. I was readying my clever salutation when I saw the woman in the passenger seat, waiting for Jack to make his way around and open the door for her. I dived inside the front gate of the neighbouring terrace, crouching behind a potted shrub and peering through the railing.

Jack looked dashing in a black tuxedo and bow tie, he would turn heads anywhere he went, but my eyes were drawn to the brunette at his side, the one he was smiling at and guiding up the steps of his terrace. She was an Amazonian supermodel; her hips swayed elegantly in her evening gown as she sashayed up the steps, her bloody delightful laughter rang out into the night air. Even from a distance I hated her, her and her fashionable, graceful splendour, following Jack into his house. I tried not to analyse my feelings, to avoid equating the unreasonable amount of rage I felt with jealousy. I didn't want to admit it, couldn't bear to even think about it as I stood up and walked through the terrace gate, squaring my shoulders and hoping that no one had seen me. I gripped my keys with white-knuckled intensity as I made quick, determined steps to my door, my focus solely on my door, not his. Not now, nor ever again.

~

A long, high-pitched ringing shunted me out of my sleep. I lifted my face from the mattress, alarmed, confused, wiping the drool from the side of my mouth.

I groaned, rolling onto my back and clasping at my temples, begging for the ringing to stop, until I realised it wasn't in my head – it was coming from my purse.

'Shit!' I dived out of bed, reaching for my clutch. 'Hello?' I croaked into my phone.

'Good morning!' sing-songed Vera.

I cringed, pulling my phone from my ear to see it was just after 7 a.m. 'Morning, Vera.'

'I'm just on my way to pick up Joy. By all reports she's doing just fine and is as cranky as ever.'

'Oh, so back to normal then.'

'Yes!'

I laughed. 'I never thought I'd be so happy to hear it.'

'Me too,' said Vera. 'So, listen, if there's anything you have or want to do, we'll probably be home in a little over an hour.'

There was one thing I wanted to do desperately – have a long, hot shower. 'Thanks, Vera, I really appreciate everything you've done. What would I do without you?'

Vera scoffed. I could tell without even seeing her face that she would have gone a shade redder, embarrassed by my words.

'All right, Vera, I better get moving. I'll see you soon.'

I was a woman on a mission. I laid out my outfit for the day: a pleated grey twill skirt and a black-and-white floral-printed silk blouse, accompanied by my rounded black cross-body handbag with black-and-white-striped interior. I searched for my favourite pair of black suede peekaboo Davie heels to complete the ensemble. I nodded, content with my choices, before continuing with my morning routine, which was going to be a severely shortened, given Nana's imminent arrival.

I didn't have time to blow-dry my hair, so rather than leave the house with half-wet, destined-for-frizzy hair, I braided it over my shoulder as I hopped down the stairs, finishing just as I reached the front door. I made my way outside, checking my watch to see I would have to make the quickest trip of my life and thinking that I hadn't made the smartest choice in footwear. Still, at least

I looked nice. Not that I was trying to impress anyone, including the person who lived behind the red door I had just passed, my heels clicking at high speed. I didn't want to be reminded of my cringe-worthy behaviour last night, cowering in the shadows, watching Jack and his super-model girlfriend come home. I closed my eyes, willing the memory, or rather nightmare, away as I turned the corner out of Onslow Gardens and towards Gloucester Road.

My few journeys outside the house had made me familiar with the landmarks of my neighbourhood. From the deep, rich red building of the Gloucester Road Tube Station, curving its way around the corner like a jewel in the street's crown, to Flowers Inc, the dainty little flower shop next to it that seemed like an old-world relic tucked among the modern hustle and bustle of coffee shops filled with commuters. The flower shop was my first stop; I wanted a cheery bouquet to take back to the terrace to freshen up the front parlour. Then I had to slip across to the Tesco Express for last-minute supplies for Nana, namely tea and milk, and then duck into Paul, a little French patisserie, for a dark chocolate cake. The sheer volume of butter, sugar and rich cocoa that made up the cake no doubt made it a no-no for 78-year-olds, but this was a special occasion. With no time to spare, I juggled my flowers, shopping and cake box, weaving through locals and tourists down Gloucester Road toward home, hoping against hope that I didn't run into Jack on the street – even if I could do with an extra pair of hands. Out of breath, I finally made it to the black-and-white tiled entrance of the terraced landing, all but falling into the foyer, both spent and relieved that I had made it. I dashed into the front parlour, dumping my cargo onto the low antique coffee table and kicking off my shoes.

'God, that feels good,' I groaned. No time to explore the damage of my blisters, I summoned enough energy for one final push. I straightened up the cushions on the couch, drew the curtains wide open and ran a tissue over the mantel for any wayward dust, finishing off with a spray of Bvlgari perfume around the room. As I went about sorting out the shopping and flowers, I remembered Nana's bedroom and bathroom. I didn't want it to seem like I had merely left everything and gone out to party (like I had), so I quickly made her bed and swept over the bathroom.

'Right, good,' I panted, clearly talking to myself. Maybe I shouldn't be left alone for too long a period of time.

As if answering my fear, I heard the front door open and the unmistakable voices of Vera and Nana filtering through the doorway. I couldn't lie, I was actually excited to see them, now realising how much I enjoyed having company, even if it was Nana's.

I grabbed the vase displaying the most amazing colours: hyacinths, tulips, ranunculus and anemones.

'Welcome home, Nana!' I sing-songed as I walked down the hall, a smile spread broadly across my pink, shiny face, holding the flowers aloft like a thing of wonder. When

I stood before her, my smile slowly fell from my face as I followed her eyeline all the way to . . .

Oh God.

'Those are your shoes, I suppose.'

Her bony arms rested on the sides of her wheelchair, her scowl resting on my black heels that sat in the middle of the parlour where, in my haste, I had shucked them off.

'You think that's funny, do you?'

'No, of course not, I just kicked them off before I went and got you these—'

'Well, maybe I'll try them on later, finish myself off next time.'

'Joy,' Vera interjected. 'Don't be sensitive. Kate didn't put them there as any kind of joke.'

But it mattered little what Vera said, Nana looked at me with a very clear and unmistakable intent. She hated me and my shoes. I felt the same old misery coming back to me, like a dark cloud had descended over Onslow Gardens the minute she had been wheeled through the front door. I took the flowers into the parlour, feeling her steely gaze following my every step as I put them on the coffee table, twisting them so their best side showed. I swallowed, repeating to myself over and over again, 'Don't get upset, don't let it show' while silently picking up my shoes.

'There's cake in the fridge, your favourite, the dark chocolate kind,' I said, without waiting to see her response. I made my way to the stairs, feeling the tears well in my eyes. I was halfway up the stairs when I heard a knock followed by a familiar voice.

'Morning, neighbours, anyone home?'

I turned to lock eyes with Jack, standing in the doorway, that familiar warmth emanating from him, and I was never so happy to see a friendly face, even if it did belong to him.

Chapter Fifteen

Despite insisting that he didn't want to intrude and merely wanted to check in on the patient, Vera had already taken Jack's coat and I had hurried down the stairs, ready to deadbolt the door behind him if I had to.

'We have cake,' I said, a touch desperately. 'I was just about to get it. Do you want some cake?'

Jack, seeming unaffected by the attention of three doe-eyed females, looked at me, his brows high. 'Cake for breakfast?'

I laughed, feeling my nervousness return as his amused stare questioned me. I shrugged. 'Why not?'

Jack went to answer but his words were cut off.

'Oh, for God's sake, Katherine, stop mooning over our visitor and leave the man be,' Nana snapped, her words turning me a deeper shade of red, a mixture of rage and mortification. Nana's ice-blue eyes lifted to Jack, her smile sickeningly sweet. 'Jack, please do come in, come sit,' she insisted.

Jack obliged, going into the formal lounge. Vera went to push Nana in behind him but Nana waved her away, annoyed, choosing to wheel herself in, suddenly Miss Independent. Vera and I looked at one another with a sigh as we followed her, ready to protect Jack in any way we could. Though, considering Nana's swift change of mood since his arrival, Jack was most likely the last person who needed protecting.

'Maybe he could stay forever,' muttered Vera out the side of her mouth.

My answer was halted by a high-pitched laugh from Nana, who apparently found something Jack had said delightfully witty. The foreign sound caused Vera and I to flinch.

'Maybe he could be her new carer?' I whispered back, watching in astonishment.

'If only, there would be peace on Earth.'

Jack glanced my way, winking before turning his full attention back to Nana, who was now blabbering; maybe that's where I inherited that from.

I couldn't help but smile, watching the scene before me, shaking my head. 'Peace on Earth? I'd settle for Kensington.'

Something had changed, like the sun had appeared from behind the clouds. As I leant against the window pane of the parlour, my attention darting from Jack and Nana out to Jack's parked car, I wondered where the Amazonian was. Was she still upstairs, stretched out on Jack's bed, wearing one of his expensive shirts? My bitter thoughts were interrupted by Nana's increasingly disturbing laughter. Jack's eyes briefly locked with mine as he sipped from a dainty teacup, which looked utterly ridiculous in his large hands. He had nice hands: big, strong, manly . . . My mind began to drift again until Vera elbowed me, causing me to mentally jump back into the room.

'Sorry, what?' I stammered, surprised she had come to stand next to me.

Vera's eyes were alight, ever watchful. 'Oh, I never said a word,' she said, taking pleasure in my awkwardness.

I folded my arms, unfolded them. Seemed like everyone was enjoying a cup of tea, maybe I needed to keep my own fumbling hands busy. I lifted my chin, and with as much grace as I could muster, crossed the room to pour myself a cup of tea from the tray between Nana and Jack. I had visions of tripping, smashing china, scalding poor, defenceless Nana in her chair, ruining Jack's pants; all manner of disasters rushed through my mind as I poured as carefully as I could. Not an easy feat when I could feel both Nana's and Jack's eyes on me, Nana's words falling away as I approached, clearly interrupting the conversation. My instinct was to apologise for it but then I thought better of it, knowing it was a ploy of Nana's to make me uncomfortable. When I glanced at her, I almost recoiled when I saw she was smiling sweetly at me.

Nana tapped the seat next to her. 'Sit down, Katherine. I was just telling Jack all about you.'

I looked at the seat like it was booby trapped, glancing briefly at Vera, who watched on with suspicion as I slowly sat down. 'Really? I hope you were being nice.' I smiled weakly at Jack, who had edged forward in his seat with interest.

'Joy was just telling me how you came to be in London.'

'Oh.' I nodded, suddenly relieved. There really wasn't anything ground-breaking or interesting about it. I had always wanted to come to London, and after years of saving the meagre wage from my dead-end job, I was no closer to my dream – until Nana asked Mum for a 'companion' and here I was.

'I said to Penny, my daughter, that I wouldn't let just anyone stay in my house. I would have to trust them, find them to be a good-natured, reliable person. Not words you usually associate with the generation of today,' Nana said, looking at me sideways. I was uneasy, worrying about where all these positive words were leading to until she finished her sentence. 'But I am lucky to have found it in Katherine.'

I paused mid-sip, looking at Nana as if she was a stranger. Maybe it was the influence of Jack's presence, but when she had said the words, I knew she had meant them. I could see it in the way she looked at me as if seeing me for the first time. My heart ached at the rare, and much-needed, moment of bonding. This was the first time she had ever said anything nice about me and I was so taken aback I could feel my eyes getting a little misty.

'Of course, I never would have believed it. Most young people are all about binge drinking and partying and all that nonsense so I was dead against her coming here at first, but when Penny assured me Katherine was different, it did give me some comfort.'

I smiled, sipping my tea and glancing over the rim at Jack, who raised his brows at me as if he were impressed by my character assessment.

'Of course, Katherine being a virgin certainly convinced me of her character.'

I spat my tea out, coughing and spluttering, my cup clattering onto the table. I could barely see through my watery vision as I tried to force my words out.

'What?' I croaked, my eyes wide with horror as Nana looked back at me calmly.

'Oh, don't get yourself all flustered, Katherine, you should be grateful to your mother for telling me, it sealed your fate.' She settled in her seat looking expectantly at Jack, who seemed frozen in place. 'So, as you see, Jack, I don't have to worry about Katherine bringing home strange men, or going out on the prowl.'

I WANTED TO DIE.

Taking advantage of the change in atmosphere, Vera interjected. 'Joy, I think we better take some of that pain medication, now that you've had something to eat.'

'Oh, bring it in here, Vera, I really don't want to . . .'

'Won't be a sec,' Vera announced, grabbing onto the wheelchair and moving her so quickly that Nana's protests were disappearing down the hallway.

Leaving me alone with Jack in stunned silence.

'I've slept with lots of men!' I blurted.

Jacks brows disappeared into his hairline.

'Oh God, no, not like that. I mean, I don't know where the hell that came from or why my mum, who I am incidentally going to divorce as my parent, why she would even say something like that, when I am most definitely not a vir—'

'Kate.'

Jack's voice stilled me.

'It's okay,' he said, so earnestly I didn't know whether to be relieved or concerned. Did he think I was lying, that I really was a virgin and too embarrassed to admit it? Oh God, there was no fixing this without digging myself into a deeper hole, which actually seemed like an attractive idea if it meant I could cover myself in dirt and hide from this mess.

'Listen, I'm going to go, can you tell your nan goodbye for me?' he said, placing his teacup onto the coffee table and standing.

Oh God, he could not leave like this.

I jumped to my feet to follow him into the hall.

'Jack,' I said, hating how panicked I sounded, and how completely blank my mind went when he turned to look at me, stopping just before the front door. I had nothing.

He broke the silence for me. 'So, are you ever allowed out on the prowl?'

I closed my eyes, grimacing. 'I'm going to kill my mother.'

Jack breathed out a laugh. 'Oh, I don't know, I wouldn't be too harsh on her. It sounds like it was a pretty genius way to get you here.'

I shook my head, more miserable than I had felt in my entire time here. 'Some days, most days, I wish I hadn't.'

Jack placed his fingers under my chin, forcing my eyes up to look at his, dark and serious. 'Well, Katherine Brown, I'm mighty glad you did.'

Chapter Sixteen

I suppose I should have sought permission. Respected the answer that I knew would be a no. I had felt the pangs of guilt in the pit of my stomach that day when I stole into Nana's secret room. But after her deliberate attempt to humiliate me in front of Jack, I suddenly didn't feel so bad about what I was about to do. In fact, I was damn well looking forward to it.

My credo: What the devil doesn't know, won't hurt her.

It raised an interesting question. As much as I was living a lie, tiptoeing around upstairs while I waited to access Nana's designer Shangri-La, I wondered: How honest was I going to be with my audience? Would a patched together, DIY vlog really build my empire, regardless of the priceless beauty at my disposal? I had seen enough endless vlogs on YouTube with bad lighting, crooked cameras, shoddy sound and cheesy cutaways and I didn't want my work to be like that. I had a unique treasure trove as my backdrop; I had to get it right. This was my opportunity, a time to

take it to the next level, to stop whining about my life
and create a new one. One that made me happy and kept
me busy, so busy that I was out of Nana's way and, more
importantly, out of Jack's.

If I wanted to avoid him before, Nana's 'confession'
of my virginity was enough to keep me away from him
forever. Simply hearing the purr of his Aston Martin
coming and going through the week was painful enough.
Another perk of Nana's secret room was that there was less
road noise, less distraction. My new normal saw me rolling
out of bed, faking my way through an elegant breakfast
spread with Nana and Vera, who had generously extended
her hours after the fall, before excusing myself to paw over
my now-typed ideas of what kind of blog I wanted 'Kate
on the Thames' to be, where I wanted to take it, and what
I wanted to achieve from it.

A tentative tap sounded at my bedroom door. I smiled
to myself, glancing at the time and knowing exactly who
it was and what the visit meant. Vera was predictable to a
fault, and I loved her for it.

'Come in,' I called, barely glancing up from my screen
as I touch-typed about vintage clutches. I heard the jingle
of Vera's tray before I saw her.

'You're still at it?' she asked, amazed.

'No rest for the wicked.'

'How about we get some fresh air in here.' Vera placed
the tea tray down before crossing the room to open up the
terrace doors.

'No, don't, it puts a glare across my screen.' I shielded my laptop, squinting at the intruding beam that appeared now that the curtains were drawn open.

'Well, turn around then,' Vera said, continuing to open the door, letting in a cool blast of air and the distant noise of street traffic. 'It's not good to be cooped up all day, every day.'

I slunk deeper into my chair with scowl. 'Well, I don't have much choice, do I?'

Vera crossed her arms and looked at me pointedly. 'You're letting a 78-year-old woman dictate your life? Really?'

I flinched at Vera's outburst, it was just so . . . not Vera.

'That 78-year-old woman just so happens to be the key to me staying in London.'

'In other words, she owns you.'

'Pretty much,' I said, directing my attention to my keyboard as I tapped away again.

'So what would happen if you walked out the door right now?'

I sighed; Vera meant well, but just because she was essentially a full-time carer now didn't mean she understood the dynamic between me and Nana, even if she had more to say about things these days. I kind of missed the days when she kept her thoughts to herself.

'It wouldn't be worth the worry, believe me.'

'So what, she would ask questions, glare at you, forbid you to go, insult you somehow?'

'All the above.'

'When's the last time you even saw the sun?'

'It's England, Vera, nobody has seen the sun all week.'

'You know what I mean,' she said, stepping out onto the terrace, shifting the chair and examining the space. 'It could do with a good clean out here, but this could work.'

I thought back to the last time I had stepped out on the terrace, and more importantly the reason why I had been avoiding it. I had managed a whole week of staying out of Jack's way, and in that week I had been more productive and more contented than ever before. I really didn't want to mess with that.

'Seems like your neighbour Jack sits out here far more often than you do.'

My head snapped up. 'What makes you say that?'

'Well, aside from the empty beer bottles, his space is quite clean.'

Curiosity told me to take a peek, but I held my ground, feigning indifference. Why should I care? I'd probably see the remnants of romantic candlelight suppers with his beloved; I was content to spare myself from that reality.

'I can't sneak out of the house like a teenager any more, Vera, those little windows of time are more exhausting and stressful than anything. I am better off just keeping out of the way and abiding by the rules.'

'And does that include raiding Joy's closet?'

I flinched, snapping my computer shut instinctively. 'Sorry, what?'

Vera sniggered, heading back to the bedroom door. 'Don't worry, Kate, your secret's safe with me.'

I slunk back in my chair, defeated. I had thought myself so clever, so secretive in my mission, and my cover was blown already. How could I be so careless? And now Vera knew – how long before Nana figured it out?

I pushed myself away from my desk, twirling around on my computer chair and moaning like a melodramatic teenager.

The doorbell pulled me out of my despair. It sounded again and I wondered who it could be, and if I should stay in my safe space.

No, Kate! You are not going to become this person. You are far too young to turn into a hermit, and your conversational skills aren't strong enough to talk to yourself forever. Get a bloody grip.

I had almost convinced myself that I was a well-rounded, confident person who was capable of anything, when Vera's voice called up the stairs.

'Kate, it's for you!'

Chapter Seventeen

I had fought so hard to avoid that smile, tried my absolute best to wipe it from my memory, and tried not to overthink the meaning in the last words he had said to me. But despite all of my efforts, Jack Baker stood at my front door, looking up at me expectantly and holding a very big box.

'Don't look so excited,' he said.

I came to stand next to Vera, my narrowed eyes trying to decipher the label, but not getting very far: it was in Chinese.

'Unless there's a puppy inside, I'll try to contain myself.'

'Well, let's hope not, I don't see any air holes,' he said, lifting and examining the box.

My attention shifted from the box to Jack, waiting for him to shed some light on the object in his arms, and his presence in my foyer. A huge mistake, because watching his mouth break into a blinding smile was enough for me to forget all about the bloody box, and his bloody girlfriend . . . well, almost.

Jack's eyes flicked to the box. 'It was left on my door-step, but it's for you,' he said, tilting it to the side to reveal 'Kate Brown' printed in black marker on the top.

'For me?' I asked as Jack dumped the deceptively heavy box in my arms. I made a valiant effort not to think about just how strong his beautiful arms must be to have held it aloft for so long. I struggled with the parcel, more confused than ever.

'Did you order something?' Vera asked, trying to examine the label.

'No, I haven't . . . ah! My lighting!' I carefully placed the box on the ground and began tearing at the gaffer tape. 'I don't believe it, I ordered this weeks ago, I'd completely forgotten about it . . .'

I paused mid-tear, looking up at my captive audience, who were poised for the big reveal. I had ordered a video studio lighting kit from eBay weeks ago. I had been so inspired and excited to do this for real, to vlog like a pro, and now it had arrived, just when I needed it the most. Now I was truly ready for my very first shoot; procrastin-ation and delay were no longer a possibility, the time was now. 'Kate on the Thames' was ready shoot!

'Lighting?' Vera questioned.

'Ah, yeah, just some heat lamps, you know, for the cold winter months ahead,' I said, standing and dusting my hands off.

Jack looked at me as if he wasn't buying it. 'Heat lamps?'

'Yes,' I said, pushing the box aside with my foot.

Jack folded his arms and leant against the door jamb. 'You have been pretty reclusive lately – you're not operating an illegal drug trade from the attic, are you?'

'Don't be ridiculous,' I scoffed.

'Well, not in the attic anyway, is it, this secret business,' Vera chimed in.

I cut her a dark look. So much for her keeping quiet. My secret didn't feel safe, not with Jack's and Vera's obvious curiosity; my anxiety only worsened when I heard Nana's cut-glass voice slicing up the passage.

'What is all this racket? Honestly, I can't hear myself think.' She limped along the hall, her walking stick clunking more heavily these days. Vera and I stepped instinctively in front of the box like a couple of naughty school children.

'Look who's here, Nana, Jack from next door!' I said, a little too enthusiastically. I watched the oily mechanics of her brain work. She was probably thinking of another humiliating story to share at my expense.

Sensing the same thing, Vera stepped forward.

'Kate was just about to head out for a bit.'

Wait, what?

My attention snapped to Vera, my eyes boring into the back of her head as she came to stand next to Nana.

'Where?' Nana asked, instantly agitated by the thought of my going out into the world, a world that, until now, I'd had no intention of visiting today.

'Oh, just with me, Joy, we won't be long.' Jack's voice from over my shoulder had me turning so fast I almost tripped over the box.

'What are you doing?' I hissed.

Jack simply winked before holding his arm out as if he wanted me to take it.

'Well, Nana Joy, you always said that unless Kate had a reliable chaperone . . .' Vera added helpfully.

Nana weighed up the image before her, as if deciding just how evil she was going to allow herself to be this morning. As much as I dreaded my forced expedition with Jack, I was relieved that she was at least distracted from the box at my feet.

'How long will you be?'

My shoulders slumped. For the first time, I had wanted Nana to object, to forbid me to go. Now she was actually going to give me permission, with the one person I had been trying to avoid? Bloody typical.

I felt Jack's hand at my arm, slowly guiding me toward the door.

'You don't have to worry about a thing, Joy, Kate's safe with me,' he said.

And as I stepped begrudgingly through the doorway, catching the cheeky grin from Vera, I glanced at Jack and mumbled under my breath.

'I don't know about that.'

Chapter Eighteen

According to Jack, there were many more ways to experience London, other than a red phone box selfie and a rushed fish 'n' chip pub lunch.

He gave no hint to our destination; we simply walked along the shop fronts of Gloucester Road, leading down onto the corner of Palace Gate and Kensington High Street. We veered away from the high street, crossing the main road and making our way through the gateway past an ice-cream stand, where, with a knowing look, Jack went over and paid for two vanilla and boysenberry ice creams.

'It's not a proper summer walk without ice cream melting over your knuckles,' he said, handing me a waffle cone.

I took a moment to sneak a look at this man, a man who was trying to win me over with ice cream. Our walk had been fairly awkward, most of it in silence, so I'd focused on taking each step, one foot in front of the other.

We walked into the park, along the gravel paths, under the trees, past all the adorable dogs and leading up to the grand, sweeping grounds of Kensington Palace, the jewel in a green crown.

'I can't believe you've never been here! The royals are practically our neighbours,' he said, standing before a circular pond dominated by an impressive marble statue of an eighteen-year-old Queen Victoria in her 1837 coronation robes.

'I feel like a such an underachiever,' I admitted, crunching on the end of my cone and staring up at the statue.

Jack laughed, his ice cream long gone, his hands pushed deep into his pockets. He tilted his head, indicating for me to follow.

'This way.'

We cut across a corner of lawn, momentarily seeking refuge in the shade of the plane trees, before walking toward ornate black-and-gold gates. Kensington was the perfect backdrop at the end of the long gravel drive. An imposing, uniform block of red-and-brown brickwork and windows galore overlooked the immaculate green, sprawling lawns that flanked either side of the drive. I gripped the gates, smiling at the majesty of the place, until I was asked to step aside so a couple of tourists could take a happy snap.

Ordinarily I would have also been jostling for a photo op, but it occurred to me: I live here.

This is my neighbourhood . . . and I don't know anything about it.

A beautiful oasis of quiet and calm in the centre of the city, west of The Serpentine, where centuries of royals had taken a stroll, and it was just around the corner from my home; did it get any better than that?

'Are you hungry?'

My attention snapped so quickly I didn't need to give an answer. Jack was already laughing at me.

'Well, all right then, this way.'

~

Surrounded by the beautiful evergreen grounds of the palace, we sat at a table in The Orangery, which was once the setting for Queen Anne's sophisticated court entertainment, with soaring ceilings and classical eighteenth century architecture. My heart and smile lifted as our Royal Afternoon Tea was delivered to the table. I tried to be cool, like it was no big deal, but my widened eyes roamed over the selection of tiny sandwiches: smoked salmon and cream cheese, Coronation chicken, roast ham and English mustard, cucumber and fresh mint; not to mention the orange and currant scones with Cornish clotted cream and English strawberry jam and the piping-hot pot of Earl Grey. The situation was made more surreal by Jack's large hands reaching for a dainty sandwich. He paused mid-chew, cocking a brow in question. I simply shook my head and smiled.

'Thank you,' I said.

Jack began to chew again, watching me. 'What for?'

'For breaking me out. I certainly never predicted my day would end up like this.'

'What? With cucumber sandwiches?'

'Not in the least.'

Jack looked at me for a long moment. 'Kate, can I ask you something?'

'Hmm.'

'Have you been avoiding me?'

I froze in the act of spreading strawberry jam on my scone, and straightened in my chair. 'What makes you say that?' I asked, trying to keep a lightness to my voice.

'Because you looked physically pained at the thought of going for a walk with me,' Jack said, filling my empty cup with hot tea.

'No, I didn't,' I said, grabbing my cup and taking a noisy sip.

'Wow, you don't even realise you're doing it.' Jack sat back in his seat, his eye tracing over me in silent assessment.

'Doing what?'

'You get this little line that pinches between your brows.' He pointed, causing me to touch the place in question.

'Well, probably because I'm constantly terrified about what will come out of Joy Ellingham's mouth. I'm going to need a serious dose of Botox after living with that woman.'

I rubbed the line I could clearly feel under my fingertips; yet another thing to worry about.

'Oh, come on, she's not that bad.'

I scoffed. 'Oh sure, for you, maybe. It's not as easy as you think, you know.'

'Nothing is,' he said.

A silence fell between us, and in spite of the beautiful surrounds and the pretty feast before me, I was angry at Jack and his lack of understanding. It was a complex situation: to be here in London, among the history and the culture and the fashion, I had sold my soul to the devil, only to be told I wasn't allowed to get out and see the city nor experience all that made it special. Lord knew what the repercussions would be when I got home after my outing.

'I'm a prisoner, Jack. She owns me, that's the harsh reality; this is the first ounce of freedom I've been permitted, and it's only because I have a chaperone. I'm like a freakin' flower in the attic,' I said glumly, looking into the milky recess of my teacup.

'Bollocks!'

My head snapped up, my eyes darting to a lady left of me, who was pursing her lips and turning away in disgust. 'What?'

Jack leant over the table. 'I said—'

'Yes! Yes, I heard what you said.' I quickly stopped him from saying it again; that word in a setting such as this was utterly disrespectful. We already looked completely out of place: me with my broad Aussie twang, trying not to stare in open-mouthed wonder at my surroundings, partnered by a giant of a lad sipping on tea and buttering scones.

Jack smirked, slow and casually sexy, as he pressed his back against the chair.

'You choose to be a hermit.'

'And why would I do that?'

Jack breathed out a laugh. 'You tell me.'

I simply stared at him, desperately trying to not let my brows knit together. I wanted to remain serene, but Jack was pushing all of the right buttons. Yes, I had been avoiding him, and it was more than just embarrassment: that had merely been the excuse. I was doing what I always did, I was shutting down and removing myself from temptation; nothing good could come from liking a man like Jack Baker, a man I knew little to nothing about, except that he had a stupidly glamorous girlfriend who was probably wondering where he was.

'I wouldn't expect you to understand,' I said, averting my eyes from his.

'Jesus, you really are throwing yourself a pity party; look around you. Take in the sunshine, bask in the glory of the vast, open spaces, the food in your belly, the ridiculously good-looking man sitting opposite you.'

I laughed. I didn't want to; I had been so used to seeing the worst in everything I didn't know how to turn that around and see past the gloom.

'Are you always this optimistic, Jack Baker?'

A boyish smile lit his face as he snared a pastry from the tray, saluting me with it. 'Only when I'm sitting across from a ridiculously good-looking woman.'

And there it was again, that flirting, suggestive banter that played with my head. I know it was a warm summer's afternoon, but it was Jack's words that were heating my face as I reached for the milk to keep my hands busy. I was at a loss how to respond.

'My point, Miss Brown, is that you have to live a little. So you had a bad day, week, month or whatever: just live in the moment, enjoy your environment, build memories worth something. Spread your wings.'

'Okay, well, I might just have to climb over to your balcony in order to do that,' I quipped.

Jack's eyes flicked up from his tea and only then did I realise how incredibly suggestive that sounded. I instantly regretted my choice of words.

'As in, a means to escape from my house,' I added quickly.

'Hey, it's okay,' he insisted. 'Any time you want to climb over my balcony is all right by me, my door's always open,' he teased, stretching back in his chair and looking at me in a devilish way that seemed just as inappropriate as saying 'bollocks' in Queen Anne's court.

My lips twitched while I looked at Jack, knowing how he loved to tease. I shook my head – it was just his way. It didn't actually mean anything.

'Oh, sod off,' I said in my best South London accent, which had Jack breaking into uproarious laughter. Most of the patrons turned in their chairs to look our way, but this time I didn't care, I loved the sound too much.

Jack leant forward, placing his elbows on the white linen. 'Well, Miss Brown, we could make a local of you yet.'

Chapter Nineteen

We strolled in comfortable silence under the warm summer sun. We made our way through the ever-green cradle walk, an arched arbour of red-twigged limes that afforded views of the sunken central garden while taking the bite out of the heat of the day. Contentment was a word I rarely had cause to use these days, but standing here with Jack, I felt it. I felt it deep in my bones, taking in the full measure of what he had meant by living in the moment, forgetting about the dramas in life and just simply living. I knew that the minute I returned home, my anxiety and gloom about my everyday reality would return, but I shook my mind away from all the things that were set to tear me down. Instead I turned to Jack, about to comment on my momentary peace, but his eyes seemed to focus on some distant concern, a million miles from here. He was definitely not practising what he preached.

'Jack?'

Still caught in his thoughts – thoughts he didn't seem to want to share – his eyes ticked over my face, searching for an anchor in my inquisitive stare.

Was he nervous? Surely not Jack Baker. But then, I had never seen him act this way before.

'Kate, can I ask you something?'

His words hung heavy in the air, and the sun seemed to go behind a cloud, causing my skin to prickle. What could make him be so intense? Was he in a witness protection program? Have a secret family sleeping on mattresses in his flat? My eyes searched his face, my lack of response encouraging him to continue, because I was too afraid to voice my assent question, worried about what he might say.

Just as I thought he might tell me, something in him shifted, the moment gone as he smirked in a way that wasn't wholly believable.

'Never mind, it's getting late, we better head back.'

And with those words, the beautiful golden hour of late afternoon fled, and I felt a little afraid: of going back home; of not seeing that usual spark in Jack's eyes; of what he had wanted to ask me; of the words still left unsaid.

'Okay,' I said, making a concerted effort not to seem worried; I wanted to keep my mood light and carefree. Lord knew I would have to put on an Academy Award-winning performance walking back into the house as it was.

Leaving the grounds to the joggers, dog walkers, tourists and bike riders, the scenery changed from lush and peaceful greenery back into uniformed London city-scapes. Though Jack chatted animatedly on the way back to Onslow Gardens, I still couldn't quite shake the memory of his troubled eyes and the fact he had wanted to ask me something. It haunted my thoughts as we finally closed in on our neighbouring terraces, pulling up short of my steps.

'Well, the curtain isn't parted, Nana's not keeping a look out for you, so she mustn't be too worried,' said Jack.

'Don't be too sure; Nana has an impressive tendency to find drama.'

'Is that where you get it from?'

I laughed. 'Oh, piss off.'

Jack laughed, so loud I was worried Nana might hear and the curtain might very well peel back. I shut down my rambling mind and tried to focus on the here and now. Gazing up at the rather lovely looking Jack Baker, getting lost in the depths of his smiling, dark eyes, I almost let all my troubles melt away, until inevitably, he opened his mouth and ruined everything.

'Do you want to come up?'

'S-sorry, what?'

'I said, do you want to come up?' he repeated, amused, as we stood out the front of his infamous red door.

'Oh, I, um, don't know, I should really be getting back.'

Jack stepped forward, his hands by his sides. 'Live in the moment, Kate.'

Looking into his challenging expression I knew that he was right. That I could either go home and be a recluse, or I could – wait a minute . . . Go upstairs . . . with him? What about the Amazonian girlfriend?

I swallowed, weighing up my options, then shook my head. He was definitely trouble – trouble that had to be avoided at all costs. I tried hard to think of a way out, even though I didn't really want one.

'I think I'll pass.'

'I must say, you're the least enthusiastic woman who has ever been offered a trip up my stairs.'

I threw Jack a knowing look. 'Been many, have there?'

Jack grinned broadly, a sparkle of mischief in his eyes. 'Well, I'm not a virgin, if that's what you mean.'

I rolled my eyes. 'Goodbye, Jack,' I said, turning and walking up my own steps, leaving Jack and his uproarious laughter behind.

'What? What did I say?' he called after me, but I didn't dare turn around, I was too determined to hide my smile, going through my front door and closing it behind me.

Chapter Twenty

The house was cast in darkness, save for the late afternoon light that filtered in through the parlour and down the hall from the kitchen. I was afraid to hear voices, because it meant Vera and Nana were around and I'd have to engage in conversation, when all I wanted to do was go upstairs and try not to let Jack dominate my every thought. With each step I took to my room on the second floor, I fought the urge to go through the forbidden door at the end of the landing and surround myself with beautiful things to lift my mood. But as I came to stand at the top of the stairs I realised that, despite everything, I already felt a warmth inside me and it had nothing to do with handbags or vintage dresses and everything to do with remembering Jack's boyish grin, the way his eyes lit up ordering an ice cream, his fussing over the Cocker Spaniel in the park and asking the elderly owner a series of questions. Jack had a way about him, a genuine warmth, a light that I just didn't see in anyone else. And although I tried to deny it, each day I hoped that, even if it was just for a brief moment, our paths would cross. He made me feel better and, on some level, that scared me. I didn't want to rely on someone to make me feel better, it was so much easier to lock myself away and seek comfort in things: things couldn't hurt you or answer back, or break your heart. This was what Tom Hanks must have felt like in that movie *Castaway*, but if I painted a face on one of Nana's designer bags and called it Wilson I suspect that would mean I had reached my limit. Yeah, probably a good idea I had gone for a walk with Jack, I thought.

Everything was going to be okay.

The day had ended well enough, rather spectacularly really, until Jack had spoiled it by inviting me upstairs. Still, I was ever so proud of myself for saying no because, despite rejecting his invitation, I really, really wanted to say yes.

Yep, you are going to be okay, Kate. Just fine. You did good.

Dropping my bag inside the door of my bedroom with a sigh and feeling the tension in my neck, I rubbed the ache as I shut the door behind me, switching on the light and . . .

'HOLY SHIT!' I jumped, clutching my heart at the sight of Nana in my chair, waiting expectantly with her wrinkled hands clasped together, sitting in the muted light like a figure from a nightmare. I glanced behind me, confused.

'How did you . . .'

'Manage the stairs?'

I nodded.

'Oh, Katherine, I am not a complete invalid, I can do things for myself.'

There was a horror building inside me at the thought; I much preferred the idea of old, frail Nana Joy. Her decrepitude kind of made her nastiness more forgivable – she was just old and jaded. But as she sat in my room, her clear blue eyes staring me down, she looked a figure of health. What had driven her up here? Was it to bond with me, to listen to me and indulge my recollections of a lovely day out? Doubtful.

I tried to remain calm, stoic even, but if she expected me to welcome her with open arms, she would be bitterly disappointed. Instead I did my absolute best to keep my eyes away from the desk where my notes and laptop sat, betraying all of my plans for 'Kate on the Thames'. I felt instantly nauseous.

'Did you have a nice time?'

Was I wrong? Could she really be up here to establish some kind of connection with me on friendly turf?

'Um, yes, yes . . . it was a nice day for a walk.' I was completely out of sorts; having Nana in my room was strange enough, but having her apparently interested in my day was just downright bizarre. Her lips were twisted and she was looking around the room as if avoiding my eyes.

'Yes, well, I've been thinking,' she said.

Here we go . . .

My insides twisted; anything that drove Nana literally to my door couldn't be good.

'Oh, what about?' I pressed, trying to keep my voice light, despite the fact that my heart was beating so fast and loud I swear Nana would be able to hear it across the room.

'Hmm?' Her brows rose as if she hadn't heard me, even though I knew she had. 'Oh, just a few things,' she said as she grabbed for her walking stick. 'I don't think it's healthy for a young girl to be spending so much time alone and inside. It's not natural.'

I had tried to keep a neutral expression but it was an impossible feat; there was nothing that could mask the look of shock on my face. Had Vera said something? I was afraid to hope that this was my chance, the permission slip, the acknowledgement that perhaps Nana had been a little overprotective.

'So, things are going to change around here, Katherine.' Nana nodded as if resigning herself to an uncomfortable truth, and my heart soared.

This was it, this was the key to the city. Oh, I couldn't wait to tell Jack, to make plans and see if he wanted to be a part of them, to have him show me the sights. 'Kate on the Thames' would reach spectacular new heights. I was so excited, only just resisting the urge to dance on the balls of my feet.

'Aw, Nan,' I said, wanting to hug the hell out of her, I was so grateful. Grateful she had gone to the trouble to make her way up the stairs, willing to let go even though I knew it wasn't in her nature to do so. In that moment, I loved her, bloody loved and appreciated her, despite everything that had happened before. Jack was right, Nana Joy wasn't so bad after all.

'I thought on Tuesdays we could go to the lunchtime bingo with Cybil, she could use some time out too. On Wednesdays we could go shopping with Vera, but that would be only fortnightly because we will over-shop and that's a waste of good money and will just encourage us to eat too much, and you certainly don't need that. On Thursdays, well, the crossword sections are particularly challenging and there is nothing like a good cup of tea and some stimulation for one's brain. Weather permitting, we might even have tea in the garden. On Fridays . . .'

And it went on, and on, and on . . . Every day accounted for, excursions here, there, everywhere. A full, almost jam-packed agenda, from morning tea to afternoon naps. With each elderly activity listed, a little piece of me died. I was going to become Nana's wingwoman; I had to fight the chunks that threatened to rise in my throat. I was about to go from a nearly contented recluse to living the life of a Golden Girl.

Sure, before I left Australia I had envisioned market shopping in Notting Hill and afternoon tea at the Ritz with my nana, but that was before, when I thought she was a glamorous socialite with a whip-smart sense of humour and a kind heart. The nana I had come to know was nothing like that. I suddenly felt hot. I pulled at my collar and moved to the balcony doors.

Nana missed nothing. 'What's wrong, are you ill?' she snapped.

'It's a bit hot in here, don't you think?' I pulled open the doors and took in a deep breath.

Oh God, this is not happening, this is not happening.

'Well, get some rest, we have a big day tomorrow.'

My head spun around so fast I almost got whiplash. 'Tomorrow?'

'Yes, the ladies from Richard and Judy's book club are coming over to discuss some ghastly book about *refugees*.' Nana pronounced 'refugees' with obvious distaste, and this was the very reason I couldn't spend any more time than was necessary with this woman. I could feel myself breaking out into hives at the thought of spending my days with her.

Nana squinted at me, her piercing blue eyes boring into me as if she was expecting me to say something, an objection maybe; surely she wasn't expecting enthusiasm? I wasn't that good an actress.

'Yes, tomorrow. Sorry, am I tearing you away from something of importance? Sleeping-in, watching TV all day, joogling?'

'Joogling?'

'Yes, joogling!' She mimed me pressing my phone.

'Oh, GOOGLING.' I laughed.

'Don't be a smart mouth, Katherine, or I'll ship you back in the crate you came in.' Her words were like acid and she glowered at me, as if looking for disobedient thoughts to burn out of me.

I sobered in an instant. What could I say? I had nothing, there was no getting out of this hell. I was more trapped than ever and I could feel my heart plummet, and a cold sweat begin at the base of my spine.

'Tomorrow sounds good,' I lied.

I saw the effect of my words: they rolled over Nana and instantly defused the bomb. Her edges softened, and she nodded her head in one curt movement.

'Tomorrow, then; now help me down the stairs, Katherine, you dragging me up here is no good for my ankle, honestly.'

I followed Nana out, repressing my sigh and the fleeting evil thoughts I had.

Help her, Kate, don't push her.

Chapter Twenty-One

'Now remember, Vera, I am coming down with something that is ghastly and contagious and I really don't want to infect anyone.'

Vera's head tilted as she folded washing, her knowing eyes taking in the baggy dressing gown that engulfed me. 'Do I even want to know what you are up to? No, actually, don't answer that, I don't want to incriminate myself any further than I already am.'

'I just don't want to be disturbed.'

Vera's eyes trailed down my robe to the pretty antique rose-coloured marcellina heels I was wearing, a stark contrast of glam against my robe. 'Oh, I think you're already disturbed,' Vera teased.

I sighed, shaking my head. 'You have no idea.'

If I was going to be subjected to Nana Joy's book club I would be more than disturbed – I'd be certifiable.

'I guess the real question is, should I be worried?' Vera

asked seriously, gathering the pile of laundry and dumping it on top of the washing basket.

'Of course not,' I said, tightening my robe and glancing at the clock, aware that the sleeping dragon would soon be stirring. 'Just having a me day,' I said, proud of myself for thinking of such an excuse to escape today's fate. As for the rest of my life, I wasn't sure what I was going to do, but for now I felt flooded with relief. That is, until an infamous voice sounded down the call.

'Vera!'

Boom-boom.

'Where's my tea?'

I flinched, startled by the shrill sound of her voice, the echo of walking stick on floorboard. I had to get out of here.

I carefully side-stepped past Nana's closed bedroom door.

'Look who's awake,' Vera said. I brought my finger to my lips, rounding the stairs, quickly and quietly making my way up, peeling off my robe to unveil the outfit I had been dressed in since the sun came up. I tried not to think about how crazy eager about my day that had made me look; still, no one had to know, and they certainly needn't know I had agonised for near on an hour over the selection of said outfit. I had finally settled on my favourite metallic multi-dot skirt and black rosette sweater, a stark contrast to the blonde braid that fell over my shoulder. My Marcellina heels might have set off my outfit but, as

I only just realised, my audience weren't going to be able to see my shoes.

My audience.

Just thinking about it brought butterflies to my stomach. I picked up my notes from my desk, bundling them into my arms and tiptoeing across my room and through the door, closing it behind me. I paused as I peered down the stairs, a new fear raising its ugly head, remembering how Nana had made her way up them despite her bad ankle. It made what I was doing all the more dangerous – she could come and find me at any time. It was what made the timing of today's shoot all the more important: I had to be in and out and done while she was distracted. I opened the door to the secret room, allowing myself a moment to take in the sight before me. The lighting stands had been erected and the lamps strategically placed and tested. I felt positively giddy, seeing how incredible the backdrop of Nana's beautiful belongings looked on camera, the baby blue of the shelves and the stark white of the cornices; the only other colour came from the twinkling golden beams of the crystals from the chandelier and the rainbow line of the clothes themselves. I shut the door behind me, and set up my station for the day. I had already taken some footage and still shots to edit for the intro, and had allotted myself four hours to make as many episodes as I could, allowing enough time to change my clothes and hair between takes and alter the setting a little, in an effort to make out each video was shot on a different day.

It was the perfect crime.

I sat in the chair that I had borrowed from Nana's dressing table in the next room; it was pale pink and incredibly plush. I felt like a queen on her throne ready to share my world with the world wide web, even if it was going to be somewhat of a lie. I decided not to mention that the pieces belonged to someone else; I was simply sitting in a room filled with beautiful things, offering case studies and 'favourites' segments in order to provoke discussion. No one had to know that my real life was far less luxe than this. None of my family or friends knew of my blog, and that was exactly the way I wanted to keep it. No one would connect my blog with the real Kate, the one imprisoned in her nana's spare room, lusting after her neighbour – the man she could never have. No, sitting down, pressing record and confidently smiling through my introduction and backstory about my love of fashion, food and travel, I knew the world would see a different Kate Brown, the one I wanted them to see. I would become the confident, know-ledgeable, interesting 'Kate on the Thames', because for now, as I held up one of Nana's brown alligator bags, which I had teamed with a pair of 1940s-inspired brown block-heeled shoes and a well-cut, inky-blue blazer, I suddenly felt alive. This was me, this was what I wanted to do, this was living in the moment.

Chapter Twenty-Two

A hand waved in front of my face.

My attention flicked up from my laptop screen, confused, until I saw Vera's angry face, her finger to her lips as a gesture to be quiet. She glanced back at my bedroom door, ever watchful, as I peeled off my headset.

'Are you deliberately trying to get caught?'

'Sorry?' I double-blinked, thinking how meticulous I had been, taking out the lighting equipment, returning everything to its rightful place, including the borrowed chair. I had even wiped down the glass vanity and cabinetry, careful to remove any fingerprints; no stone was left unturned. It was like I had never been there, despite the evidence I was now editing on my computer.

'Could you slam the door any louder?'

I blinked, trying to cast my memory back, and how I had stumbled through my bedroom door with my arms full of the clothes I had changed into for each episode, frantically kicking the door closed behind me. 'I did, didn't I?' I winced.

'Ah, yeah, the whole house shook; I had to make out that I didn't hear anything.'

'Oh, right, sorry,' I said, still in a bit of a daze.

'Are you okay?'

I looked back at Vera, my eyes wide and my smile broadening as I sat forward in my chair and took the headphones off my neck, trying to contain my excitement.

'Oh Vera, I had the best day!' I said.

The sternness etched across Vera's face melted away. 'Well, I am pleased to hear that. It was worth sacrificing the book club, then?'

I cringed, thinking about the event I had managed to escape.

'Did Nana ask about me? Was she desperately concerned for my welfare?'

'Well, she didn't say a lot.'

'You can tell me, you know, I have developed a rather thick skin.'

'Well, not according to Nana Joy, who said you were just like your mother and your grandfather: no backbone, just soft underbellies.'

I laughed, thinking back to all of my near-on meltdowns in the face of Nana Joy's wrath. I certainly wasn't as strong as her, or as well put together as my mum, or likely to be held in such high esteem as my granddad, but I liked to think I would go down in history for something more than histrionics. Maybe that was why I was passionate about blogging, about leaving a mark on the planet no matter how superficial it may seem. Or maybe I was just hopelessly materialistic and desperately vying for attention like Nana.

God forbid.

'Well, I'm glad you had a good "me" day.'

'I did!' I beamed, excited at the possibility of making this all work, that I could be truly happy here, in my own way.

'All right, but maybe try to have some dinner downstairs tonight, I can only keep Joy at bay for so long.'

The smile fell from my face. 'I'm pretty sure I would still be deemed highly contagious.'

Vera tilted her head. 'Kate, please.'

'Okay, I'll come down.' I sighed, feeling suddenly weary.

'Oh, and Kate.'

'Hmm?'

'You might want to wash the make-up from your face and look a little bit more . . .'

'Miserable?'

'Yes, let's go with that.'

I nodded. 'Give me two-point-five seconds in Nana's company and I doubt I will even have to pretend.'

~

I cleaned my room, showered, and dined with Nana, who was in fine form, sipping on her small glass of sherry.

'I am not going to lie, Katherine, but when you were born, I was bitterly disappointed.'

Vera choked on her water, glancing at me as if she regretted subjecting me to this. But something was happening, some new strange feeling was growing inside me that had me grabbing for my own drink.

'Is that so, Nana? Well, that's no good,' I said, relaxed and unconcerned. Vera was looking at me as if she was afraid that I might snap at any moment: the calm before the storm. But it wasn't like that – I just felt nothing. Nana's words couldn't hurt me anymore; instead, my mind would simply go back to my happy place, the world of my blog. And any time I thought about the beautiful world I'd constructed, there was nothing Nana could say to alter my mood.

'Katherine, are you still unwell? You have the most frightfully dopey expression on your face – are you on drugs?'

'I'm just high on life, Nana; in fact, what have we got planned for tomorrow? Bridge with the girls, a matinee at the theatre perhaps, or are we knitting mini jumpers for orphaned penguins?' I asked, leaning my elbows on the table, knowing how much it annoyed her.

Nana seemed a bit unsettled when she looked at me. 'Katherine, I think you should go lie down, you're not well.'

'Maybe you just need some fresh air, Kate, you have been cooped up all day,' Vera said, wiggling her brows.

Maybe that's what I needed. Perhaps I'd had a little too much artificial lighting for one day. I glanced at the time. It was near on six; Jack would be home soon and fight it as I might, even on a good day he dominated my thoughts. It was going to take some time to shake him from my mind. Still, there was a part of me that wanted to tell him that I had been living in the moment, and I was more than happy for him to flash me that sexy smirk and tell me 'I told you so'; in fact, it would kind of be the icing on the cake.

I stood up from the table. 'I think I might just sit outside for a bit, read a little maybe. Can you recommend a good book, Nana?'

Nana scoffed. 'Well, Richard and Judy certainly have no idea.'

I stifled my laugh. 'Fair enough, I'll just grab something from the shelf then.'

'Why don't you read in the back garden, it's much safer,' Nana called after me.

'Oh, it's okay, I don't mind watching the world go by,' I said, choosing a random novel and heading for the door.

It wasn't until I was settled on the little stoop out front that I started to doubt everything. Would I seem like a complete stalker if I was sitting out front waiting for him?

No, no, I was on my doorstep, not his. A girl is allowed to read random literature from the comfort of her own doorway, for God's sake. I quite looked forward to reading . . . I flipped the book over in my hands.

'Oh, dear God.'

It was some kind of pirate romance novel; the cover featured a shirtless Fabio and a buxom blonde pawing at his trousers, looking up at him longingly.

'Jesus, Nana. You dark horse, you.'

This would not work, not at all, my street cred would not recover from being found reading *Shipwrecked Hearts*. But I couldn't bear the thought of going back inside to find a replacement, and figured it might at least prove amusing, so I opened to the first page, clearing my throat and sceptically reading on.

By chapter three I was hooked; by chapter six I was biting my thumbnail, turning the page eagerly to see if Calypso Chesterfield would be thrown in the ship's dungeon in shackles by the evil Lord Roman, or be rescued by the dashing dark lord of the seas, Alessandro Riviera.

'Come on, Alessandro. She can't live without you!' I mumbled to myself.

'Who's Alessandro?'

Jack's voice made me jump, and I instinctively slammed the book closed and chucked it into the pot plant next to the door. My attempt at subterfuge was unsuccessful; it took Jack the longest time to tear his amused eyes from the pot plant, while I tried to give off an air of cool detachment, inspecting my nails and crossing my legs.

'Oh, hey, Jack,' I said, inwardly screaming at how ridiculous I allowed myself to be.

'You all right?'

I loved how his Londoner accent came out at times like this, making me unsure whether he was saying hello or legitimately asking if I was okay. I went with the latter.

'Yeah, you all right?'

Jack stood there, holding a plastic shopping bag at his side. He looked tired, breathing out a weary sigh as, to my surprise, he came up the steps and sat next to me.

Here was Jack Baker, clad in a dark grey suit, loosening his tie while deep in contemplative thought. I couldn't help but feel my heart skip a little at the sight of him, even if he seemed a little out of sorts.

'Please don't tell me you've locked yourself out,' I joked.

He gave a small laugh. 'Now wouldn't that be something,' he said, without lifting his eyes. My own smile fell slowly, a chill running over me that came not from the night air but from the cold feeling of Jack's dark mood. I didn't know him, not really, but there was something unnerving about his mood, and in the way he didn't look at me. Maybe he was just tired from work, or maybe he'd had a fight with his girlfriend, but it just didn't feel right; the longer the silence drew out, the more concerned I was.

I titled my head to the side, trying to gain his attention. 'You okay?' I asked, seriously. I knew it was none of my business, and I should probably just leave him alone, but when I saw his shoulders rise and fall as he inhaled deeply, I knew I wasn't going anywhere.

Like approaching a wild animal, I had to move carefully, not wanting to spook him. I slowly crossed my ankles while my eyes took in the darkened shadows of his face before quickly turning my gaze to the street.

Don't stare, Kate. This isn't the Spanish Inquisition.

I had no idea if I was overstepping a mark or making a fool of myself, but it didn't seem right to leave.

'Bad day?' I pressed, dreading how lame it sounded.

Say something smart, Kate, something funny but insightful.

'Something like that,' he said, without so much as a sideward glance. Maybe he just wanted me to be quiet?

'Well, at least you didn't have to fake a sickie to get out of Richard and Judy's book club,' I joked. I got no response, not even a chuckle. Nothing was breaking through the wall he had put up. I didn't know what else to say, I was out of lame jokes and the silence was just painful.

I looked out across the street. We were lucky enough to have the Onslow Gardens at the front of our terraces, an urban green space plunked down in the middle of the city. There were little patches of such glory throughout London and this one was ours.

Moments passed and for the life of me, I couldn't think of anything that would lift the mood. I settled for chatting randomly to the point where he probably wished I would shut up, even if he didn't say as much; he just sat in silence, staring at his hands, listening. Well, at least I think he was listening.

'I have a sister, Catriona, it's just me and her. She's seven years older than me, living in Canberra. Married, two kids. Maddy and Oliver.' I rattled off the information, dying a little inside as I cemented my place in history as the most boring person alive. Before this evening, at least I had a bit of mystery about me, but now I was revealing myself as either batshit crazy or incredibly dull. Clearly my socialising skills were desperately lacking – perhaps I could do a class? But I couldn't help it, Jack made me nervous and it just wasn't his silence, it was him. His presence was intense, the way his broad frame filled the majority of the space on the steps. We were tucked in a little alcove out of the elements and I could feel the heat of his body next to mine, and when he shifted, the side of his leg would press against mine and I would lose my train of thought. The feeling was so intimate that I began to blabber nervously about my dad's rainfall readings from last winter and then I really, truly wanted the ground to open up. God, how was he still here, how could he stand my blathering? I fell silent again before the next pearl of wisdom hit me.

'My sister's married. A nice, sensible banker named Paul, who is very strait-laced if not slightly emasculated by my sister. You see, she is very strong-willed, independent – she even hyphenated her maiden name with her married name, which turned out to be most unfortunate.' I smiled to myself just thinking of it. I was ready to let the silence fall on my chatting, I was getting used to it now. Then I heard Jack's voice.

'Why was it unfortunate?'

I turned to him, and for the first time that night he looked at me. His eyes stared into mine and I wanted to blush from it, feeling that he was looking right into me.

'My sister married a Chinese–Australian whose last name is spelt Ai but pronounced "eye",' I said, waiting for his reaction.

Jack's eyes narrowed as if he didn't understand.

'My sister is now Catriona Brown-Ai.' I grinned because I couldn't help it; thinking about it always made me laugh, even after all these years. It seemed Jack wasn't immune either; as realisation dawned on him he smiled, big and beautiful. Finally, my interminable ramblings had the desired effect.

'Mrs "brown-eye"? Now, that is most unfortunate,' he agreed, chuckling. And just like that, I saw that the old Jack was back . . . for now.

I revelled in the victory of his smile, and decided not to push any further. Again, Jack Baker, the very person I swore I would stop thinking about, managed to find out more about me, while he became ever more enigmatic. It was beyond frustrating, not to mention completely humiliating, that after an hour of complete rambling he knew all he could ever want or need to know and I was left with more questions than ever. Questions that, even this morning, I had sworn I cared little about. I really didn't want to feel this way – to have my heartrate spike every time I saw him, to feel my mouth dry whenever his arm brushed against mine. I hadn't felt this way in a long,

long time, not since the unrequited love of Jake Miller in Year Twelve, the very boy who had broken my heart when he pashed Cassandra Barton after the valedictory ball. Sure, there had been other boys since then, but not until now did I feel that same, unmistakable tingling inside. I was doomed.

Jack rustled through the plastic shopping bag at his side and produced two brown bottles of beer, twisting off the tops and handing me one. I pressed my lips together, feeling like a sixteen-year-old once again, sneaking a beer from the boys before a school social. Taking it felt wicked, exciting – ridiculous, considering the many drunken nights I'd had back home. I tried not to think about the feel of my fingers brushing Jack's as I took the beer from him, confidently taking a deep swig of it. I could feel his eyes on me as I did so, watching to see if I enjoyed it. Despite the amount of time we had spent on the doorstep this evening, me telling Jack every meaningless detail of my life besides my tax file number and shoe size, the beer was still surprisingly cold, though bitter. I was more of a cocktail or sweet wine drinker, but I was determined not to wince at the hoppy aftertaste. I'm an Australian girl after all – I have a reputation to uphold. I used the beer as fuel, liquid courage to finally voice my thoughts.

'We should have a balcony party!' I blurted out, apropos of nothing and nowhere near the subject matter I had hoped the alcohol would give me the strength to raise.

I blamed the proximity of his strong thigh, the feeling of it touching mine, and how difficult I had found it not to think about that fact. But once the words were airborne there was no reeling them back in, no turning back the time, no matter how desperately I wanted to.

Jack looked at me closely, his expression a mixture of confusion and amusement as he tried to understand what I had said. Oh God, please don't make me repeat it, I couldn't bear it. My cheeks were red enough, and the way he was smirking at me made me want to die a thousand deaths.

'A balcony party?'

I glanced down at my fingers peeling the label off the beer, trying to disguise my embarrassment.

'Yeah, I actually had a really good day today,' I confessed with a small smile. Despite my random ramblings, somehow I'd managed not to mention about my act of 'living in the moment', which I may not have had the guts to do if not for his pushing. I was proud of all I had achieved today and wanted to share it with him, to thank him, but there never seemed to be a right time.

So what? You suggest a balcony party? How is it the right time for that?

Jack took a swig of his own beer, his mind working as he tapped out a light tune on the bottle.

'Maybe some other time, yeah?' he said, looking at me for a long moment. I'm sure I stopped breathing as I tried desperately to read him. Just when I thought I saw something in his eyes that suggested he might actually close the distance between us, Jack stood, offering his hand to help me up.

'Yeah, sure,' I said, placing my hand in his and making sure my dress didn't ride up as I stood. I was on the steps above him now and we were, for the first time, face to face, which felt odd and strangely intimate as we looked at one another.

'Maybe some other time,' I said.

Jack smiled while I continued to stare into his eyes, looking for some kind of meaning. I didn't realise I was still holding his hand until he squeezed it.

'Goodnight, Kate,' he said. I blinked out of my trance, slipping my hand away from his.

'Goodnight, Jack.'

Jack reached for his bag just as the front door opened, casting us in a strip of light from inside. I quickly turned to hide my beer – if Nana Joy saw me drinking on the step, out of a beer bottle no less, I'd never hear the end of it – only to catch a knowing smile from Vera.

'Oh, sorry to interrupt. It's time for me to head home.'

'Of course, yes, thank you, Vera,' I stammered, still flustered and foggy from the miasma of Jack's gaze.

'Nana's in bed, I think she'll be sound asleep by now. The mundane affair of book club really took it out of her; in fact, I dare say she will be out cold,' Vera said, glancing between the pair of us in a not-too-subtle hint.

'So have a nice night, you two. Kate, I'll see you in the morning, maybe sleep in a little, until you fully feel better, that is.' Vera winked, tapping me on the arm before walking down the street.

Jack's brow furrowed, turning away from Vera to look at me. 'Are you not well?'

I bit my lip, excitement coursing through my veins.

'Actually, I've never felt better,' I said, a devilish twinkle in my eye.

Jack gave a cautious smile, like he didn't quite know how to take me.

'What are you looking so smug about, Miss Brown?'

I took a deep breath. 'Jack Baker, do you want to see why I had such a good day?'

'Okaaay.'

I smiled, wondering if it was the beer or the knowledge that Nana was off in the land of nod that made me so brazen. Either way, Jack seemed to be affected, too; I sensed a new lightness in him as I pressed my back against the door and grabbed the handle. 'Do you want to come up?'

Jack's brows lifted as he looked from me to the terrace behind, a little crooked curve to his mouth.

'Geez, you don't have to beg, Kate,' he said, stepping up to the door with a glint in his eyes. The old Jack was definitely back.

My stomach flipped; I was nervous and excited all at the same time, knowing that once I invited him in, there was no going back. I twisted the handle and looked up at him.

It was all he needed. He slung his bag over his shoulder and followed me inside.

Chapter Twenty-Three

I felt like I was sixteen again. Sneaking a boy into my bedroom, leading him up the stairs, wincing as I forgot to avoid the squeaky step, and putting my finger to my lips for Jack to be quiet. Holding his hand, I led him into my darkened room, quietly closing the door. Jack was merely a shadow next to me, albeit a very imposing shadow.

'Wait here,' I whispered, padding my way to my bedside, turning on the lamp and filling the room with a glow. I turned around, wringing my hands together as I felt the nerves return. Sure, I had been confident on the doorstep but now I had him here, in my room, standing next to my bed . . . well, that was a whole other story.

Jack placed his bag on the floor next to the door and, holding my eyes, clicked the lock on the handle. 'Just in case,' he said. 'Not that I think old Joy will be barrelling through your door in the middle of the night.'

'Don't be so sure, she can get around when she wants to,' I said, glancing at the very chair I had found her in last night. A shiver ran over me.

'Are you cold?' he said, standing next to me and tugging inquisitively at the thin fabric of my tee. By all rights I should be, but if anything, I was burning up next to Jack, scalded by the way he was looking at me. In my fantasies, Jack and I would have barely made it up the stairs; instead, we would have been clawing and kissing and pulling our clothes off, or tumbling against the bedroom door and having crazy, passionate door-sex. But the reality was somewhat different, mainly because, in my fantasy, Jack didn't have a girlfriend and I was a different person: a femme fatale who wasn't afraid to undress with the light on. For all my insecurities, I might as well have been a virgin. I felt so stupid. I couldn't even look up at him without blushing furiously. Jack must have sensed the change in me; gone were the sexy smiles and arched brows.

Sure, do you want to come upstairs to . . . what? Stand awkwardly in my bedroom? Rock 'n' roll.

I blinked, trying to gain some momentum in my mind; what had I planned to show him? I knew what I wanted *him* to show *me*, but mentally slapped myself, brushing past him to get to the opposite side of the room, the somewhat safe zone. I placed my beer on top of my desk and flipped open my laptop, typing in my password and clicking into my folders.

'It's not very good. I mean, I've only done a quick edit on the first episode,' I lied, vividly recalling how many hours I had spent agonising over every minute detail. 'So it's still pretty rough.' Another lie, I was actually really proud of the end product. I brought up the video, aware that Jack had placed his beer next to mine and had his hand on the back of my chair, the other resting on the desk as he leant over my shoulder, peering at my screen.

God, he smelled good.

'So this is the blog?' His words snapped me out of my daydream.

'Ah, yes! Yes it is, here,' I said, reaching for my headphones and plugging them into my laptop. 'Sit,' I said, standing and stepping away from my chair, holding them out to him. Jack's gaze flicked down to the headset with interest, before slowly taking it from me. I couldn't let the headphones go, my hand refusing to release as the nerves and doubt threatened to overtake me.

'The thing is, um, I've never done anything like this before, I mean, like, vlog; I mean, I have blogged, but, like, nothing serious, nothing that meant anything. I don't really have a following yet, I know I said I was a writer, but I guess it's more that I *want* to be a writer, and maybe I was trying that whole *The Secret* thing, where you will something into being by saying it . . .'

I was rambling again, I knew I was, when what I really wanted to say was, 'Please don't mock me and crush my dreams.'

I don't know if Jack got that vibe, but he gently peeled my fingers off the headphones with a wink. 'Grab another beer.'

I nodded, yes, of course. Great idea.

'Do you want one?'

'Please,' he said, pulling on the headphones and making himself at home at my desk. I walked back to the plastic bag by the door, pulling out two beers, my back still turned as I twisted the tops off, trying to keep my breaths even.

What are you doing, Kate? Why are you showing him, of all people? You might as well wake Nana up and get her to come have a look too, you bloody lunatic.

I straightened and turned, all but ready to tell Jack I had changed my mind when I realised it was too late.

Jack's beautiful face was lit by the flickering of my computer, his dark eyes fixed to the screen, a smile across his face. I didn't dare move, for fear of distracting him from the show. I slowly placed his beer in front of him but he was oblivious, so I edged away until the back of my legs hit my bed and plonked myself down, sipping on my beer. I watched Jack's face transform from thoughtful to intrigued to, dare I say, compelled. He even laughed, twice, and I had to think back to what could have been so funny. Was he laughing with me or at me? I shifted on my mattress, thinking how incredibly long my video was; it certainly hadn't felt that long when I was editing it, nor, for that matter, when I was in front of the camera. Maybe he had reduced the window and was watching funny cat videos on YouTube instead? As self-doubt continued to spin my brain into fairy floss, Jack pulled the headphones from his head and sat back in his chair, looking at me like he'd never seen me before.

I rolled my empty beer bottle in my palms, waiting for him to say something, anything. 'Don't give up your day job' or words to that effect; instead, he was laughing, shaking his head.

'Oh God, what?' I said, straightening my back and preparing for the blow.

'Where did you film this?'

I bit my lip, cringing at the question. 'Do you want to see?'

~

It was a big risk, but all the same, with my finger pressed against my lips, I gestured for Jack to follow me through the bedroom door and up the hall, stilling before the secret room. The one place that worked to calm me like nothing else, even if it was with the one man who had quite the opposite effect on me. I carefully turned the handle, smiling over my shoulder as my heart beat out a frenzied tattoo.

'This is intense,' he whispered, which only caused me to smile even bigger.

'Behold a thing of beauty,' I said, before pushing the door open, flicking the light on and revealing 'Kate on the Thames' HQ.

I thought that maybe I had been enamoured by the space because, well, I was a girl and I like pretty things, but as I watched Jack edge his way into the room, his eyes trailing along the shelves and to the glass-topped counter, I could tell that even he was taken aback. The constant wonderment I experienced in this room was reflected in his wide-eyed gaze.

'No wonder you've been missing.'

I grinned, a weight lifted from my shoulders; for the first time I was able to share this with someone, and funnily enough, it was the last person I ever suspected.

Jack moved to peer over the jewellery under the glass in astonishment.

'Is all this yours?' he asked.

Oh shit. How to kill happiness with one question.

I gently closed the door behind me. 'Ah, no, not exactly.'

'Nana Joy's?'

'Yeah.'

'Please tell me she has all this insured.'

'Um, I don't know the details, I just use this room and these things as a form of inspiration for my blog. I know I shouldn't but—'

'Be damned you shouldn't! Do you have any more videos?' Jack turned to me, his eyes alight with excitement.

'Um, yeah, I have been filming all day, but I haven't edited them or anything.'

'Kate, you've got to get them out there, you have to show the world "Kate on the Thames".'

I could feel the heat creep up to my cheeks. 'Well, I've only shown you so far.'

Jack came to stand before me, looking down at me intensely. 'Well, that's got to change.'

'Yeah, I know but—'

'Kate.'

My eyes flicked up to his, and I was once again lost.

'Your vlog is brilliant.'

I smiled blindingly wide. 'Really?'

'Really. It has everything it needs to work, Kate; if you want, I can help you.'

'Know much about beauty and fashion, do you?'

Jack laughed. 'Not so much, but editing and video content? Now *that* I know.'

I folded my arms. 'Do you work in IT then?'

Jack smiled. 'Something like that.'

'What is it that you do exactly, Jack?'

Jack rubbed the line of stubble at his jaw; the question seemed to put him on guard. 'Oh, you know, a typical white-collar job that affords enough stress to down a few beers on the neighbour's steps after hours.'

It was as good an answer as I was ever likely to get. He was lucky: ordinarily, I would have pressed for more, but right now I was distracted, excited.

'So you're pretty handy with web content?'

'Very.'

'And you really want to help?'

'You said you had more footage?'

'I do.'

Jack nodded. 'Well, let's see it.'

'What, now?'

'Weren't you listening to my speech the other day? Do I have to say it all again?'

I breathed out a laugh. 'No.'

Jack reached for the door. 'Then let's get "Kate on the Thames" on the map.'

Chapter Twenty-Four

had been so deeply impressed with my own editing prowess, but my skills were nothing next to Jack's. He turned the bones of my first episode into something slick and polished while discussing the importance of having a website and social media presence outside of my blog.

'We'll get you on Facebook and Twitter so we can link it to your site and blog as well.'

'Well, I have an Instagram account.'

'Excellent, this stuff was made for Instagram,' he said, his hands dancing over the keyboard, his eyes flicking frantically across the screen. 'Do you have a business model?'

'What's that?'

'Like a plan of what your goals are, what you want to achieve.'

I smiled, leaning in front of him to retrieve an array of scrap papers and the smudged coasters from the Stanhope Arms from my desk drawer, plonking the pile down in front of him. 'Somewhat, yes.'

Jack laughed, picking up a scribbled-on serviette and examining it. 'Well, it's something.'

I studied Jack's profile, marvelling in his enthusiasm, his apparent belief in what I was doing. He had energised me in a way that had me thinking that maybe this could be something. Then my enthusiasm dampened a little as I realised I hadn't told Jack what I was doing was a secret.

'Jack, my nan mustn't find out about this. I know you probably think it's ridiculous being so paranoid and secretive when it comes to her, but this is the one thing that's my own, it's something that I can do that she can't touch, or make me feel bad about it. I would kind of like to keep it that way.'

I thought he might have argued the point; instead, he shook his head. 'She won't find out. The world will know, but we'll keep Nana in the dark.'

I blew out slowly, nodding in relief until my attention strayed to the clock on the screen.

'Holy shit, Jack, it's three a.m.'

'And so it is.'

'You better go get some sleep, you have work tomorrow.'

Jack rubbed his eyes, stretching his arms to the ceiling. 'Indeed.'

'I'm sorry, I didn't mean to enslave you into working on fashion blogs all night. I'm sure you had better things to do.'

'It's fine. I'm excited for you. I think you have the foundations of something really good here, Kate.'

'You really think so?'

'You care about the content, the attention to detail and the product you're putting out, all the key ingredients for a successful blog. But there's just one last thing.'

'What's that?'

Jack grabbed my hand and pulled it across the desk, placing it over the mouse. 'You gotta press publish.'

I swallowed. 'Maybe I should just go through it one more time . . .'

'Kate, push it.'

'Really?

Jack slid his hand over mine, entrapping it and watching as I closed my eyes, silently counted down and pushed 'publish'.

'Kate on the Thames' was out in the big bad world!

~

'Where are you going?' I glanced back from the bedroom door to where Jack was opening the terrace doors.

'Taking the shortcut,' he said, as if it were the most obvious thing in the world. I closed my door and quickly followed him, always nervous of more death-defying climbs on the ledge.

'Be careful!' I said, perhaps a bit too loudly.

Jack lifted one leg over the barrier, then the other, looking back at me with a huge smile.

'Why, would you miss me if I fell?' he teased, edging sideways, but still waiting for my answer.

I folded my arms. 'No, but your girlfriend might.'

Jack stilled, his brow creasing as he looked at me.

'Watch it,' I said, snapping him back to his task. Now was definitely not the time to be distracted.

'What are you talking about?'

'I saw the Amazonian brunette going into your house.'

Jack appeared genuinely perplexed, like he was searching through the archives of his mind. God, how many supermodels did he take home that he had to think about it? I was starting to get mad and was ready to call it a night – or rather a really early morning – when a sudden flash of realisation lit his face. 'Oh, her.'

'I don't know; is "her" a six foot bombshell with legs up to here?' Seriously, how could he forget her? I know she haunted my memories.

Jack laughed, really loud, hooking his legs back over the divide, until he sat precariously on the edge.

'Jack,' I said, pleading for him to keep it down, but all he could do was shake his head and howl with mirth, rocking back and forth. Against my better judgement, my instinct had me moving forward to grab his jacket, tugging it with great annoyance.

'Stop it, you'll fall.'

Jack's smile curved into something else, his eyes searching my face, and a sudden stillness came over him as he sobered at my words.

'Maybe I already have.'

'What?'

Jack stood then, towering over me, forcing me to look up into his eyes. Dark and stormy they were, studying every line of my face as if committing it to memory, while my blood heated under his gaze. I so desperately wanted to kiss him, for him to kiss me, here on the terrace, the early morning still covering us in darkness, but with just enough light flooding the balcony so I could read every gorgeous line of his face. Right in that moment I had never wanted anything more than to have his lips on mine and the flicker of something mischievous in his eyes had me believing that he had somehow read my mind. I could tell by the way his cocky, sexy mouth creased at the corner as he moved closer, lowering his head, never taking his eyes from me as he hovered so, so close I could feel the heat of his breath against my lips. So agonisingly slow was his approach I almost expected him to pull away, but he didn't, though it gave me just enough time for the rational part of me to object.

'Jack, I really don't think—'

Jack kissed me. Cutting off my words, pulling me against him, he kissed me so passionately that I found myself gripping the edge of his jacket with a white-knuckled intensity, anchoring myself in case my legs went from underneath me. Jack's hands moved to cup my face to gain better access to my mouth, coaxing me to open for him. And I did, gladly, letting him taste and tease and take what he wanted, before he pulled back, allowing me to draw in some much-needed air. My eyes searched his, wondering if he regretted what he had just done, afraid that I might see something in him that would tell me as much. So when his mouth curved in all the right places, I was overcome with relief. The butterflies in my stomach danced as his thumb brushed against my cheek; his erratic breaths falling over my face.

'I don't have a girlfriend,' he said, before moving to kiss my forehead and pulling away, walking backward with a knowing smile, clearly amused by my shocked face, kiss-swollen lips and flushed cheeks. I watched him step over the side and manoeuvre his way across to his balcony like a seasoned trapeze artist. I didn't dare breathe until his feet hit the floor of his terrace and he turned around, wiping the invisible dust off his pants and elbows with a huge grin.

'Sweet dreams, Kate.' Jack winked, opening his door and disappearing inside, leaving me standing there in complete and utter bewilderment, staring at Jack's closed balcony door. I slowly lifted my hand to touch my tender lips, barely believing it was real, before breaking into a smile, my mind rolling the event over and over again on a constant loop of disbelief.

Jack Baker didn't have a girlfriend.

Chapter Twenty-Five

And so my life changed, though not in the way you might have guessed. I was not ensconced in a fairy-tale romance with Jack, nor had Jack's kiss magically turned Nana Joy into a frog. In fact, from the outside, you could argue that everything looked much the same; my days consisted of 'bonding' with Nana, ignoring her nasty remarks and putting up with her temper tantrums (often at the crossword – 'the puzzle-writers aren't what they used to be, Katherine. Twitter is what birds do, not people'). And yet, even at her worst, her words seemed to merely roll off me; I refused to let them lodge themselves in my mind and erode my confidence like they may have done before. I simply smiled and ignored her, which I am sure just made her more determined to upset me but, try as she might, I was untouchable. Because, come night-time, she went off to Nana Napland and I became 'Kate on the Thames' and the fulfilment it gave me was life-changing:

blogging, editing, building my networks on social media, working on my business plan; I finally had a purpose.

And of course, I was also kept rather busy daydreaming about Jack's tongue in my mouth – oh yeah, that! Kind of hard to forget. For the entire week following, I found myself reading on the front stoop, waiting for Jack to get in from work so I could update him on my progress.

Wednesday: 'Twenty-four followers, Jack.' I beamed, sliding Nana's embarrassing romance novel into the pot plant as I stood.

Jack smiled. 'Excellent.'

Thursday: 'Thirty-one followers and two comments.'

I wasn't entirely certain that Jack was as excited to hear about my daily updates as I was to tell him; I'm sure he didn't come rushing home from work to find out the goss, and come Friday, when I was all ready to update him that I had an amazing fifty followers (halfway to triple figures!), he was nowhere to be seen. Six p.m. rolled into six thirty, then seven; by 8.40 p.m. I had resigned myself to the fact that he was either not coming home, or maybe had drinks after work, most likely with people far cooler than me. He hadn't mentioned anything last night when we'd sat on the steps, talking about when I was going to upload my next video. He seemed interested, engaged in my conversation, but then doubt set in. Maybe I was being too forward, too obsessive – he probably dreaded coming home after a long day's work (wherever that was) to have me pounce on him with me-me-me. And since the night on the balcony he never moved to kiss me, or invite me up to his, or sneak into mine once Nana had gone to bed; it almost seemed like the kiss never happened, like it didn't mean anything to him. Maybe it didn't, maybe I had finally gone mad. I sat there, torturing myself with those very thoughts, and inhaled a deep, steadying breath.

Nope, it was time to back off a little. And as the weekend went by, I busied myself with more filming and editing, and planning out the next week. Come Monday, I didn't sit out the front of the terrace, despite having reached a hundred followers and wanting desperately to tell Jack about the milestone. I held strong; instead, I sat stoically at the dinner table, watching Nan as she scowled and grimaced, pushing around her food like a fussy toddler.

'This is awful.'

'Nana,' I warned.

'Oh, don't worry about my feelings, Kate; according to Nana Joy, I don't have any.' Vera gave me a sly little wink. I was glad to see that Vera was being a little more feisty these days; between the two of us, we were determined not to let Nana get away with being so rude. Well, not entirely get away with it.

'How can I be expected to eat this? It has no flavour,' she complained.

I rolled my eyes, sinking my fork into the creamy and flavoursome mashed potato, when my phone vibrated in my pocket.

Eek, new follower!

My spirits were instantly lifted. Even though I knew better than to take my life into my own hands by checking the notification at the dinner table, curiosity got the better of me when the phone vibrated once more.

'Excuse me, I just have to go the bathroom,' I said, sliding out from my chair.

'Are you finished, Kate?' Vera asked, reaching for my plate.

'Yes, and thank you, Vera, it was utterly delicious,' I said, throwing a pointed look at Nana, who simply harrumphed.

Things had slowed down somewhat over the past few days; I had only hit one hundred and four followers. Despite my newly uploaded vlog exploring vintage accessories and the perfect shade of red lipstick to keep on hand, there wasn't anything happening, no new comments or likes. I tried not to be disheartened about it; after all, this was always about me and my passion – sharing it, yes, but if people weren't interested, would I stop? No, of course not. I started to believe that maybe Jack's earlier enthusiasm might have been a little misguided; despite doing all the things I had set out in my business plan, including developing a website, Twitter account and Facebook page, and investing a tiny amount of my savings in Google Adwords, things were still pretty quiet. Maybe the fashion and travel scene was just too crowded for a newbie voice like mine to be heard. After all, what did I really have to offer? A great wardrobe, sure, but not one that I had any part in creating, some nice lighting and a dearth of industry experience. I was lucky to have found one hundred and four people interested in listening to me.

Well, I'd be grateful for every last one of them, and I couldn't resist looking at my phone to see if I'd found one more like-minded soul. I closed the bathroom door behind me and leant against the vanity, clicking into my email notification to find that my blog had a new comment.

'Ooh, hello, anonymous,' I said, following the link that guided me to the comments section.

'Oh my God.'

I blinked, once, twice, my gaze lifting up to see the reflection of my mouth agape as I reread the message over and over again, barely believing what it said.

'Surely not,' I said, reading it once more.

Anonymous says:

Balcony now!

~

'Honestly, you are the most sickly child I have ever met; then again, maybe Vera gave you food poisoning.'

I blew out an impatient breath and turned away from Nana. 'Vera, you did not give me food poisoning, I assure you.'

Vera lowered her voice so Nana couldn't overhear. 'Let me guess, some "me time"?'

I hid my smile, thinking how well Vera could read me. 'Something like that.' Or at least I hoped so as I excused myself from the dinner table and bounded up the stairs, skipping every other one. Breathless, I burst through my bedroom door, turning on the light to see that everything was as I had left it, but it wasn't the room that held my interest. Intrigued and fighting to control my breathing, I went to the terrace door, edging the curtain aside and opening the door just wide enough for me to step through, then stopped.

There, on top of my small balcony table, was a line of flickering tea candles, a cold beer placed on either side, and a small plate of biscuits, soft cheese and strawberries. Silver ribbons fell down from the roof, brushing against my face – they were attached to at least a dozen balloons, one of every colour.

'I thought it was about time we had a balcony party.'

I turned toward Jack's balcony. There he stood, holding a singular red balloon with '100' written on it. I laughed, covering my mouth, barely believing that any of this was real. Jack once again climbed over to my balcony with the greatest of ease, closing the distance between us and handing me the balloon with a huge grin.

'Happy one hundred followers,' he said.

'One hundred and four, actually.'

'Oh bollocks. See what happens when you're not around to keep me in the loop?'

'You want to be kept in the loop?'

Jack pulled a balloon string away from my face and

stepped closer. 'I don't party on balconies with just anyone, you know.'

I stared into his eyes for a long moment and, maybe it was the sparkle of the candlelight, but there was something reflected there. I turned away from him reluctantly, taking in the scene before me.

'Wow, this is amazing. I am very impressed, and slightly horrified, at how you managed to cart all this over here.'

'Well, don't worry, I stashed nothing down my pants,' he said, lifting up a small esky from under the table.

'Oh, happy days!' I said.

Jack pulled the chair out for me, like it was our first date, while I move around him, awkward and nervous. On the other hand, well, Jack was as confident as ever. I could never imagine him being unsure of himself.

'Are there plenty more where this came from?' I asked, lifting my beer up.

'Why, yes, there are.' Jack reached for the esky, drawing out another bottle.

I knew I would have to pace myself; I was by no means a tank when it came to alcohol, but I did need a little help to loosen my inhibitions. I could already feel it taking effect as I snared a strawberry from the bowl and bit into it, looking at Jack all sexy and suggestive, until juice ran down my chin.

'Oh shit,' I said, wiping it away with the back of my hand and cringing at the mess.

'Yeah, they're pretty juicy.' Jack laughed, finishing the last of his beer and reaching for another.

'I'm sorry, I just don't know how to do this.'

'Do what?'

'This, us, any of it.'

Jack seemed troubled, like something was rolling around in his mind but he didn't know how to put it. 'Kate, are you . . . a virgin?'

'What?' I said, my voice high enough to shatter the glass on my balcony doors.

'Because, you know, it's totally okay if—'

'No, Jack, I'm telling you, I am not a virgin!'

Jack looked at me as if he wasn't totally convinced.

'I'm just awkward. And when I'm around you, I can't think straight, and when I'm not I . . . I . . . I have very impure thoughts,' I said, taking a deep swig of my beer, mainly to prevent myself from talking. Christ, since when had this turned into a confessional?

Jack grinned broadly. 'Do you?'

'Oh, don't sound so pleased with yourself.'

Jack looked delighted, and I knew that I had said too much. Running my mouth off was one of my more painful quirks and one that, unlike pimples and a love of boybands, I unfortunately had not left behind at high school. I was mortified, and braced myself for Jack's laughter. But he didn't laugh; instead, he placed his beer down and turned to me, his eyes dark and heated. It was enough to make me shift in my seat and hope that he would say something, make a joke to ease the tension. I simply sat there staring back at him. Maybe it was the alcohol, or an attempt to regain some ground after my humiliating confession, but when he pushed his chair back, crooked his finger and said, 'Come here,' I lifted my chin defiantly.

'You come here.'

Jack rolled his eyes. 'Must everything be an argument with you?'

I giggled, admittedly loving the game we were playing. I placed my hands on the table slowly. The sound of my chair legs scraping across the floor was painfully loud, but I didn't care; instead, I walked around the small table, never once taking my gaze from his. I came to stand beside Jack's chair, running my hand across his forehead to brush the hair from his brow, looking into the face of the man I couldn't get out of my head. I felt the warmth of his hand slide up my outer thigh, drawing me closer to him as I brushed my finger along the soft bow of his gorgeous mouth, watching it break into a sinfully sexy smile. Only then did I realise something that I had dared not hope for, something I felt with the utmost certainty when I looked into Jack's eyes.

I wasn't afraid anymore.

Chapter Twenty-Six

moved to sit on his lap until his hand stilled me, touching my hip. My heart stopped.

Oh god, had I misread the signs?

But no, it seemed that Jack had a very different interpretation of lap-sitting, as his hand ran down my thigh to the back of my knee, pulling my leg over his so I was straddling him. Sliding my hands over his shoulders and linking them around his neck, I could feel the searing heat of his hands on my hips, and the hardness pressed between the junction of my thighs, my breath hitching at the pressure as Jack shifted in his seat. Reading my reaction, he did it again with a big grin, a movement that incited the most delicious kind of torture, and he damn well knew it.

I breathed out. 'You're a bad man, Jack Baker.'

'A bad man who can do very good things,' he said. He slid his hands down my thighs, and up again, this time skimming a slow, deliberate line under the material of my skirt, just enough that his fingertips grazed the elastic edge of my panties, only to pull away again, in an agonising dance. It was like he was playing me, watching my face and reacting accordingly. I bit down on my lip, locking down my traitorous body and trying my best not to let him see how he was pressing my buttons. But who was I kidding? If he wanted to play games, then game on.

Without taking my eyes from him, I lowered my lips to brush against his, so close but not touching, as I moved to his earlobe to whisper,

'What kind of things?' I rocked a little, feeling his chest expand, giving me a surge of power, knowing that I had incited an almost painful pleasure in him.

Hmm, this was fun.

I lifted my head and saw the rawness in his eyes, felt it in the way his hands gripped harder at my skin. Jack went to answer, but instead I placed my finger over his lips and shook my head.

'Don't tell me,' I said. Lowering my hands, I reached for his, sliding them up my thighs, under my skirt and to the edge of my dampened panties. 'Show me.'

And with those two simple words Jack sat upright in his chair so fast the legs scraped against the floor, his mouth on me like a brand, his hands digging into my hip bones, drawing me closer to grind against the hard length of him. All inhibitions were gone. It was like the fantasy had become a reality, except so much hotter, feeling Jack's tongue in my mouth and his eager hands peeling my panties aside, sinking one finger, then another, inside me and capturing my gasps with his mouth. My body demanded his touch, encouraging him as I rocked against his hand. There was nothing innocent about me now, nipping at his mouth and encouraging him with words I couldn't quite believe were coming from my mouth.

Who was I? What wanton soul had taken over me? I couldn't get enough of him, and thankfully he was eager to please.

He pushed deeper inside me, his rhythm faster; I had to grip his shoulders to anchor myself, begging for him not to stop, to go faster, deeper. And Jack obliged, looking up into my face and drawing me down to him, stifling my cries with his mouth as I came hard against his hand. My body went limp and I draped my arms over Jack's shoulders as I panted against the dampness of his neck. The only thing that I was truly aware of was the throbbing between my thighs and the beating of our hearts.

If foreplay was that good with this man, what would sex be like? A breeze blew across my sweat-dampened skin and despite the warmth of Jack against me, I shivered. Jack pulled his hands from between my legs and wrapped his arms around me, cocooning me in his embrace. I sighed, completely contented by the after-orgasm glow and the buzz of a few beers. I had found a new happy place, and it wasn't locked behind a secret door filled with pretty things.

I closed my eyes and nuzzled against Jack's neck.

'Kate?' My name sounded deep, and vibrated against my cheek.

'Hmm?' I managed with a smile.

'I've got to go.' And just like that the record of birdsong in my head scratched and came to a complete stop.

I lifted my head, looking into his eyes. 'Why?' What was it with this man and running off? Was this whole evening some kind of elaborate booty call? Cop a feel and then go off into the night, with a don't-call-me-I'll-call-you? Was he really just one of the lads after all? I tried to stay calm, even while my insides twisted.

Jack smiled. 'Because if I go back into that room with you, it's not sleep that I'm going to want.'

My insides unravelled a little. I played the innocent card, although I don't think he bought it. 'Why, what do you want to do?' I teased, and as I shifted a little I could feel the hardness underneath me. I bit my lip and waited for him to reply.

He breathed out a laugh, gritting his teeth as I moved again. 'Oh, the things I want to do to you,' he confessed. 'So either I go or stay.' He swallowed hard. 'The choice is yours.'

I tilted my head and looked down at him. He was so desperately trying to control himself, to make out that he would be cool one way or another and, as much as it was fun torturing him, I couldn't deny what I wanted, nor what I knew he wanted. I felt it pressed between my legs. So as I got up from his lap, watching him wince as if in pain. I didn't say a word; I simply grabbed his hand and pulled him up, leading him through the balcony doors and over to my bed.

~

Keeping quiet was an impossible task. I could only pray that Nana had taken her hearing aids out. There was no way I was able to control what was coming from my mouth, or the sound of my bed. Just when I would begin to worry about the noise we were making, Jack would do something wicked to my body and the ability to care was lost in my own cries.

'Shh,' Jack whispered against my thigh.

I lifted my head from my pillow. 'Well, if you're going to put your tongue there, there is no way I am going to be silent.'

I felt Jack laugh against my leg, before crawling up my body, his arms caging me in with his hands resting on either side of me. 'How about we change tactics?'

'What, you think you can do a better job at keeping quiet?'

'Oh, I know I can,' he said cockily.

'Right, we'll see about that,' I said, pushing against his chest so he rolled onto his back. Giving him no chance to adjust, I took him into my mouth, deep.

'Holy shit!' he cried out, his hands fisting in my hair, his chest heaving in shock as he looked down on me taking in the long, hard length of him.

'Oh Christ, Kate, I'm going to come if you keep doing that,' he said, pushing at me to stop before he did. I smiled, feeling rather victorious at just how much he couldn't keep it together.

'Wow, that was so weak,' I said, laughing at his 'efforts' to be quiet.

Jack shook his head. 'Is that so?' he said, snaring me around the wrist and pulling me down the mattress, tickling at my rib cage and making me squirm and kick.

'Jack, please, no no, stop it, stop it!' I cried, now more fearful that my begging and cries could be heard back in Australia, let alone downstairs.

Jack's laughter died down as he caught his breath and stopped tickling me. He lay between my legs, the rise and fall of my breasts pressing against his bare chest, pushing my hair away from my flushed face as I looked back up at him. A silence fell between us but, unlike our evening on the steps, this time it wasn't awkward and I didn't want to fill the space with distractions. I was happy to let it linger, to look into those brown eyes and be lost in them. Aside from our laboured breaths and pounding hearts we lay there, unmoving, until Jack slid his hand down my rib cage in a touch that was slow, tender. His hand traced the curve of my breast, squeezing the bud, and watched me as I pressed up into his fingers, wanting more, needing more. He pulled away quickly, reaching for his pants, and before I could wonder at his departure,

Jack pulled out his wallet from the crumpled trousers, retrieving the square foil tucked inside.

He wasted no time tearing it open with his teeth, glancing up at me briefly before he sheathed himself with the condom. Jack came back to his previous position on top of me, staring down at me, studying my face, making me feel so wanted just with a single look. And then he kissed me, softly, delicately, like he was committing the curve of my mouth to memory, before exploring deeper. My fingers combed through the waves of his hair, losing myself in the kiss, until I felt him press between my thighs, pushing ever so gently. He edged his way deeper, inch by inch, causing my breath to hitch, before, in one smooth glide, he thrust inside me. He captured my cry with his mouth, as he stilled his hips to let me adjust to the size of him as my nails embedded half-moon crescents in his hips.

Jack rested his forehead against mine, seemingly overwhelmed by the connection, adjusting as much as I was; he slowly slid out of me, all the way to the tip before thrusting gently back. Looking into my eyes as he fucked me, so deeply. I felt it build deep in the pit of my stomach as his pace slowly built to a faster rhythm. He tore his eyes from me only so he could watch where we were connected, the slickness of our bodies, the way he looked inside me as I rocked my hips up into him, wanting it harder, faster, and begging for him to not stop as I felt myself move close to the edge. I knew he was close too, the veins in his neck bulging as he pistoned his hips faster, crying out and grabbing onto my breast, squeezing and fucking me into oblivion. The bed head thumped loudly against the plaster, and I came so hard I didn't think I could take it, his satisfaction tipping me over to my own. In his final frenzied pumps I bit into his shoulder, stifling the cries, crashing, falling so deeply into a chasm of sensation that I didn't think I would ever get myself out. Any ability to think, talk, move was all but lost to me as the weight of Jack's body anchored me, still connected in the most delicious way, thinking I could so easily come to love a man like this.

And just as quickly as the thought came I brushed it aside, instead choosing to live in the moment, lying in the arms of Jack. Tomorrow, and whatever might come with it, seemed a whole world away, so for now I would stay right here and breathe.

Just. Breathe.

Chapter Twenty-Seven

awoke with a kink in my neck and a smile on my face. The sun had decided to shine today and a small strip of light illuminated my bed covers. I rolled over to touch it, feel the warmth of it against my skin and on my bed . . . my very empty bed.

I sat bolt upright, clutching the blankets over my breasts, half-asleep, the sunbeam hitting me right in the eyes.

'Shit.'

The only clothes that were strewn over the floor were my own, there was no rose on my pillow, or note on my bedside, nothing except an empty feeling in my heart and soreness between my thighs, the only evidence of Jack being here. I edged out of bed, struggling to twist the sheet around my naked body, tripping and swearing and generally hating on the world as I went to the balcony, ripping open the curtains, and flinging open the doors to find . . . nothing.

No empty beer bottles, no burnt-out candles, no snacks. Surely last night wasn't a dream? There was no way a dream could be that real, with so many multiple orgasms. I checked underneath the table to see if maybe a note had blown there – nothing. Maybe there was something on my desk that I hadn't seen, or on my dresser; there was just no way Jack would have left without saying goodbye. We had even had dawn sex, the memory of him all the more vivid for the presence of daylight. The recollections of our night together only deepened my despair as I collapsed on the edge of my bed, feeling numb and hollow. He had got what he wanted, and left. My hopes raised a little, thinking maybe he'd just left for work and didn't want to wake me. But then I remembered that, after our third round, he'd said he was grateful he didn't have to work tomorrow, because he wouldn't be able to function. Well, he functioned all right, up and out of my room, and I had never felt so stupid. He was just another bloody typical lad, probably made all the girls feel special until daylight came. I pulled my sheet tighter, taking comfort in the pain of the edges digging into my skin; it distracted me from the pain that burned deep within me. I fell back into bed, lifting the covers over my head, curling into a ball. I was fine until I smelt Jack on my sheets, then my eyes went misty as I thought about how utterly stupid I had allowed myself to be.

I wanted to wallow in self-pity for all eternity, but then I heard the doorbell ring. Oh God, maybe I could suffocate myself with the same pillow I had dragged over my face to muffle my cries. Today was crossword day, and if that was Cybil and her thesaurus, I didn't think I could take it, knowing that I no longer had means to escape, no source to uplift me when I felt trapped or hopeless. I think that's what got to me most of all, that the person I thought Jack was didn't actually exist, and my only ray of hope in this miserable place had turned out to be an illusion. It felt like all the air had been knocked out of my lungs.

I heard the familiar thud of Vera's footsteps on the stairs and I knew things were about to go from bad to worse as she knocked on my door and announced Nana's request for an audience.

'Kate, are you awake?'

I pulled the pillow from my face. 'No!' I called out like a moody teen.

'Well, best get dressed and come downstairs, I've just boiled the kettle.' As if I could possibly be lured down by a hot cup of tea.

'It's crossword day, isn't it?' I said, waiting for her confirmation that would be the final nail in the coffin.

Vera paused. 'Well, yes, but that's not the reason you should come downstairs.'

'Give me five good reasons why I should.'

'No, but I'll give you one: Jack Baker's here to see you.'

I sat up so fast that I rolled out of bed, falling to the floor with a thud. I scrambled and tripped, trying to unlock the bedroom door but only scratching at it like a wild animal; the commotion from the other side must have entertained Vera no end. I whipped the bedroom door open, dressed in a sheet with bloodshot eyes and severely matted bed hair.

'What?'

'Didn't you hear the doorbell? Jack's downstairs in the parlour, so I suggest you get down there quick smart before Nana starts telling him stories of when you got your first period – you know what she's like.'

'Oh God.' She was right. 'Give me two minutes,' I said, closing the door and letting the sheets fall to the ground, doing a nudey run to the wardrobe. With no time to agonise over my outfit choice, I chucked on a fitted grey T-shirt and some jeans; the one luxury I allowed was brushing my hair.

'Ow, ow, ow, ow.' Sex hair was the worst! Though admittedly I had never had a night quite like last night.

I sprayed some perfume into the air and spun into it on the way to the door, where I took a moment to gather myself, taking in a deep breath. I walked onto the landing, squaring my shoulders as the sound of Jack's deep voice and Nana's answering laugh floated up the stairs.

What are you playing at, Jack Baker?

I tried to put a bounce in my step, as if I hadn't a care in the world. I did a quick run through in my head, practising how I would handle this utterly unexpected situation.

Oh, hey, Jack. How are you doing? Thanks for the

mind-blowing sex last night. Nana, would you be so kind as to pass the sugar?

Yeah, maybe not.

I spun around the banister at the bottom of the stairs, bracing myself to enter the parlour where Jack sat opposite Nana on the couch. They both turned to me, Jack standing as I entered the room. I made a particular effort not to make eye contact with him.

'Morning,' I said to the room.

'Oh, there you are, Katherine – I told you she was most likely sleeping her life away.'

'Rough night, Kate?' Jack asked, causing my attention to snap to his smug face.

'No, rather forgettable, really.' I watched something flash in his eyes as I sat in the armchair. Jack sat once more, looking anxious. He never looked anxious, not even in the presence of Nana.

'Jack has something he wants to say, but said he would wait for you. Sorry you had to wait so long, Jack, my grand-daughter's punctuality leaves something to be desired.'

Already on high alert, her words grated even more than usual and it took considerable effort to maintain my composure.

Jack cleared his throat. 'There's been something I've been meaning to ask. Kate, remember the other day I was going to ask you something but didn't?'

I thought back to the sunken garden at Kensington Palace: he'd been mulling over something, something that it seemed he'd wanted to share with me but then decided to keep to himself. It had played on my mind since then.

'Yes, I remember.'

'Well, the reason I didn't ask was because I know you wanted to spend more time with your nan since the fall, and I know you've not been feeling the greatest.' He glanced at Vera, who was nodding her head like she was watching her child perform at a beauty pageant.

I narrowed my eyes as I watched Jack lie so effortlessly. What was he up to?

'You see, Joy, I know this is your house and I want to respect that, and I didn't want to step on anyone's toes, and I know you care and worry for Kate, but you see there's this thing and I—'

'Oh, for God's sake, spit it out, man!' Nana snapped. I was on the edge of the overstuffed armchair.

Jack laughed. 'There's a fundraising ball in a few weeks, and I would very much like to take Kate as my date. If she would like to, of course.'

For the first time I met Jack's eyes; was he asking my nana's permission to take me on a date? My heart squeezed; this was better than any rose on a pillow.

Nana slumped back in her seat. 'Oh, is that all?' She sniffed. 'A silly little ball. Really, Jack, I seriously doubt that Katherine—'

'I'd love to!' I cut off Nana's words, ignoring her scowl and seeing only the warmth in Jack's eyes. I broke away from them reluctantly, moving to sit by Nana.

'Do you think you could handle me going out in the big city for one night, Nana?'

Nana lifted her chin like she was mulling over the thought. 'Well, what would you wear, Katherine? All your clothes are hideous.'

I smiled, not from the insult but the fact she seemed to be warming to the idea.

'Well, I'm sure I could come up with something.'

'No,' she said quite adamantly, causing Jack and I to look at each other. Of course, the lack of Nana's blessing meant little; I would be going to this ball, come hell or high water, even if it meant tying bed sheets together and climbing down off my balcony. It would, however, be easier with her agreement, which was obviously why Jack had undertaken this ruse; you had to give him an A for effort.

'No, it just won't do,' she said. 'No granddaughter of mine is going to a ball wearing a sack of potatoes; what's the dress code for this event, Jack?'

'Evening formal.'

Nana nodded. 'Well, in that case, I will have to lend you something of mine. I have a few evening gowns swimming around the house, I am sure we could find you something.'

My chest tightened, knowing damn well she had some gowns 'around the house' – she had Aladdin's bloody cave! But more exciting than the chance to wear vintage couture was the fact she'd said yes! No sneaking around, no lying. I was going out with Jack, to a ball, in London. Eat your heart out, Jane Austen!

'Aw, thanks, Nana.' I hugged her, feeling her recoil from my touch.

'Yes, well, we'll have to get the gown taken out of course; I was much thinner than you in my heyday, so naturally the dress won't fit you.'

The jibe bounced right off. In fact, I didn't care if she insulted me for the rest of her days, which she probably would. I turned to Jack with a big, goofy grin on my face. He replied with a wink and stood up from the sofa.

'Thanks, Joy. I promise I'll look after her.'

'Well, you better, Jack Baker, the world isn't what it once was, you know.'

'Oh, I know, that's why I need Kate to chaperone me.'

Nana scoffed, waving Jack away.

'Bye, Joy, Vera.' He nodded, then caught my eye. I stood and followed him to the front foor, the tension between us palpable. I opened the door and Jack lingered on the edge of the step.

'A ball, eh?' I said, trying to look nonplussed.

'And you don't even have to try to climb over your balcony in a long dress and heels.'

'Thank God.'

Jack watched me, studying my face, my smile mirroring his.

'You could have asked me that day. I would have said yes.'

'No, this was the right way to do it: no sneaking around, so we can just enjoy the night.'

'You're an ideas man, Jack Baker,' I mused.

He laughed. 'I try my best,' he said, beginning to descend the front steps before pausing. 'Oh, before I go, you might want this.' He reached around his back, pulling something out from underneath his jumper and handing it to me. It was a book.

There in the palm of my hands sat *Shipwrecked Hearts*, the book I had read nightly while waiting for Jack, my dirty little secret. I blanched, my eyes darting up to his in horror.

'I see where you learn all those moves of yours,' he said with a cheeky grin, bounding down the steps as if afraid I might throw the book at him.

'Very funny!'

Chapter Twenty-Eight

had to play it cool.

I hadn't seen Jack since this morning's surprise visit and, as the evening wore on, I had to seriously resist the urge to climb over to his balcony. There were two weeks until the fundraising ball, and I really didn't want to come across like I had already chosen the names for our firstborn, though Zoe and Michael were definitely my preferences. I had to just not think right now; I was fully aware of how crazy I was being and I didn't want to analyse why that might be. But no matter how I tried, everywhere I looked in my bedroom brought back vivid memories from the previous night. I went out onto the balcony, hoping that maybe some fresh air would clear my mind, but seeing the chair that Jack had been sitting in reminded me of all that we had done there, so I couldn't be out there either.

As a last resort, I walked down to the rose garden, deciding to take in the cooled evening air with my weathered copy of *Shipwrecked Hearts*, my go-to when serious distraction was needed. I was dying to know if the marriage of convenience between Alessandro and Calypso was going to lead to an explosive honeymoon night.

I read on, hungrily turning each page until being utterly shocked by the plot twist.

'No way! Alessandro is Lord Ramon's long-lost brother?'

'I could have told you that,' Vera called out from the opened door of the kitchen.

'Don't tell me you've read this too?'

'Well, I have to pass the time during Joy's naps somehow. Seems like it's been a good time killer for you as well.'

I folded the page at the top corner, thinking there were far more interesting ways to kill my time as another memory surfaced. I could only hope Vera linked my blushing cheeks to the contents of the book. I sighed, chucking the book on the table and making my way to the kitchen, wincing as seldom-used muscles protested after last night's workout. I had to see him again, to know that last night meant something; sure, he had invited me on a date, but that was an eternity away.

'Well, I've had my free time, best get back to my blog.'

'See, hot date planned, fresh air with a good book, some blogging: who says you can't have it all?'

I thought about that for a moment: the way I was feeling and what had happened in the last twenty-four hours. Try as I might, I couldn't fight my smile.

I relented. 'Life is pretty good.'

Vera paused from her carrot peeling. Leaning her hip against the cabinet, she looked at me expectantly, her own little smirk in place.

'Well, it's about to get a lot better,' she said.

I straightened. 'Alessandro and Calypso live happily ever after?'

Vera burst out laughing. 'Well, that's not what I was referring to but yes, they do.'

'Oh, then what?'

Was bingo cancelled with Nana?

Vera turned her attention back to the sink. 'You better go check your room,' she said cryptically. I peeled away from the kitchen and legged it up the stairs. All I could think about was whether I had managed to clean up everything from last night's antics. I had disposed of condoms and emptied my rubbish bin, washed up and put away the water glass Jack had used, straightened my sheets and even opened my windows in case the smell of sex still hung in the air. I'd been so thorough, it was like I was cleaning a crime scene, but had I missed something? Why was Vera telling me to check my room? I opened my door, fearing the worst, when I came to a complete standstill.

There, laid out on my bed, was a beautiful midnight-blue gown, with silver heels, an ivory white clutch, and a mother-of-pearl-and-diamond hair comb.

'Oh my God,' I breathed.

I knew this dress, all right. It was a Pierre Balmain couture, a dress that I had looked at longingly on more than one occasion. My hand traced over the satin of the dress. The Parisian designer, along with a few select others, was responsible for reigniting French fashion after the Second World War. His sumptuous ball gowns and luxurious wedding dresses seduced the most glamorous of Hollywood's queens, so it was little wonder that his pieces attracted the likes of Nana Joy. And she had chosen this for me. I felt a lump in my throat. I held myself together for the most part when it came to Nana Joy, but as my hands skimmed over the silken layers of the dress, I could not control my feelings. Without thinking, I ran from my room and down the stairs, bursting through the parlour in a loud, clumsy commotion to throw my arms around Nana Joy, jolting her out of her sleep.

'Thank you,' I whispered, pulling back and looking into her blue eyes, wanting her to see how much her gesture meant to me. 'I love them.'

Nana was annoyed, squirming at my words and looking like she wished she was anywhere else. 'Well, like I said, you probably won't fit into it – you're far too hippy, like your mother.'

I would live on water and crackers and wear four pairs of Spanx if it meant fitting into that dress. Where there was a will, there was a way.

'You are the best!' I beamed. No such words had ever left my mouth in reference to Nana, but in that moment

I saw her in a new light; somewhere under the harsh, weathered exterior of this bitter woman, deep down – okay, so deep, deep, deep down – there was something good.

Nana winced, as if my words physically pained her. 'Oh, don't be so dramatic, Katherine, really.'

Some small part of me might have hoped for a 'you're welcome', but nothing could bring me down. I was on cloud nine, having finally found a happiness that I didn't think possible in this house, in this city.

I took the seat next to Nana, fighting against my instinct to run back upstairs and swan around with my stunning new gown and elegant accessories; instead, I took in a deep breath, smiled and addressed Nana.

'So, what are we doing tomorrow?'

Chapter Twenty-Nine

I closed my laptop screen and sat there, not daring to believe what I was thinking.

Kate, you can't.

I unravelled my hair from its bun, delighting in the feeling of running my fingers over my scalp as I lost myself in thought.

Seriously, don't even think about it.

I edged off my bed, stretching my arms to the ceiling and placing my hands on my hips, twisting from side to side, glancing at the terrace doors.

The sun had long gone down and my room was lit with the usual golden lamp light, a cosy refuge from the hustle and bustle of the world and all that lay beyond the doors I walked toward. I skimmed my hands along the lace curtain material. It had been a long day; having just pressed publish on my new post, a sick feeling clawed at my insides. What if people hated it? What if people thought that I was just a pretentious, materialistic twat? I glanced at the beautiful strapless Balmain gown hanging on my door, biting my thumbnail, too wired to sleep, anxiously wearing a track on my rug. I needed a distraction and I knew the very best person to provide me with one.

Kate, NO!

Sorry, inner voice, there is no winning me over right now.

I let my adrenaline push open the balcony doors and stepped out into the night air. I climbed over the edge. *Holy shit, do not look down, Kate!* The edge of the terrace felt grimy and flaky under my hands. I gripped the window ledge desperately, my feet slowly side-shuffling over to Jack's side. It was only now, halfway across with the night air whipping my hair into my eyes, that I started to really doubt what I was doing. I tried to remember to breathe and move, breathe and move. *Don't look down, you are almost there!* But Jack's ledge felt a mile away and there was nothing to do but glance down.

Big mistake.

I froze, paralysed and angry at my stupidity; seriously, what was I doing? But then came a memory of Jack's burning eyes, and the way his mouth felt against my skin, and I was moving once more, a new determination slowly overriding the fear. I hooked my right leg over, anchoring myself to Jack's balcony before summoning the courage to throw my arm over, followed by my left leg in a ghastly dismount. I was grateful that Jack wasn't around to see my inelegant display, rolling and falling to the floor with a yelp. I clapped the dust from my hands and rubbed at the small graze I had gained on my knee for my efforts. How Jack made it look so effortless was beyond me.

I stole a moment to catch my breath and take in my surrounds. So this was what life looked like from Jack's world – oddly similar in aspect, if not in actuality. Making my way to the door, I summoned enough courage to tap lightly on the glass, while fighting the urge to head back over the balcony to my own bedroom. I remembered Jack joking that his door was always open. I tested that theory by twisting the handle and gently pushing it—

Oh God, it was open.

I pushed a little more and stepped inside.

I didn't know exactly what I expected of Jack's flat, but it certainly wasn't this: neat, sparse and tasteful, and, unlike my first impression of the home's occupant, nothing obnoxious. After seeing his beautifully tailored suits, square-tipped leather shoes, expensive watch and James Bond-esque car, I'd expected something . . . flashier. There was no doubt, however, that Jack Baker's flat was impressive, just like the man himself, who was currently in front of me, asleep, or at least I thought he was. He sat on the couch, arms crossed, head tilted back with his headphones on. The light of his ridiculously huge flatscreen highlighted the beautiful angles of his face, so peaceful in repose, like a little angel, which was fairly ironic given his performance in my bedroom. My eyes skimmed the walls for any tell-tale clues about Jack's life. A framed doctorate, or law degree maybe? Something that would hint at his chosen career, the one that had him in suits all week, that paid for the V8 engine that revved down the streets early in the morning and returned late in the night.

Charcoal and light greys accented the stark white of the glossy, modern kitchen and white leather sofas in the lounge room of the open living-style apartment, so clean and sleek, it made my room look like it belonged to Angela Lansbury, with its scalloped curtains and herringbone flooring. An organised selection of books and DVDs ran the length of the far wall and there was even a potted plant in the corner, looking healthy and cared for; could he be into Feng Shui?

You are full of surprises, Jack Baker.

Having finished my snooping for now, I looked back at Jack. Was he asleep or listening to music? I crept forward and gently lifted the edge of his headphones up, peeling them off. Jack stirred from his recline, sitting up and blinking in surprise.

'Hey,' he said, rubbing his eyes and seemingly getting his bearings. He looked tired, but I was pretty certain I knew how to wake him up. Running on the dregs of my adrenaline and shutting down the voice of reason, I pulled off my T-shirt then took off my bra, throwing it in Jack's lap. His eyes moved from the bra up to my breasts, which were only partially covered by my long hair. He swallowed hard; he was wide awake now.

'Am I dreaming?' he asked.

I giggled, shaking my head and edging his legs apart with mine, before straddling him on the couch, making fast work of his belt and reaching for his zipper.

Jack shook his head. 'You're a bad woman, Katherine Brown.'

I lowered my mouth against his. 'A bad woman who can do very good things.'

Jack laughed, the warmth of his breath burning my sensitive lips before he kissed me, his hands on my hips, holding me in place. He looked up at me, his eyes ticking over my face. 'It's that book, isn't it?'

I burst out laughing, linking my hands around the back of his neck. 'It's definitely a page-turner.'

Jack moved his hands to undo the buttons of my jeans, one pop at a time, but never once moving his gaze from mine.

'Of that, I have no doubt,' he said, his mouth pressing against mine, his hands sliding up to cup my breasts.

How had I ever thought that seducing him was a bad idea? Or was he seducing me? The way his hot, wicked mouth kissed a path down to my breast, sucking it into his mouth, eyes looking up at me as I arched into him, grabbing and pulling at his shirt, I wasn't sure who was seducing who.

'I want to feel you against me.' My words were breathless, desperate; the barrier between us, however thin, was too much – I needed to feel him, all of him.

Jack took his mouth from me and grabbed the back of his T-shirt, pulling it over his head and tossing it aside.

He brought my mouth to his once more, filling, tasting and teasing me with his tongue, then biting softly on my bottom lip. I moved back from him, smiling, and trailed my fingers down his chest, watching him intently as I went lower, and lower. Jack looked at me with interest, as if curious to see where I would stop, but I had no intention of stopping.

'Fuck!' He sat back, watching me take the long, hard length of him in my hand.

'I want to taste you like before,' I whispered against his mouth. Jack's hips bucked against me, caught between pleasure and pain as I pumped him in long, agonising strokes.

Jack shook his head. 'On your knees.' His voice was hoarse, like it had taken an incredible amount of effort to speak. I bit my lip, ready to slide down his body and take him in my mouth, but Jack had other ideas, slipping out from underneath me and pushing me forward onto the couch. My palms were splayed on the soft leather, my breath hitching in my mouth as I felt Jack behind me, edging my legs apart with his knees, pulling my shorts down, inch by agonising inch.

Oh God.

I felt the couch shift and the heat from my back was gone; I went to protest but then saw Jack's reflection in the hall mirror, rolling a condom down his long, hard length and returning to his position behind me. I gripped the couch, anchoring myself to the edge, anticipating what was to come. Last night Jack had gone hard and deep, so when he took me slowly, filling me gently and sliding his hand along my spine, my eyes lifted to the mirror to watch him watching me, our eyes locked with each thrust. There was something about the connection that changed us in that moment; reading my face as I saw the need in him, Jack quickened his pace. Digging his fingers into my hips, he drew me against him with a new urgency, pounding into me so hard the legs of the couch scraped along the floorboards. Never before had it seemed so real, the way we watched each other come, lit by the muted TV screen, colours dancing across our naked skin. Jack pulled me up against his chest, cupping his palm over the most intimate part of me, pumping into me. I came so loudly it was enough for Jack to lose his mind, his teeth grazing my shoulder, cursing and groaning into my skin. But it wasn't enough, it was never enough, and until we climbed and fell and came so completely unravelled – then and only then did we stop. Jack's body slumped over mine, pinning me to the couch, our sweaty skin sticking to the leather. But we were too spent to care; for now, breathing was all that mattered. In, out, in, out. It was all I could focus on, simply bringing myself back into my body.

Jack rolled onto his side, his eyes closed, his chest expanding. 'Is that a book club book?' he asked.

I pulled myself up onto my elbow, giggling. 'No, it's not.'

Jack swallowed, shaking his head, still fighting for breath. 'Well, it bloody should be.'

Chapter Thirty

I stirred under my cover, the soft cashmere cosy and warm against my skin, my very naked skin. I blinked, disorientated by the light streaming in through the window into my eyes. I put my hand up against the sun and—

'Oh shit.'

Sun? Sun meant daytime. Daytime meant—

'OH SHIT!' I sat bolt upright, wrapping the throw rug around me, the leather groaning against my every move as I searched for my clothes. They were nowhere to be seen, despite my increasingly frantic scrabbling under cushions and, a little desperately, the couch.

Laughter echoed in the kitchen and I sat up, brushing my dishevelled hair out of my face to see Jack clinking a teaspoon against his cup.

'Morning,' he said, bring the steaming tea to his mouth.

'Why didn't you wake me!' I said, attempting to stand and walk while wrapped in the rug without falling flat on my face. Panic spiked in me as I looked at the clock: ten past nine.

'I tried, but I guess that balcony climbing really tuckered you out . . . among other things. Tea?' Jack sipped on his cup once more before stirring the other. Oh, he was so bloody cocky he didn't even attempt to hide it! A late-night urge for distraction and pleasure was going to result in a shaming I would never live down.

'Where are my clothes?'

Jack's brows drew together as if he was thinking deeply about my question. 'I'm not sure, they didn't exactly stay on for long.'

I sighed, trying to decide between throwing a cushion at him and demanding my clothes or wrapping the cashmere throw around me like a toga and climbing out the window, giving the residents of Onslow Gardens a sight they were not likely to forget. Either way, this would be the first and last time I climbed over Jack Baker's terrace.

'Jack, please, if Nan finds out I'm—'

'You'll what? Be sent to bed without any supper? Be put under house arrest? Oh no, that's right – you're a consenting adult, not a prisoner.'

'I just . . . I don't want to complicate matters. Things have been improving somewhat and I just want to keep it that way.'

'Is that why you were in such a good mood yesterday?'

I rolled my eyes. 'Yes, Jack. That's why I climbed over your balcony and set upon ravishing you last night:

because of my improving relationship with my nana. Do you seriously think that's the reason I came?'

'Not at all, just nice to have it confirmed.' Jack took another sip of tea, quite a feat considering his lips were rather busy smirking. 'Checked your stats lately?' Jack sat down at his sleek glass dining table. He was dressed casually, no suit, just a nice navy polo and dark jeans, his hair damp from the shower.

'Well, my routine has somewhat altered this morning, but as soon as I find my clothes and get back home I'll be sure to look.'

'Fair enough.' Jack tilted his head to the left of me; I followed his eyeline to the chair, upon which sat my neatly folded clothes.

'Oh.' I blushed. 'Right, thanks.'

Jack smiled graciously. 'Are you sure you don't want some tea?'

I bundled my clothes into my arms, trying my best to not let the blanket slip. 'What is it with you Brits thinking everything can be solved with a nice cup of tea?'

Jack shrugged. 'It's kind of our superpower.'

I smiled, shuffling an awkward path over to him. He watched with great interest. I pecked him on the cheek. 'Where's your bathroom?'

Jack simply shook his head.

'What?'

'Oh, you're going to have to pay a bigger toll than that, I'm afraid,' he said, hooking his finger into the front of my blanket and pulling me to him, stealing a sweet, gentle kiss. I could feel the heat creep up my skin; the edges of my mind that were so determined and clear only a moment before now seemed foggy and confused when I looked into his deep brown eyes. I would have stayed forever, I really didn't care about anything as I watched a slow smile spread across his face. I blinked out of my trance when he finally spoke.

'First door to your left.'

~

I picked up my phone from my bedside table. 'Oh, you have got to be kidding me!'

My phone was dead, deader than dead. I followed the charger cord to the powerpoint only to find it wasn't switched on.

'Perfect!'

In my eagerness to see Jack last night I had literally plugged and run. It was all his fault, the way he was always derailing my thoughts. I pulled the charger from the wall socket, not wanting to delay my arrival downstairs a second longer.

How do you disguise the 'I've just had sex' look when walking into a room?

I was about to find out.

'Good morning!' I sing-songed; it was a better alternative than cringing at the no doubt stone-cold breakfast Vera had fixed for me.

'Sorry I'm late, Vera, I do love your full English spreads,' I said, moving to the sideboard and plugging in my phone charger before taking my seat and avoiding Nana's searing gaze.

'Looks great!' I said, flicking out my napkin and placing it over my lap.

'You look different.'

My head snapped around to meet Nana's interrogative gaze, trying my best to look innocent.

'Different? How so?' I laughed, busying myself by lifting the lid from the bacon tray.

'Just, different,' she said, chewing thoughtfully on the edge of her toast. I had psyched myself up for a dressing down, a chastising over being late, but it never came. It left me even more uneasy, wondering if this was the calm before the storm.

'Kate, we're heading down to High Street if you want to come for a walk. I know you said you wanted to get some exercise.' Vera smiled at me.

I tried not to choke on my toast, thinking about how many calories I had burned on Jack's couch last night. My answer was saved by the buzzing of my phone.

'What is that noise?' asked Nana, her pinched face looking around the room.

'Oh, it's just my phone charging, Nana.'

'Ugh, vile things.'

'It's on silent.'

But in the still morning of Nana's breakfast room even the vibrations of a phone on a sideboard seemed painfully loud, and there were certainly a lot of vibrations.

'Someone's popular,' said Vera, sipping her juice, brows raised in interest. I would like to think that the buzzing signified multitudes of text messages from Jack, professing his undying love for me, but I was pretty sure he didn't have my number. He'd been inside me but, no, didn't have my number.

Buzz, buzz, buzz.

'Oh, for God's sake, Katherine, turn it off!' snapped Nana.

'All right, all right,' I said, throwing aside my napkin and moving to my phone. I was keen to see what was going on, anyway. Was my phone faulty, or was it in need of an app update? Either way, I had to admit that, even for me, the sound was pretty annoying.

'Okay, let's see what we can see,' I said, tapping in the password. 'Oh my God.'

'Kate, what is it?' Vera asked. I blinked, looking up from my screen, remembering that I the captive audience of Vera's worried eyes and Nana's sneer. My pulse jack-hammered and my knees shook.

'Um, I . . . I think there's something wrong with my phone.'

'Oh no, is it not working?'

I glanced down at my screen, reading it once more and shaking my head.

'Throw it away then; nothing good can come of those things, if you ask me,' Nana said, but all I could hear was white noise. The conversation that carried on between Vera and Nana didn't register with me as I blinked and stared, blinked and stared.

'Earth to Kate.'

'Sorry, what?'

'Did you want some more tea?'

Tea, yes, tea solved everything, right? Maybe a magical cup could give me some answers. Instead, I yanked my phone from the wall.

'Actually, I think I might go see if I can troubleshoot my phone.'

'But what about your breakfast?' Nana asked, perturbed.

'Oh sorry, I'm really not that hungry.' And before another question could stop me, I walked slowly to the doorway, after which I legged it to the staircase. Running up to my room so fast that I misstepped twice. I steamed through my room until I hit the terrace doors, I was ready to jump from my balcony to the next if need be, but instead I came to a skidding halt as my eyes landed on Jack, sitting on his balcony and looking up from his newspaper expectantly.

Wheezing and coughing, unable to speak, I rested my hands on my knees, shaking my head. God, I was seriously unfit.

Jack lowered his newspaper and leant back in his chair, watching me as the corner of his mouth curved up.

'I'm guessing you checked your stats, then?'

I shook my head. 'It can't be.'

Jack took his phone from his table and read his screen. 'Seven hundred and forty-one shares.'

'Are you sure?'

Jack laughed. 'As sure as I'm sitting here.'

'My post has gone nuts.'

Jack shook his head. 'No, love, your post has gone viral.'

'Viral? How?'

'I ran a search. Have you heard of a magazine called *London Bound*?'

'Are you kidding me? Everyone knows that magazine, it's huge.'

Jack thumbed over his smart phone, before holding out it out to me. 'I think you'll find that this had something to do with it.'

Jack's balcony was close, but not so close that I could read the screen. 'What is it?'

'Charlotte Whitakers' Top Five. You've hit her movers and shakers list in *London Bound* and that's all you'll ever need.'

'Holy shit, Charlotte fucking Whitakers?'

Jack laughed. 'You know her then?'

'Well, no, but I know of her, and I know how much of a big deal this is – I mean, *London Bound*? Are you for real?'

'Doors are going to open for you, Kate, to places you can't even begin to imagine.'

I felt a lump in my throat. 'But what did I do?'

Jack smiled at his screen. 'Near on eight hundred shares.'

'Oh, shut up!' I screamed, refreshing my phone, scrolling down the screen. 'Oh my God, Jack, look at all the comments.'

'You're in for a busy night.'

'I don't even know where to start, I can't even fathom—'

'Kate.'

My eyes flicked up from my screen.

'You got this.'

It was nice of him to think so, but in that moment I felt like I most definitely did not have 'this'. I couldn't even begin to conceive of what 'this' is. I felt like a fraud.

'Will you help me, you know, until I find my feet with all this?' I asked, grimacing with embarrassment.

Jack smiled reassuringly. 'Every step of the way.'

Chapter Thirty-One

'Why am I so nervous, Vera?'

I stood in front of a full-length mirror, marvelling at the job Cybil had done, adjusting the waist and hips of the dress to better fit my frame. It didn't need a dramatic alteration, but I wouldn't tell Nana Joy that: whatever made her feel better.

'Oh, you'll be fine once you get there, just make sure you enjoy every minute of it. You look absolutely lovely,' Vera said, patting me on the arm. It was all well and good to feel glamorous and special in my beautiful vintage dress, but the real test would be Nana's appraisal, one I was definitely not looking forward to. It felt like walking the green mile – I wish I had a priest saying a prayer beside me.

The dress swished as I made my way down the stairs. I wished I could have saved this entrance for when Jack was here, but it was important to get Nana out of the way to save embarrassment and/or potentially spoiling the moment. Concentrating on walking in the unfamiliar shoes, I lifted my skirt as I entered the lounge where Nana sat, heels clicking across the foyer.

She cast her cold eyes over me from top to bottom. I psyched myself up for: 'Have you put on weight?' 'You really are quite hippy, aren't you?' 'Are you really going to wear that shade of rouge?'

I had put on a mental suit of armour, telling myself that, no matter what she said, I wouldn't let it spoil my night. So when Nana said, 'You look lovely,' I near on fell over.

'I do?'

'Of course you do, I have excellent taste,' she sniffed, and there was the Nana Joy I had come to know.

'Well, you most certainly do; out of all of them I am so glad you chose this one,' I said, spinning around, only to lock eyes with Nana, her expression stormy.

'All of them?'

Oh shit. Shit, shit, shit.

'Ah, yes, well, I mean, I assume this is one of many . . .' I stammered, hunting around for a way to talk my way out of the mess I'd landed myself in.

'You went into my room, didn't you.'

'I-I discovered the room by accident; you see, I was looking for an umbrella . . . it really is the most incredible collection, Nana Joy, I've been obsessed with beauty and fashion and I can tell you it's absolutely—'

'Did you touch my things?'

'Um, yes, but nothing has ever left the room or the

house and I have been nothing but respectful, I know how valuable your collection must be.'

'You know nothing.'

I stood frozen in the middle of the lounge, terrified beyond measure. I had seen Nana's eyes ablaze, heard her clipped tones before, but never had I seen such a rage burn under the surface as it did now. I could imagine her stripping me of my dress and kicking me out into the street. I couldn't think of anything to say that might appease the apparent betrayal. I wished Jack would hurry up and get here; if anyone was going to save the day, I knew he could.

Right on cue, the doorbell rang. I had never been so grateful for anything in my life.

'I'll get it,' I called, leaving Nana to quietly fume. I ran to the door, opening it up and coming to a stop, my mouth agape. Any worry I had left my mind, along with the ability to speak coherently.

In the doorway, dressed in a black tuxedo and bow tie, hair slicked back like a forties' movie star, stood Jack. He'd never looked more handsome and I could barely think of an appropriate compliment; instead, he beat me to it.

'You look beautiful, Kate.' His dark eyes drank me in from head to toe, saying far more than his words.

'Oh.' I blushed, looking down at my dress. 'Thanks.'

'I'll be the envy of every man at the ball.'

'Oh, I don't know about that,' I said, glancing behind me and desperately wanting to leave.

'Oh, Jack, don't you look right handsome,' said Vera, waddling down the hallway. 'Come, come, show Joy what a fine couple you two make.'

I closed my eyes, cringing at the thought and bracing myself for the worst. So when Nana was, instead, sickly sweet and complimentary to us both, I was incredibly unsettled.

'Well, have a good time, you two; remember, take plenty of pictures.' Vera waved us out the door.

I slid my arm through Jack's and he led me to the front door, but not before seeing Nana's smile fall away in the reflection of the mirror in the foyer; it was enough to give me chills. I was filled with guilt, and trepidation about what would greet me when I returned home. But I was unable to do anything about it right now, so I chose to concentrate on the warmth of Jack's arm, the excitement of the evening ahead, and my recent success with the blog.

By the time the ball had come around, my blog post on Nana Joy's wardrobe had been shared over two hundred thousand times. My website had been viewed nearly seven hundred thousand times, with four hundred thousand unique visitors. I was overwhelmed at first, but Jack had been a rock, navigating the social waves and making sure my site didn't crash, my links worked, and even finding a way for me to make money from it, using affiliate links and sponsored posts.

'Hey, I've got something to show you,' Jack said, slowing his step as we walked through the foyer and reaching into the inner pocket of his tux. He handed me a folded piece of glossy paper. 'For the scrapbook,' he said, watching as I unfolded the article. My spirits instantly lifted. There was my name, a link to my blog, a photo and bio under the heading 'Movers and Shakers' by Charlotte Whitakers.

I laughed. 'This is amazing. I meant to I tell you – she emailed me!'

A line pinched between Jack's brow. 'When?'

'This morning. She wants to meet with me – actually meet me at *London Bound* HQ – can you believe it?'

Jack took the article from my hands, removing the distraction and placing it on the sideboard, apparently annoyed. 'Why didn't you tell me?'

'I am, now. I was just so crazy busy getting ready for tonight that I guess it slipped my mind. I did reply.'

'Oh Jesus.' Jack rubbed the side of his face. 'Right, and what did you say?'

I frowned. Now I was getting mad. 'I did just as you told me to do: I was myself. I gave her some background on me, told her I love her work and that I can't wait to meet her in person.'

I thought that the fact I had taken his advice might have pleased him, but he didn't seem convinced.

'Just tell me when things like that happen.'

I gathered up my gown, stepping around him. 'Why, are you my agent now?' I snapped, regretting it the moment I said it.

Jack sighed.

'Let's just have a good night, yeah? Put all this aside, not think about likes or shares or views, just for one night.'

I nodded in agreement, admitting, to myself at least, that my blogging had taken up a lot of airspace lately. And Jack had supported me every step of the way. Looking into his dark brown eyes, I knew I loved him. I wouldn't tell him as much just yet, though. I slid my hand into his and smiled.

'There is nothing I would love more.'

~

Jack led me into the lobby of the Corinthea, a luxury hotel and former British Government building that was located on a triangular site between Trafalgar Square and the Thames Embankment. The façade of the building had been sympathetically restored, but inside it was jaw-dropping, modern luxury throughout. It was a place that felt buzzy and lively yet, by some magic, still managed to exude a quiet calm. The soft colour palette of muted greys, lilacs and creams was interspersed with pieces of modern art, and seasonal floral lobby displays; the result was stunning. Jack squeezed my hand, diverting my attention back to him.

'I'll check us in,' he said.

'Wait, check us in?'

Jack laughed. 'You'll see,' he said, leaving me to stare in awe at my surroundings. Maybe this explained my fascination with goods from another world: like my couture dress that had a life lived way before mine, in this moment, in this place, I could pretend to be someone else, stepping into an alternative world where I was someone fabulous. A princess maybe? Hollywood royalty, or who knew, maybe a blogging sensation? Yeah, let's not get too carried away, I thought, laughing quietly to myself. Maybe tonight I would be a Katherine, standing in the stunning lobby lounge with its soaring ceilings, anchored by a spectacular Baccarat chandelier I was completely enamoured with.

'Can you spot the red crystal?' Jack's voice was smooth against my neck, causing me to startle a little.

'The what?'

Jack pointed. 'A fitting heart to such a beautiful display, don't you think?'

I spotted it then, one singular red crystal glowing among the bright masses; it was a wonder I had missed it before.

'Are you going to show me lots of things tonight, Jack Baker?'

'So many things.' A wolfish smile spread across his handsome face. To a bystander, he looked so innocent, but I could see the wicked sparkle in his eyes, a promise of things to come, and I could feel the butterflies dance in my tummy at the thought.

Jack led me through the lobby lounge, a perfect, elegant setting for traditional British afternoon tea; it was a tragedy that we wouldn't have the chance to try it on our visit. The baskets of fresh strawberries, beautiful delicate cakes and chilled bottles of Laurent Perrier champagne looked enticing, but the real clincher came from Jack.

'I've heard that the scones served here are some of London's best.'

My mouth instantly watered and I shook my head. 'You are such a tease, Jack Baker.'

Jack laughed, far too loudly for such a refined space. 'You have no idea.'

Chapter Thirty-Two

I had built up in my mind what I thought a typical fundraising ball might be. A small dance floor, helium balloons, spinning charity wheel to win a frozen chook maybe, but walking into the grand ballroom of the Corinthea was something else. With its Victorian splendour fit for aristocrats, debutantes and the bejewelled crowns of Europe, this was not like any ball I could have possibly imagined. With my arm hooked in Jack's and my gown swishing against the gold and magenta swirls of the floor, I struggled to take in the beauty of the high ceilings, towering columns and mirrored walls that reflected sparkling chandeliers.

Jack leant into me. 'You're going to have a sore neck by the end of the night if you keep looking up like that.'

Leaning into him, I said, 'I'm used to all manners of aches and pains after a night with you, Mr Baker.'

Something hot flashed in Jack's eyes and I loved that I put it there.

'Come on, I see a nice table of well-behaved ladies who have no chance of corrupting you any further.'

'What if I corrupt them?'

'Behave yourself, Lady Katherine.'

I giggled, letting him lead me to the table in question and pull out a chair for me, smiling at the apparently abandoned wives and girlfriends seated there.

'I'll be back in a minute,' Jack whispered, kissing the top of my head, causing me to turn in alarm.

'Where are you going?'

'Ah, secret men's business, won't be long,' he said, and if it wasn't for that cheeky wink I might have been annoyed. I turned slowly to see all eyes were on me, roaming my dress, their over-manicured brows curved as they turned their attentions away from me. If Jack had planned to sit me at the bitchy table of isolation, then well done, he'd succeeded.

~

Forty minutes after our arrival, I sat slumped with my head leaning on my hand, opening one eye, closing the other, making the wine bottle move from side to side on the table like a kid's magic trick. I sighed, rolling my neck, bored out of my mind. I caught the eye of one of the socialites, who was staring pointedly at my elbow on the table; my reply was to place my other elbow on the table top with a loud thud, in a silent 'fuck you'. I was all but ready to round up a search party for a Mr Jack Baker when he suddenly appeared, as if conjured by my imagination.

'Ah, excuse me, ladies, I am under strict orders to show Miss Brown a good time, and I'm afraid I have been failing rather miserably.' Jack reached over and took my hand, rescuing me from the judging looks and bitchy whispers of the miserable wallflowers. He led me through the crowd, weaving around the tables and leading me out to the dance floor.

'Oh, Jack, no, I'm really not in the mood to—'

'Come on, Kate, time to tear up this dance floor. There are far too many sad sacks here – you're not going to be one of them.'

And without taking no for an answer, Jack swung me around on the dance floor, clearing a bigger space for us in the middle as Hozier's 'Someone New' started up. Jack took me into his arms, surprising me by knowing all of the lyrics as he swung me around the floor, taking great delight in dipping me and making me squeal. By the end of the song, we were the only two left on the dance floor and the spotlight was on us for all the wrong reasons but I didn't care. Jack had a way of making me embrace the moment and by the next song, I was dancing with complete abandon, turning and spinning and returning into his arms, accidentally stepping on his toes and trying not to laugh as he went cross-eyed from the pain. By the third song we had settled down a bit, and I linked my hands around the back of his neck and looked into his eyes, into him.

'I really like you, Jack,' I said, not knowing where exactly that came from but feeling it nonetheless. Jack smiled; the dimple in his left cheek appearing to let me know he was pleased.

'And what if I told you I really, really like you?'

'Well then, I would say, I really, really, really like you.'

'Well then, I really like you, times infinity . . . no returns.'

'No returns?'

'Well, maybe a little.'

I giggled, resting my head against his chest.

'Hey, Kate.' I felt his lips press against the top of my head.

'Yes, Jack?'

'There's something I want to tell you.'

Before I could speak, the piercing wail of feedback through the PA system got everyone's attention.

'Apologies, ladies and gentlemen, that'll teach me to get too close to the speaker. Presentations and entrées are about to commence, if you would please be seated,' said a stocky, well-dressed man, reading off a card with his glasses at the edge of his nose.

I turned back to Jack, panicked. 'Do you think I have time to go to the restroom before it starts?' I hadn't exactly worked out the logistics of my impossibly tight bodice and floor-sweeping train when it came to toilet breaks.

Jack looked equally worried. 'You'll have time, but before you do . . .'

'Jack, I really have to go,' I said, kissing him on the cheek and gathering up my skirt to make a run for it. I felt kind of bad abandoning him on the dance floor, but, hey, that would teach him for abandoning me earlier. Weaving through chairs and leaving the echoes of the PA system behind, I had never been so happy to see the ladies' toilets, and without a queue, no less! Pure class, all the way down to the lavs. After relieving myself, I made my way to the basin to wash and primp, touching up my red lipstick then pouting at my reflection and dropping the lipstick into my clutch. I stepped back for one last inspection before making my way to the door, only to stop dead in my tracks at the sight of a very familiar someone.

It couldn't be.

My eyes trailed up the long-legged Amazonian brunette, the same woman I had seen walking into Jack's terrace. Stranger still, she looked back at me curiously.

'Kate?'

She knew my name?

'You're Kate Brown?'

All I could do was nod. 'Um, yes . . . I—'

The Amazonian thrust her long, slender hand out to me. 'I am so happy to meet you. I'm Charlotte, Charlotte Whitakers.'

I took her hand; my handshake was woefully limp as the reality of the situation washed over me.

Charlotte Whitakers?

'Jack has told me so much about you! Is he coming on Monday for our meeting, do you know?'

'I, um, I don't think so.'

'Oh well, just us girls then,' she said, smiling. 'Well, I won't fangirl over you tonight, but I just adore your blog. You have an amazing space there and I just love your voice and vibe. I can't wait to learn more,' she said, sidestepping to the marble vanity.

I blinked, confused, trying to piece it together, but hoping against hope that I was wrong.

'Sorry, Charlotte, just out of interest, how did you find out about the blog?'

Charlotte shrugged, turning from her reflection in the mirror. 'Jack told me, said he had a sure thing. He wasn't wrong,' she said, smiling confidently and turning her attention back to the mirror.

I wandered dazedly back into the ballroom amongst the commotion of guests rushing to their seats for the presentations, finding myself back at the table but unable to recall how I got there. Avoiding Jack's eyes I sat in my seat, brushing the crinkles out of my skirt and reaching for the napkin, readying myself for my entrée to be delivered.

'Kate.' Jack's voice seemed even more urgent now and I couldn't help but turn to him, looking directly into his dark, seemingly honest eyes.

'Yes, Jack, you had something to tell me?' I said. He swallowed hard, readying himself to speak. Just as he did, a voice came over the PA system again, the same irritating man drowning out Jack's words.

'Good evening, ladies and gentlemen. I would like to call on the opening speaker, someone who is not only one of London's leading entrepreneurs, bringing his energy and boldness to every facet of his long and impressive career, but whom also devotes his time to worthy causes within and outside our community, including being a tremendous supporter of our own Brighter Futures charity since 2014. It is my great pleasure to welcome back a true icon of the industry, the founder and CEO of one of London's largest fashion institutions, *London Bound* magazine. Please give a warm welcome to Mr Jack Baker.'

And there it was: the truth played out with an audience and the soundtrack of deafening applause. The white noise surrounded us, and the spotlight shone over us to capture us in our moment of discovery, a moment that should have been explained in private well before now. We simply stared at one another, Jack's eyes locked with mine even while he slowly stood. Who was this man who had occupied my mind for these last few weeks, who I had let into my bed, into my heart? He was a stranger to me now.

'You're the founder of *London Bound* magazine?'

Jack's jaw clenched. 'Yes.'

I didn't know what else to say. I continued staring at him, the only person in the room not clapping. Pain flashed across Jack's face, torn between wanting to explain and having to fulfil his CEO duties, finally walking regretfully toward the stage. I suppose it was my chance to finally learn about this man, the man who had given so much of his time to help me achieve my dream but shared nothing of his true self. Perhaps I should have listened to Jack's speech, heard about all the wonderful things that he had accomplished in his working life, and what he still hoped to achieve. But I couldn't stay, couldn't sit there looking up at someone I had felt so close to and now didn't know at all.

I stared down at the tablecloth, trying to remember how to breathe, trying not to let the tears that threatened fall down my cheeks. I focused on the glossy cream-coloured card that sat on the table near Jack's wine glass. The key to the room Jack had booked. I stared at it, my eyes shifting from the key to Jack, flawlessly commanding the stage; had I not felt so numb I might have been impressed. I looked back to the card, then calmly opened my clutch purse and placed it inside. Smiling at the gentleman next to me, I stood up, pushed my chair out and started toward the exit without so much as a backward glance.

Chapter Thirty-Three

The word 'room' was misleading. In a room you might expect a queen-size bed, built-in desk, a bathroom with a spa if it was really luxurious, free wifi if you were lucky. And while the Corinthea was no roadside motel, when I swiped the keycard against the door sensor, I didn't expect to be greeted with the bloody Taj Mahal of suites.

The Royal Penthouse was set in the curve of the hotel, spread over two floors, and had spectacular river views. Exploring every inch of the 500-square-metre space and marvelling at the expanse, I felt like royalty. There was a private spa suite and hidden den, as well as a butler's pantry and walk-in wine cellar, the surfaces a mix of panelled walls, leather-lined shelves and oak parquet floors. Each piece gleamed with opulence, from the dining table of highly polished Makassar ebony to the bed frames of walnut with leather detailing to the marble honey onyx bathrooms that were bigger than Nana's back garden.

I walked from room to room, deciding against the private lift and instead using the grand staircase, the satin of my dress swishing as I walked. Lost in the beauty of my surroundings, I stepped out onto the roof terrace, my emotions shifting from awe to sadness as I took in the vista before me.

I knew the moment I stepped outside why Jack had chosen this penthouse; the roof terrace had the most breathtaking panoramic view of London, stretching as far as St Paul's Cathedral all the way to the Millennium Wheel. Champagne rested on ice in a fluted metal bucket, and a richly textured white card sat folded in front of it on the table. I tentatively lifted the card, hoping against hope that it contained directions for the TV or maybe the password for the wifi. No such luck.

First London – then the world.
Jack x
P.S. Now this is what I call a balcony party.

I felt like my heart was breaking all over again.

I closed my eyes, the wind brushing against my face and the hot tears burning under my lids. How had my life come to this? I had achieved all of my goals: living in London; dream career; dream man; standing in couture; champagne at the ready with the most spectacular views of London. But it all felt wrong, I was living a lie: I was dating a man I barely knew and enjoying success that I hadn't earned, a success that had been created by my boyfriend's connections and my nana's wardrobe. Never had I felt more alone, more miserable.

I read the note over and over, lifting my eyes to the city. Bugger this – I'd spent too much of my time in London unhappy, and I wasn't going to waste a magical evening in a vintage gown because of some lying lad.

I needed some answers.

I took a deep swig of champagne straight from the bottle, wiping my mouth with the back of my hand, every bit the lady I was.

'Okay, Kate, let's go see what Mr Live-in-the-Moment has to say for himself.'

I let the anger fuel my steps, though Lord knows running in a ball gown was no easy feat – no wonder Cinderella had lost her bloody shoe. I nearly fell on my face a number of times. It seemed that every possible obstacle was in my path, threatening to take me down. I was a blue streak of lightning, flashing through the hotel halls, an elegant but rage-filled vision slicing its way through the opulence, causing raised brows and annoyed tuts as I whizzed past.

The ballroom was in full party-mode now, most guests had abandoned their tables and were mingling, networking, dancing and drinking up a storm. I weaved through the tables, searching all the faces, praying that he hadn't left, that he was above all a business man and would be disciplined enough to stay at the ball and see out his duties. I spotted the statuesque line of Charlotte

Whitakers' back and made a determined path toward her. I felt so completely out of place; wisps of blonde hair had fallen out of my intricate hairstyle, my cheeks were flushed and a light sheen of perspiration sat on my skin. I didn't feel worthy of her presence, and utterly embarrassed to be interrupting her conversation.

'Sorry, Charlotte, have you got a minute?'

Charlotte's green eyes turned to me, so bright and intoxicating up close that I couldn't believe I hadn't noticed them before.

'Kate, is everything all right?'

She was far too polite to tell me I looked a sight and I was grateful for that. I offered an apologetic smile to the beautifully dressed couple opposite her, who examined me critically. I stepped aside and Charlotte excused herself from the couple, coming to stand beside me.

'Have you seen Jack?'

Charlotte smiled sympathetically. 'Bad night?'

I laughed, because if I didn't I would cry. 'Not great.'

'I saw you leave during Jack's speech.'

'Yes, not my finest moment,' I said, retrieving the security card for the penthouse. 'Can you do me a favour and give this to him if you see him?'

She took the card from me, her perfectly made-up face expressing her surprise. 'Wow, the royal penthouse, he must really like you.'

'Yeah, well, probably not anymore.'

'I tell you what, how about you give this to him, instead,' she said, handing it back to me.

'If I were Jack Baker, where would I be?' I spoke mainly to myself. The truth was I had no idea because, at the crux of it, I didn't really know who Jack Baker was.

'Leave it to me,' said Charlotte, lifting up the edge of her gown and sashaying toward the stage, smiling and laughing with people along the way in a far more dignified display than I could ever hope for. I watched, confused, as she walked onto the stage, confidently picking up the microphone.

'Good evening, ladies and gentlemen. Sorry to interrupt your night but if anyone could point me in the direction of Mr Jack Baker, I would greatly appreciate it – he has left the lights on in that beautiful car of his.'

Charlotte didn't have to wait long before a slurred voice yelled out, 'He's in the Bassoon Bar.'

Charlotte leant into the microphone, flashing a blinding smile. 'Thank you, Graham.'

Graham saluted her with his glass. 'It's a bloody good bar, that one.'

Charlotte looked at me and winked.

I mouthed, 'thank you.' Outrageously beautiful *and* kind, Charlotte really did have it all. Wondering at the biological lottery she had won, I made a determined path to the exit, my destination set for the Bassoon Bar, wherever that may be.

~

The Bassoon Bar was the perfect moody setting for Jack Baker, who sat casually at the bar. He stared into a tumbler of a whiskey, his bow tie unravelled, his hair dishevelled by the weary fingers he continued to run through its thick locks. Despite the sight, I smiled, relief overriding my anger as I walked into the bar. I nearly reached him without detection, but then he lifted his eyes and stilled and it was enough to make me want to stop in my tracks. I drew in a much-needed breath and urged myself to keep walking, to ignore the frightened, vulnerable side of me that whispered to run home. I stood beside him, placing the keycard on the bar and sliding it across to him.

I shrugged. 'It's a bit big for one.'

He motioned to the barman for a refill. 'Didn't think you would appreciate the company.'

'Well, I was hoping to share it with the Jack that I've come to know these past few months.'

Jack looked into my eyes, curiosity burning within them.

'But I don't know where he went.'

Raw emotion filled Jack's face as he said, 'It's still me, Kate.'

'Is it? I don't want to be that person, suspicious and ungrateful. I see it in my nana, a bitterness, an unwilling-ness to trust, and it's starting in me. I'm keeping secrets myself and it's just so bloody toxic. But you – all this – why didn't you tell me?'

'Kate, I didn't tell you because when I'm with you I'm not Jack Baker of *London Bound*, I'm just Jack, a nobody. You saw me for me, not my empire. And when I found out you were a blogger in the fashion world, it made me more determined for you to know the real me first, without my career.'

While he may have hoped to appease me with his honesty, the result was quite the opposite. 'Do you really think I would have propositioned you to help boost my career?'

'You wouldn't have been the first.'

'Then I guess you don't know me at all.'

Jack stood, towering over me. 'I know you, Kate, and I know you know me. I helped you because you worked for it, didn't expect it. Yeah, I slid your stuff under the right noses, but Charlotte contacting you, and all the other magazines and websites that have featured you, that was their decision, not mine. I'm sorry I didn't tell you, and, knowing you as I do now, if I had my time again I would have told you. But I've learned to be careful about the people I surround myself with, and every single person in my life is there because I trust them to be there. You've earned that space in my life . . . in my heart.'

He gestured to the lobby. 'It's like that bloody chandelier, surrounded by thousands of glittering white crystals, but you're that rare piece, the red crystal, the colour that I've been waiting for.'

Jack lifted the fresh tumbler to his mouth but I stopped him.

'Probably shouldn't be mixing whiskey and champagne.'

Jack looked at his drink, confusion lining his face. 'But I'm not . . .'

I took the drink out of his hand and placed it back on the bar, then slid the room key over to him. 'You will be.'

Jack looked at the card as if not daring to believe.

'I'm not saying I'm not mad, and I kind of get why you did what you did. But don't ever keep anything from me, Jack; if we're going to do this it has to be all or nothing.'

Jack moved toward me, gently cupping my cheek, his thumb brushing against my skin. 'I'll bore you with every single minute detail since my birth. I'll tell you whatever you want to know.'

'Somehow I think that there wouldn't be a boring moment in the life of Jack Baker.'

'Boring? No, probably not, but there's something that you need to know about me, Kate.' Jack slid his arms around me; the warmth, the familiarity of him felt so good, so right. It was hard to think, to breathe.

'Oh, what's that?'

He pulled away a little, a small smile forming. 'I have never lived till now.'

My brow curved. 'Until now?'

'Well, actually, the moment I nearly hit you with my car.'

I burst out laughing at the memory of what seemed like a lifetime ago.

'Oh, yes, that! You never did say sorry.'

Jack grinned. 'The day Kate Brown came bursting into my life.' He shook his head. 'No, I'll never be sorry about that.'

I looked up into Jack's deep brown eyes, lost to him. 'Neither will I.'

Chapter Thirty-Four

Pulling up to the kerb outside our terraces, I took a moment to look at the houses. The first day I arrived here, looking up at their imposing rooflines, I would have never imagined that my life would quite resemble this, arriving home in an Aston Martin with a couture ballgown draped over my arm. My attention turned back to the impressive cockpit-like interior of the car.

'Is it even possible to leave your headlights on accidentally in a car like this?' I asked, mainly to myself.

Jack laughed. 'What?'

'Oh, nothing,' I said, opening the door and extending the handle on my overnight bag, the one that Jack had sneakily got Vera to pack without my knowledge; an incredibly sweet gesture, but one that also accounted for the rather dowdy mismatching attire of faded jeans and out-of-shape grey V-neck. Apparently Vera had sold the idea to Nana that staying where the ball was being held would be a much safer, more responsible solution, as it meant avoiding a late-night commute. She was an absolute genius.

I stood on the path, waiting for Jack to make his way around to me; smiling, he pulled me into his arms, kissing the top of my head, resting his chin on me. Our lingering moment of affection was so very different from the first time we met on this very spot. I recalled the cocky, incredulous look on his face and how I had hated finding him attractive. I pulled away from his embrace to look up at his handsome face.

'I'll be in in a sec,' he said.

'Balcony?'

'Ah, I think it's time to start coming through the front door, yeah?'

I smiled. 'Wow, that's a big step.'

'No more secrets, remember?'

My smile fell away, recalling our pact. 'No more secrets.' The only way we could move forward was to be honest in all aspects of our lives, which included telling Nana about using her secret room for my blog posts. Remembering the way she had looked at me last night, when she thought I'd merely looked in her room, made me feel sick about what I had to do.

'Hope Nana's in a good mood,' I said over my shoulder, pulling my case up the steps.

Unlocking the front door to the terrace and swinging it open, I picked up the mail from the floor and plopped it on the side table.

'Nana, Vera, anyone home?'

'In the kitchen,' called Vera.

'Okay, well, I'm just putting the dress away, be down in a sec.' I wasn't going to lie, the sooner I got Nana's dress safely back where it belonged the better; wearing it last night, worrying about spillage and tearing, had made me more than a little anxious.

It felt nice to actually have a reason to visit the one place, aside from Jack's arms, that calmed me. Now that Nana knew I knew about the room, I felt a step closer to being more honest about everything in my life. As I walked toward the room, my bone-deep dread melted away, letting in a new-found optimism. All the stars were aligning, and with a meeting with Charlotte Whitakers planned for tomorrow, I was never more determined or excited about 'Kate on the Thames'. Jack had assured me that he would only help if I asked, that he wouldn't interfere, but I didn't care all that much. The nights I had worked with Jack on the video editing and my social media strategy had been some of the most memorable moments of my life; we shared a core vision, a deep love for beautiful things and the passion to present them in a way that could be appreciated by the masses. It wasn't CEO Jack whose advice I sought out, but the Jack who had sat on my front doorstep with a cold beer listening to my follower updates. I smiled to myself, barely believing how things had turned out. I juggled my bag and the dress and managed to twist the door handle, pushing it open and switching on the light.

I froze, my mouth falling open, my blood running cold.

The room, though still its glorious light blue, with beautiful white cabinetry and sparkling chandelier, had one very obvious difference. The room was completely empty, devoid of any vintage splendour or designer collectables; the entire room had been stripped of belongings. I let the dress in its plastic carry bag crumple to the floor, moving to open the double doors to the adjoining room, hoping that maybe they had been relocated, but there was nothing. Even the dressing table was barren. The only object in the room sat on top of the glass cabinet: the article from *London Bound*, the one that Jack had brought over last night, that had a photo of me holding up a Louis Vuitton to the camera against the backdrop of Nana's shelves, with the caption 'One to watch – "Kate on the Thames". I cast my mind back to last night, the heated words Jack and I had had at the door, him taking the article from me and leaving it on the sideboard.

Oh God.

I felt gutted, both ashamed for accepting kudos for something that wasn't even mine but also devastated that Nana had taken away the one of the few things that gave me joy.

I shook my head, barely believing, as I marched a determined line to the door, ripping it open and heading directly for the stairs.

'Nana!' I called out, opening the door to her bedroom then bathroom – both empty. Beside myself at the loss of my secret happy place, I was ready to start a full-scale war. I blindly ran into Vera in the hall, almost knocking her over.

'Kate, what on earth—'

'Where's Nana?'

'She's in the back garden.'

'It's gone, Vera, all of it, every single item has been cleared out,' I said, brushing past her to head through the kitchen to the back courtyard where Nana sat in the sun, crumbling pieces of bread for the birds dancing around in the garden. The scene would have been as pretty as a picture had I not been so upset.

I came to stand before her, but her attention never broke from her task.

'You didn't have to do that.'

'Oh, I see old Mother Hubbard went to the cupboard and the cupboard was bare.'

'Do you really hate me that much?'

Her ice blue eyes lifted to me, disregarding my obvious state of distress with a hard look. I felt like a small, wilful child about to be reprimanded for her selfish behaviour.

'I know I should have asked, I know what I did was wrong. I was going to tell you about the blog, but then it exploded, and I just didn't know how to tell you; I waited for you to be in a good mood, but you never are. Every day I try not to upset you, to please you, while you seem to live to be nasty and to put me down. Do you know how exhausting that is?'

Nana looked away from me, continuing to crumble bread for the birds as if I wasn't even there.

'Well, if you wanted to teach me a lesson, well done, you have. You win, you've taken all my joy – Joy, is that why you're called that? Because you suck the life out of people? You grind them down to dust by being so hateful and hurtful? And if saying this gets me kicked out, then so be it. I know I was wrong, I admit it. But you're wrong too, Nana. You're wrong too.'

I didn't wait for her response. Instead, as hard as it was to pull away from her searing gaze, I stalked inside, ignoring the shrill calls of my name.

'Get back here, Katherine Elizabeth . . . Kate!'

I walked past Vera in the kitchen, going down the hall, feeling myself shaking. I was so upset, so terrified of the consequences of my words.

'Kate, wait!' Vera called after me, but I was not stopping, I was out of here and would never look back. I opened the door and slammed so hard into Jack that he had to grab my arms to steady me from falling over.

'Whoa, what's wrong?' His brows knitted together, looking from me to Vera, who was now standing behind me. 'So Nana's not in a good mood then?'

I wiped my eyes. 'Take me away from this place, Jack.'

'What's going on?' he asked.

'A family trait, Jack: short wicks. I'm afraid she gets her short fuse and knack for jumping to conclusions from me.'

I turned to Nana, who stood next to Vera behind me. She sighed as if bored, leaning on her walking stick. Despite knowing how upset I was, there was not an ounce of sympathy.

'I'm nothing like you,' I said. I felt the press of Jack's hand at my back as he tried to halt my words, but I didn't care. If anything, I was relieved; no more secrets, everything was out in the open. I would cancel my meeting tomorrow with Charlotte and just start again, somehow.

Like it's that easy.

Vera stepped forward. 'Kate, I think there's something you should see.'

'I think I've seen enough.'

'Trust me, you are going to want to see this. Joy?' She turned to Nana as if expecting her to chime in, but if she wanted her to beg me not to go, then Vera really didn't know her at all. As expected, Nana rolled her eyes.

'Oh, for God's sake, let's put her out of her misery, my tea's getting cold.'

'What are you talking about?'

'Jack, answer me this: is she like this with you?' asked Nana.

I shot Jack a warning look, cringing about what had happened last night. I could tell he was thinking about it by the way his lips twitched, stifling a smirk.

Jack shrugged. 'I don't know what you're talking about.'

Chapter Thirty-Five

I don't know why I followed, there was nothing for me to see, nothing that I could have possibly cared about. Nana had made sure of that. But we went up to the second floor and down the hall, following Nana at a glacial pace. Vera, Jack and I stood behind her as she approached the closet door. The only thing I was certain of was that there were no umbrellas in that closet, and that it was far too small to house any rare vintage garments. Joy opened up the closet door, revealed just what I suspected – linen.

Nana looked proud, actually smiling, as was Vera; Jack's confusion and my annoyance aside, I started to wonder if there was a slow gas leak filtering through the terrace, making everyone mad.

'Well, if it's storage you're worried about, I am sure you have ample of it now: two rooms, in fact.'

Including mine, as soon as I left this place.

'Well, you certainly don't get your smarts from me, that's for sure.' Nana laughed.

Vera winced. 'Joy, honestly.'

I was all but ready to walk away when Nana scoffed. 'Fine then, open sesame,' she announced, pushing the shelving with her bony hand, flinging it aside and revealing—

'Holy shit.' Jack spoke the very words I was thinking.

There, in the poky little cupboard, behind the slender shelves that Nana had pushed open like a door, were a set of stairs leading up into darkness.

My eyes shifted to Nana, unable to voice all the questions whirling around in my head.

Nana smiled, pointing her stick toward the stairs. 'Go on then.'

My eyes strayed from Nana, to Jack, then to Vera, uncertain. 'Are you going to lock me in the attic, Nana?'

Nana laughed. 'Don't tempt me, child. Now go; take Romeo with you if you're so scared.'

'There's a drawstring light at the top of the stairs,' said Vera.

I tentatively edged forward, ducking my head and moving through the dusty opening. Jack's hand was on my back, letting me know he was right behind me. I slowly started up the small, narrow, seemingly endless steps, the light coming from the hall behind us the only guide.

'Well, if we're locked up here for all eternity at least we'll be together,' Jack teased.

'I know that's supposed to be a comfort, Jack, but it's not working. I'm trying to rack my brains for any missing cousins in my family.'

'Any you can think of?'

'Not that I can recall,' I said, coming to an opening, my hands sliding along a banister leading me into more darkness.

'Look for the light.'

'I am,' I said, my hands searching in front of me, waving around until my hand touched a string.

'Ah-ha! I got it!' I yelled, yanking on the cord and flooding the room with brightness, blinking and smiling at my little victory; the relief of having got up here safely soon left me, however, as my widened eyes took in the room. The only thing I could do was grab Jack's hand, squeezing so tightly my knuckles turned a yellowy-white.

'Jack! Pinch me!' I said urgently, needing him to prove that I wasn't dreaming, that this was real. He pinched my bum so hard I swear it bruised instantly, but it was his laughter that had me tearing my eyes from the sight before me to him.

'Fuck me!'

And before I could repeat those exact sentiments, a shadow rose from behind Jack, bearing down and striking him on the arm.

'Jesus, what the hell?'

'Language, young man!' Nana lowered her walking stick; there will be no such language in the presence of Prada.

Or Chanel, Saint Laurent, Vuitton, Dior.

An entire room, chock-full of racks and racks and racks of clothes, boxes and shelving, full to overflowing, far more than what could have existed in Nana's room.

'W-what is this place?'

'Storage,' said Vera.

'It's where I keep the really good stuff.'

'The really good stuff?'

Nana shrugged. 'I mean, the stuff in my room was all right but if you want to be serious about fashion then you'll need to work with quality.'

I blinked, completely confused. I didn't understand a word of what she was saying.

Vera must have guessed as much. 'I showed Nana your blog; well, actually she bullied me into it after finding the news clipping.'

Oh God, she had seen my blog, the videos of me touching her things. I turned to Nana's steely blue gaze, so serious and mean, bracing myself. But then something unexpected happened: her brows lifted, and she leant into the light with a small but genuine smile on her face.

'I loved it.'

What? Nana didn't love anything or anyone – surely she was just being cruel?

'R-really?'

Nana shrugged. 'I did. Made me think that it was time to wipe the dust away and give my belongings to someone who not only admires, but respects fashion and the memories and culture attached to it. I mean, Lord knows your mother would have them in an auction house if she could; no, they belong to you, Kate. I couldn't think of a more worthy owner.'

I shook my head, still struggling to register what I had just heard. 'I think that might just be the compliment of my life.'

Nana scoffed. 'Well, Jack, you better lift your game; if you're going to date my granddaughter, you're going to have to pull out a few more stops.'

I thought back to last night, Jack kissing me and dancing with me under the Baccarat chandelier at the Corinthia, how we had drunk champagne on the roof terrace and made love until the morning sun lit the murky waters of the Thames. Jack was off to a fine start.

'So I have your blessing then, Joy? To date your granddaughter?'

Jack's words snapped me out of my daydream, bringing my attention to Nana, who assessed him with a cold, hard stare.

'Can you lift heavy things?'

Jack laughed. 'Yes.'

'Good, help Kate set up her room with whatever she wants,' she said, making her way slowly back down the stairs.

'Wait, what, Nana . . .' I called out, going after her until we re-entered the hallway and stood face to face. 'Are you serious?'

'Deathly serious, otherwise I wouldn't have nearly broken poor Vera's back clearing out the room for you.'

I could feel hot tears brim in my eyes.

Nana fidgeted, clearly uncomfortable with my emotion. 'It's a blank slate now, choose what you want, set it up how you want just . . . keep the noise down,' she said, breaking away before I had a chance to reach out and hug the life out of her.

'Nana,' I called out after her, causing her to stop at the top of the stairs.

'I'm sorry that I said I was nothing like you; I am like you, more than I ever realised. And I'm very proud to be.'

Nana smiled mockingly. 'Oh, don't be ridiculous, Katherine, you and I both know that there's only room in this life for one of me,' she said, before returning to her slow descent down the stairs.

I watched her go, feeling Jack come to stand beside me.

'She's one of a kind, your nan, that's for sure.'

I shook my head. 'She most certainly is.'

Chapter Thirty-Six

I wasn't sure what Nana was whingeing about, I thoroughly enjoyed Richard and Judy's selection. But after meeting Cybil, Jean, Rose, Margaret and Carol – the lovely ladies of the book club – and while being wary of ruining the deep-thinking, literary sensibility of the club, I couldn't help but feel they needed some spice in their lives. Sitting in a loose circle in Nana Joy's parlour, I decided to take a chance, producing a copy of *Shipwrecked Hearts* from my bag. Seeing their eyes light up, I could see my instincts were right on the money.

'Now, I have read this and unfortunately it is out of print, but I'm sure I could hunt down some copies on eBay, maybe, or I—'

'Yes!' said Jean cutting me off. 'I think that would be a fine idea.'

Carol took it from my hand, adjusting her glasses and looking rather scandalised at the cover. 'Oh yes,

I think a change is certainly worth a try – what do you think, Joy?'

Nana, whose lips were pursed, looked around the room with condescension. 'Oh, honestly, who would bother with such smut?'

I looked pointedly at her, knowing damn well that she knew where I had found the copy.

Nana deliberately turned away from me. 'But if that's what you ladies want to read, who am I to say no?'

Rose clapped excitedly. 'Pass it over here, Carol.'

'In a minute, I'm just reading the blurb.'

'Ha! Like you care about the plot,' teased Margaret. 'Hurry up, don't be a hog.'

Yep, I would have find more copies before all hell broke loose.

By the end of the afternoon's excitement, Nana excused herself from the riff-raff.

'I think I might lie down, Vera, you ladies always manage to exhaust me,' she said, grabbing her stick and moving slowly to the hall.

'You okay, Nana? Do you need some help?'

She placed her hand up, cutting me off. 'I'm all right,' she snapped. 'Just see the ladies out, would you?'

'Okay.' I smiled, relieved that she was back to her old rotten self.

I couldn't really blame Nana this time around. I wasn't making excuses for her, but even I was exhausted by an afternoon with these ladies and I was all too happy to show them the door.

'Do you think you could get me two copies, Kate?' asked Rose, as I helped her with her things out the door.

'Leave it with me and I'll see what I can do.'

Ushering the last of the ladies out the door, I crashed into the back of Rose as they all stopped suddenly on the porch.

'Ladies, what's the hold-up?' I followed their eyeline, confused and slightly annoyed, until my attention locked onto a six-foot-four man standing at my gate.

'Oh, my word,' said Cybil. They slowly descended the stairs, whispering and giggling like a group of schoolgirls. Jack stood aside to let them through.

'Ladies,' he said, flashing them a winning smile.

More giggles erupted and I couldn't help but shake my head as Jack moved up the front steps to the door.

'What can I say? I have a way with the ladies.'

'Well, I'd be careful if I was you, they're about to read the book I was reading.'

Horror wrote itself across Jack's face as he turned to watch the old ducks shuffle down the street. 'Jesus.'

'Yep, there goes the neighbourhood,' I said, folding my arms and leaning against the door.

'Speaking of neighbourhoods, do you want to escape this one for a while?'

I glanced behind me, stepping out onto the porch and closing the door behind me.

'Well, Nana's having a nap, so I could probably break away for a bit.'

'You don't have to ask permission anymore – you know that, right?'

'Old habits die hard.'

'Well, clearly, seeing as you climbed over my balcony last night when you could have just used my front door.'

'Ah, yes, but where's the fun in that?'

'Well, if you want to keep things spicy, come with me right now.'

'Jack, if you're taking me to a curry house, you should know I'm no good with chilli.'

Jack laughed. 'You are something else, Kate Brown.'

'I'm serious, I don't want—'

'I'm not taking you to a bloody curry house.'

'Oh, well, what then?'

Jack stepped forward until my back hit the door.

'I'm going to take you to so many places, and show you so many things, every single chance I get, starting from now.'

My mouth twitched. 'Oh yeah, and where are you taking me now?'

Jack grinned, taking me by the hand and pulling me into motion.

'You'll see.'

~

I could honestly say that, aside from the view from a luxury penthouse suite, a river cruise was the second-best way to see London, though for someone who had barely been out their front door, the recommendation may not mean a whole lot. The Thames River spanned over three hundred kilometres straight through the heart of the city, dividing the north and the south sides of London, and the dinner cruise that Jack had booked took us through the very best parts.

I kept my hair pulled back at the nape of my neck. Long blonde strands still whipped around my face wildly, but I didn't care, for that afternoon I was unashamedly a tourist, standing and pointing, smiling and basking in the glorious sunshine that the London clouds kindly let through for our voyage. Jack didn't say much, he didn't need to, content to watch in quiet amusement at my excitement. Being here with Jack, gliding past the London Eye pier, down from Big Ben, the Tower of London and my favourite, the iconic Tower Bridge, I thought my heart would burst. Along the way down Bankside we passed the historic Shakespeare's Globe, a replica of the old one that burnt down in the seventeenth century, or so the PA system informed us. Feeling the wind against my skin and the sun burning brightly above, it was anyone's guess if I was more likely to suffer from an acute dose of windburn or sunburn, the latter not something I would have ever thought would be an issue in England. Spying on the banks lined with eateries, bars and theatres, I could completely imagine my

life here; I finally felt a sense of belonging that was hard
to explain. Maybe it was due to my heritage, or my deep,
unabiding love for full English breakfasts, but this was
definitely home.

I stretched my legs out and folded my arms, momentarily distracted from the awe of my environment by
a niggling thought that popped into my head. 'I can't
believe you haven't asked me,' I said, turning expectantly
toward him.

'Asked you what?'

'About my interview with Charlotte.'

'Oh, that, well, hey.' He held his hands up. 'Nothing
to do with me.'

I rolled my eyes. 'Don't you want to know? I mean,
you probably do, or you'll no doubt find out, but I
mean you don't have to be like that, I just thought that—'

'Kate.' Jack laughed. 'What happened?'

I didn't know if it was the choppy surface of the river,
or just my nerves that were making my insides twist, but
I bit my lip and watched Jack's face expectantly. 'Charlotte
offered me a position to write content for her website,
a home for "Kate on the Thames". I could talk all things
fashion and do interviews and write a column if I wanted,
it would be great exposure, a dream job really.'

Jack's face was unchanged as he looked at me.

'I said no to her offer.' I winced, and started to twist my
hands. 'It's not that I'm ungrateful, it's just that I kind of
want to see where this goes now that there are no secrets

and I have all this inspiring content at my fingertips, and a space where I can be creative and not trapped in an office or answer to anyone but myself. I know that it's an amazing chance I'm passing up but I just think I have to go with my gut on this one . . . I'm sorry.'

'Kate, what have I told you?'

I remained silent, trying to recall what he had told me about my career, but then Jack broke into a slow, brilliant smile.

'My door is always open.'

'To *London Bound*?'

'To everything that is mine.'

I blinked back tears, turning my gaze to the skyline of the city, seeing it from angles those on land would not be privy to. I felt blessed, more so when I felt Jack's hand slide over mine, linking our fingers and lifting my hand to kiss it.

'Are you afraid Joy might change her mind?'

I laughed. 'No, Vera and I won't let her.'

'I believe that.'

I turned to him. 'So, Jack Baker, looks like we're going to be neighbours for the foreseeable future.'

'Well, it's a good thing I really, really, really like you then.'

I smiled, leaning into him, resting my head against the crook of his neck, shielding myself from the river breeze.

'You haven't worked it out yet, have you?'

I shook my head. 'Worked out what?'

'Why I took you on this particular cruise.' Jack laughed, leaning into me and whispering into my temple. 'Now you're quite literally Kate on the Thames.'

I straightened and looked around, my smile cheesy and bright as I turned back to Jack, giggling.

'And so I am!'

Acknowledgements

To my loving husband Michael, for taking me around the world in the winter of 2015. For comforting me in moments of horrific turbulence and bouts of food poisoning, and for all the shopping centres I managed to drag you through without complaint. I am a nightmare and you are a saint to travel with, but more importantly, if we hadn't gone on this adventure together then this series would never have been born. It might be my imagination that creates these worlds, but it is always your support that makes what I do possible.

To my wonderful publisher Hachette Australia for their passion, support and encouragement: working with you all (Fiona, Laura, Essie, Haylee) is a sheer joy.

To my wingwoman Kate Stevens for working so tirelessly to guide me through every story with your vision, compassion and professionalism. I want to grow old writing books with you.

To Anita, Keary, Jess and Lilliana, for always pushing me and helping me to the finish line even when it seems impossible. Your friendship, patience and smarts are what help govern my success; I cherish each and every one of you.

To my amazing family and friends for putting up with my lockdowns and never-ending deadlines, for constantly reminding me of things I tend to forget; you remind me to live and be balanced. Your love is the best anchor I could wish for.

To all the readers, bloggers, reviewers of my stories, for taking something away from my words and for loving and embracing the characters; for wanting to read Australian voices, no matter what city they may stand in.

And lastly, to London, who stole my heart and inspired me on one singular bus trip where I first had the idea for the 'Heart of the City' series. Everyone has a place away from home where they belong – London, you were that place for me.

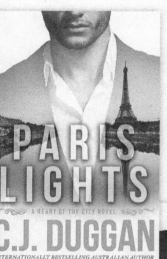

READ ALL THREE
STANDALONE TITLES
IN C.J. DUGGAN'S
HEART OF THE CITY SERIES:

READ ON FOR A PREVIEW

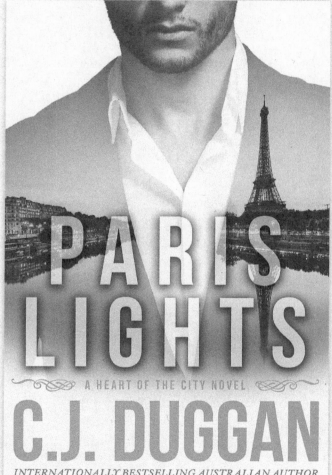

PARIS LIGHTS

A HEART OF THE CITY NOVEL

C.J. DUGGAN

INTERNATIONALLY BESTSELLING AUSTRALIAN AUTHOR

Chapter One

genuinely believe that aside from your place of birth there is somewhere else you belong: a place you're guided to by your heart. Some people might spend their entire lives in search of such a place, but all my life, throughout my travels, I knew which place was waiting for me.

Paris.

I had fed my love of Paris by having the Eiffel Tower plastered on my bedspreads and cushion covers, by buying kitchen accessories and placemats with *Rue Du Temple* scrawled across them, and hanging a cute *Bon Appetit* sign in my kitchen. I'd tried to explain to my boyfriend, Liam, that it wasn't really an obsession, I had just adopted a French Provincial style of decorating for our home. He seemed unconvinced.

Everyone wants to go to Paris. To fall in love, eat smelly French cheese and drink good local wine while toasting to the Eiffel Tower. It was more than just our home's décor and my Chanel lipstick collection that strengthened my bond. Paris is the art capital of the world, with tourists flocking from near and far to catch a quick glimpse of Da Vinci's *Mona Lisa* and wander the vast halls of the Louvre. But, while many people believed the Louvre to be the pinnacle of the Parisian art museum scene, there were so many other museums to see. With much excitement, I had rattled off the list of must-see locations to Liam as we'd planned this long-awaited weekend in Paris.

'We could head to the Centre Pompidou, Paris's bastion of modern art. We'll need a good couple of hours to wander through all the amazing rooms with world-famous works of – oh my God, we'll be able to see Picasso, Klimt, Miro and Kandinsky!'

Liam's face had twisted in horror, and he'd said, 'Claire, I would sooner claw my own face off than spend an entire weekend in art museums.'

I had laughed it off, but my heart sank knowing that he wouldn't budge on this. I would have to settle for compromising on the art so we could both enjoy the trip.

Liam had insisted we save the Eiffel Tower until our last day in Paris. He'd said we shouldn't conform to the typical tourist itinerary, that we should discover other parts of the city first. He was so smart, so romantic.

We battled the crowds at the Louvre for a date with Mona Lisa, strolled hand-in-hand through the Jardin de Tuileries, dodged pigeons and love-lock sellers near Notre Dame, and, of course, no trip to Paris would be complete without a visit to the famed Moulin Rouge.

And this morning, stepping from the bus, our heads had craned upward, my mouth ajar as Liam clicked away on his expensive Canon camera, snapping the iron beast before us. Except it wasn't a beast. The Eiffel Tower was a lady – strong, imposing, beautiful – but I couldn't have said so to Liam. He would have just rolled his eyes.

We'd lingered around the edge of the crowds, taking it all in. It was incredible how something that stood still could evoke as much excitement as a themed rollercoaster at Disneyland. Hordes of tourists surrounded us in a blur of excitement and delight. Despite the wonders around me, though, my attention remained on Liam. I only had eyes for him.

I tilted my head, admiring my gorgeous boyfriend: his dark, unruly hair, his five o'clock shadow, his charcoal-grey jumper and dark jeans that made him look like he belonged here; a true Parisian. Liam had been acting strange for days. Twitchy, antsy, a bit snappy. As he stood beside me, rubbing his unshaven jaw, I could see the cogs turning in his head, no doubt wondering what to say, how to do it. He is such a stickler for details; it's one of the things I love about him.

My chest expanded as I breathed deeply. I tried to hide the knowing smile that twisted the corner of my mouth. *This is it; this is really going to happen.* It was all clear to me now: the impromptu visit to Paris; saving the tower till last.

This is my moment.

Wait until everyone back home finds out about this.

I stood in the heart of the square and waited for Liam to speak. Waited for him to ask the big question, to go down on one knee in front of all these people, and ask me to be Mrs Liam Jackson.

My chest tightened as he turned to me. His focus was on me and me alone. In this moment, under the massive iron structure, the world around us didn't matter. It was as if we were the only ones on the planet and that the tower had been built for us alone. I could feel my skin prickle despite the warm air that swept over us.

'Claire.' Liam swallowed nervously. I could feel my eyes watering as he reached out and grabbed my hand, a hand that had been nervously tapping my thigh.

'Yes?' I breathed out, my heart beating a million miles an hour. *Yes, yes, yes* had been echoing in my mind all morning.

The dark, hypnotic pools of Liam's eyes made me breathless as he gazed intently at me.

This is it! This is what I've been waiting for. The perfect end to a perfect weekend.

He squeezed my hand. 'I think we should see other people.'

I didn't think I'd heard him correctly; the sound of a record scratching in my head might have prevented me from understanding. Or maybe it was the tourists, talking and pointing animatedly as they took selfies with the tower. Even the traffic noise seemed painfully loud right now. I tilted my head as if to listen more intently, my eyes blinking in confusion.

'Sorry?'

Liam's eyes seemed less romantic now, and his face was twisted in pain. But it wasn't pain caused by the inner turmoil of working on romantic perfection like I had thought. It was another kind of pain entirely.

'I said, I think we should—'

'No!' I shut off his words, afraid that he would only repeat himself. 'No, no, no, no!' This was not how it was supposed to go.

I had planned it all in my mind: Liam on one knee, a box appearing from his pocket (preferably from Tiffany), applause ringing out across the square as I cried and said, *Yes, yes, YES!* I had envisioned how to pose with my ring for Instagram, adding the witty caption: 'I said oui oui.' I had even picked out the appropriate filter for our selfie. It was all so perfect – in my head.

'Claire, I'm sorry.' His brown eyes were sorrowful, as though his heart was breaking. It was like I had just said the words that would tear us apart, not him. 'I never meant to hurt you.'

I felt my fists clench. My shock, my disbelief, was morphing into something else, even as the hot tears pooled in my eyes.

He never meant to hurt me.

'You're breaking up with me!'

Silence.

'In *Paris.*'

He looked away.

'Under the Eiffel fucking Tower!' I screamed, attracting the attention of those who were unlucky enough to be standing nearby.

Was there any feeling worse than this? A punch in the face on a gondola in Venice maybe? He might as well have punched me – it felt like all the air had been sucked from my lungs.

My admiration for him, my total and utter besotted and blind obsession with Liam, died. I could feel my heart darken; my soul was so black it scared me. We had been together for eighteen months, had moved from Melbourne to London so Liam could follow his path in life – whatever that had meant; he'd never actually clarified it. If he meant we were both always strapped for cash and working double shifts in the dimly lit London pub, then we were following his path all right. Living the dream! We had been so determined to find our way and make a new life in a foreign land, despite Liam's rather lacklustre path in London. I had been certain we knew each other's dreams and fears. And that's what was burning a hole in my heart, because at the crux of it, I don't actually think Liam knew me at all. Because anyone who ever did know me knew that coming to Paris had been my lifelong dream. I had mentioned it often enough. The city was so close to our new home, but until this weekend we had been too busy to make the trip: there was an excuse, there was always an excuse. So when Liam not only agreed, but instigated this trip, I had convinced myself that this was the moment. Why else would he bring me here?

I shook my head. 'How could you?'

I broke away from his hold. He was trying to explain, but I couldn't listen to his reasoning. I stumbled away, skimming past people as I made my way toward the bus that would take me back to the hotel. Everything was a blur. I sat on the top level of the double decker, my eyes forward, staring aimlessly at a balding Italian man and his wife. I couldn't look back to the tower for fear of catching a glimpse of Liam. I didn't hear Liam calling my name, pleading for the bus to stop as it pulled away. I'm not sure if I was more relieved or hurt by the fact he didn't pursue me, but I guess those kind of dramatics only happen in movies.

The sky was grey and ominous. I swear it had been blue when we arrived. That's how quickly things had changed. My bus rolled on, pausing only to give happy, snapping tourists one last chance to take a shot of the tower. I couldn't even bring myself to look at it, not that I would have been able to see it anyway through my bleary vision.

Maybe one day I would forgive Liam for breaking my heart. But tainting Paris, and ruining my experience of this city, that was something I could never forgive – ever!

~

Apparently Paris is especially magnificent in the rain. I had yet to experience the pleasure in my short stay, but as soon as I stepped off the bus, the heavens opened up, soaking me to the bone. It seemed a fitting finale to my disastrous afternoon. In a moment of complete self-indulgence to my misery, I had refused the complimentary plastic poncho from the tourist bus, opting instead to let the rain pummel me. Ordinarily a person might squeal, laugh and run for cover, delighting in the glorious downpour in a foreign city. It was, dare I say it, romantic. But let's face it, romance was dead, as was my ability to feel anything.

I walked along the pavement from the bus stop to a pedestrian crossing, squelching a slow, sad path in my ballet flats, my pleated skirt clinging to my thighs, my long brown hair plastered to my face. Mercifully, the droplets of water disguised my tears. Our hotel was a few blocks away on Rue Lauriston. We were ideally located between the Arc de Triomphe and the Eiffel Tower. It only seemed like yesterday that we had booked the last room available with great excitement.

Our hotel that *we* had booked.

I guess I had to stop saying things like that now. In one afternoon, the life I'd thought I had had become completely redundant. Was that even possible? Had I stayed to face Liam's explanations I might have found out more. If I'd challenged him, fought, screamed, demanded answers. But 'Let's see other people'? That was like a dagger to the heart, almost as bad as 'I'm seeing someone else'. I tried not to entertain the thought that that could have been the reason behind his decision.

I let my feet guide me along the narrow path, through the neighbourhood that seemed amazingly familiar to me even though I'd only been here for a short time. The past three days I'd been wide eyed, drinking in every detail of the impressive Haussmann-designed apartments and buildings; watching the locals go about their daily rounds to the butcher, florist or bakery in their effortlessly stylish way. The air felt thick. I fixed my gaze on the ground, willing my feet forward, telling myself that my reward would be to lock myself away in my hotel room and let my defences crumble down and scream and cry into my pillow.

The red sign of our hotel was mightier than any beacon. I battled on, each step becoming more perilous as the soles of my shoes fought to gain traction on the wet footpath. It took immense concentration to quicken my pace without breaking my neck, but I was determined. That's when I heard the distant sound of a fast-approaching car.

It slid around the corner, the revving engine of the black Audi echoing in the small street, disturbing the peace and quiet, slicing its way through the dying light. It was enough to distract me, annoyed as I was by the reckless-ness of its approach as it sped along like a rally car, and in wet conditions too.

I made sure to glare at the driver.

'Bloody maniac,' I grumbled.

Stepping back from the kerb, I gasped as the car sprayed up a wave of putrid gutter water. Now I was mad. Madder than hell.

I watched as the very same car pulled up in front of my hotel.

'Right,' I said. I was in just the mood to give the flashy lunatic behind the wheel a piece of my mind. And sure, there was a good chance that he wouldn't understand a word I was saying, but if all else failed, flipping the bird was a pretty universal gesture. I neared the car, sleek and beaded with droplets of rain, the windows so heavily tinted it was impossible to see inside.

'Hey!' I shouted, knocking on the driver's window angrily.

There was no response; the only sign of life was the heat that radiated from the vehicle itself. I glared at the window where I imagined a person's head might be. Feeling pretty satisfied at showing my displeasure, I sacrificed the unlady-like gesture of flipping the bird and thought it best to just head into the hotel, leaving a watery path behind me.

And I was about to do exactly that when the unexpected happened. The driver's window slowly edged its way down, revealing a pair of intense, angry blue eyes that seemed to stare right into my soul.

Yep, my day was about to get a whole lot worse.

Chapter Two

If I could have, I would have glued all Liam's undies to the floor and set his favourite pair of jeans on fire, all the while tossing his other possessions over the balcony. Instead, with much less drama, I quietly spoke in a croaky voice to the doorman by the front entrance.

'Can you please come and collect some bags from room twenty-five?'

I was wet and deflated and completely rattled from the death stare the Audi driver had given me, which had sent me fleeing into the hotel. Guess I wasn't as tough as I thought. I certainly didn't feel it right now. What's French for fragile?

If it hadn't been for Cecile, the warm, bubbly lady at reception, I would have sworn everyone in Paris hated me.

'Bonjour!' she said, beaming, showing the gap between her extremely white teeth. Her bright blue eyes lit up and I knew I had her full attention like always. 'Oh, Mademoiselle Shorten, you got caught in the rain?'

I sheepishly examined the squelchy footprints I had trekked through reception.

'Next time, take an umbrella by the door,' she added helpfully.

Ha! Next time. There won't be a next time. I am done.

Despite the bitter edge to my thoughts, I smiled. It was strained, but no matter how bad I was feeling I could never take it out on sweet Cecile; she had, after all, been one of the very few highlights of my weekend.

'Merci,' I said, one of the very limited words I knew the meaning of, even after listening to the audio translator on the Eurostar from London three days ago. My memory for language was not great; I had managed to remember that paper in French was 'papier', and the door was 'la porte'. Neither was going to get me out of a bind.

My watery trail followed me across the foyer to the lift. Pressing the button to summon the slowest lift in Paris, if not the world, I brought the edges of my soaked cardi together, the chill from my wet clothes starting to work its way into my bones. The screeching, rackety shoe box–sized lift groaned its way down to reception, the door struggling to open as the tiny cavity of doom presented itself to me. I tentatively stepped in and, like every other time I had done so, I wondered if this would be the time I would be trapped in here. Would today be the day the lift gave up the ghost? With my current track record, I wouldn't be surprised – it would be the icing on the bloody cake.

The lift screeched its way up to level four, its doors sliding painfully slowly to the side, releasing me to freedom on the narrow landing. I couldn't get out quickly enough. I would live to see another day.

I walked down the narrow carpeted hall to our room. The dated, awkward spaces that had once seemed so quaint to me now just seemed dingy. It made me feel less bad about leaving marks on the already worn, rose-coloured carpet. In the short time that I had stayed here, I had realised that our door required a particular lift-twist-and-shimmy action in order to open it. Still, it took me three goes to get it open, with a few swear words to aid the cause. After finally hearing the magical click of the lock, I shouldered my way through, the door hitting one of the suitcases in the light, tidy yet small room. I negotiated my way through the mess of our bags and clothes to the bed. Side-stepping around it I went to the balcony door, wanting nothing more than to let some fresh air in.

As I opened it, the balcony door hit the edge of the bed, allowing barely enough room to go out; it was something Liam and I had laughed about when we opened it the first time. Every new, quirky discovery had been met with care-free laughter because, after all, it was Paris: there could have been a rodent watching TV on our bed and it would have been okay. WE WERE IN PARIS! But now, as I shifted awkwardly through the small opening and onto the little rain-dampened balcony, I didn't feel any form of whimsy or lighthearted joy at all, even though my heart never failed to clench at the sight of the beautiful apartment buildings lining the street. Opposite me, a slightly damp black cat lazily washed himself on the balcony, the window left ajar for him for whenever he was ready to return.

Despite the traffic noise and the sound of a distant police siren, my mind was alarmingly quiet. My legs, which had felt like jelly, no longer shook, and although a breeze swept across me I didn't feel cold. If anything, my cheeks felt flushed and my heart raced; was I getting sick? Was this a normal reaction to heartbreak? I couldn't tell as I had no experience with being dumped, apart from David Kennedy ditching me in Grade Four for Jacinta Clark. Liam had been my first serious boyfriend and heartbreak was new to me, so I didn't know if what I was feeling was normal. I felt like a robot. Was I completely devoid of emotion?

My question was answered the moment I glanced down to the street, my eyes narrowing as I saw the black Audi that was still parked out the front of the hotel. The sudden rage I felt bubbling to the surface proved I wasn't a robot. I was all right, just as furious as I'd been on the pavement, meeting those steely blue eyes boring into me through the slit of the car window. Without apology they'd stared me down, and it had worked.

'Cocky bastard,' I mumbled, my voice causing the cat opposite to pause mid-clean and look at me with his yellow eyes.

'Shut up. I wasn't talking to you,' I said, smiling as he went back to his bath time. My humour was short lived. Hearing voices echo off the buildings, I gripped the edge of the railing, leaning over to get a better look at the commotion below.

A man in a dark navy suit strode out of the hotel entrance. He seemed determined, purposeful and intent on ignoring the struggling doorman who ran after him with an umbrella in a bid to keep him dry. The man ignored him, clicking the button and walking toward his . . . black Audi. He was talking on his phone, loud and robust, as he argued with someone on the other end. He seemed passionate, and manic, his free hand gesturing animatedly, before turning to aggressively wave and dismiss the doorman, who backed away with what looked like a thousand apologies.

The suit, whose face I couldn't see from this angle, opened his car door, ended his conversation abruptly and threw his phone inside.

What an arrogant bastard. I had seen it in his eyes, now I'd heard it in his voice and watched it in his stride. I almost wished that he would look up now, willed him to do so, so I could give him the finger this time, send him a 'screw you, buddy' scowl. The thought of doing such a thing almost made me feel giddy, but of course thinking and doing are two different things, and just as I stared down at him with a knowing look on my face, the last thing I actually expected to happen, happened.

He looked up.

I didn't give him the finger. Instead, I yelped and stepped back so fast I tripped on the lip of the door and went hurtling through the narrow opening, crashing rather mercifully onto the bed, before slipping onto the floor and collecting the side table on the way, pulling the curtain down with me, the rod narrowly missing my head.

I groaned, feeling the sting of carpet burn and a healthy dose of humiliation as I sat on the floor, the sheer fabric of the curtain draped over me like Mother Teresa.

'*Sacré* fuckin' *bleu*,' I said, half laugh, half sob.

Yeah, I showed him all right, I thought gingerly, and picked myself up, using the mattress as support. I hadn't even gotten a chance to really look at his face, all I remembered was meeting those same steely blue eyes and panicking. I heard the loud engine of his car speeding down the narrow road, probably taking out women and children along the way without a care in the world. Men like that belonged on an island; an island that should be set on fire.

I got to my feet, pulling back my curtain veil, and rubbing my arm, wincing at the bruises that were sure to come. I sighed, glancing out the window. The cat was gone. It had probably been spooked by the unco tourist flailing about and disturbing the peace, just as mine was suddenly disturbed by a knock at the door.

'Luggage, mademoiselle?'

Oh shit! Shit shit shit shit.

I stepped once to the left and twice to the right, a dance that continued as I tried to get my head together.

'Ah, just a second,' I yelled a bit too frantically. I picked up the side lamp from the floor, trying to straighten the skew-whiff lampshade and wrestling with the curtain cape over my shoulders. I'm sure I looked like some demented form of the Statue of Liberty. Shoving the curtain and pushing the rod behind the bed, I quickly drew the drapes. *Nothing to see here!*

Flustered, I gave in to the one fantasy I'd had walking back to the hotel: I grabbed every piece of Liam's belongings and shoved them into his bag. Quickstepping to the bathroom I dumped his toiletries into his bag too. It kind of felt good, packing him away piece by piece. By the time I opened the door to the doorman I was breathing heavily, my hair was half dry and fuzzy and my clothes were patchy and creased. If the doorman wondered what a hobo was doing in residence on the fourth floor, he didn't say anything. He smiled and gestured to take my bag, seemingly confused when he looked over my shoulder at where my stuff lay strewn all over the room.

'Ah, just one?' He lifted his finger.

We weren't leaving until tomorrow, heading back to London on the 11.05 train. I hadn't thought beyond just wanting Liam away from me – I couldn't even face him right now. I thought that his bag at the front door was a good enough hint as any; I only hoped he didn't see the need to come and talk to me.

I nodded. 'Just one.'

The door closed behind the doorman, leaving me standing in my room, my heart beating so fast it felt like it was robbing me of breath. I felt hot and manky, claustrophobic, so I peeled my clothes off quickly, hoping that would alleviate the feeling. I sat on the edge of the bed in my bra and undies, hands on my knees, shoulders sagged in defeat. What had I done? A knee-jerk reaction was typical of me, and in this moment a new kind of panic surfaced. Didn't I owe it to us to talk? To try to work it out? After all, the biggest change in my life had been moving to London with Liam. Was I simply going to let everything go?

My thoughts were interrupted by a muffled chime coming from the crumpled pile on the floor. I bent over, searching through the damp mess, feeling the lump in my cardi pocket that was illuminating the thin fabric.

Mum.

Quickly swiping the screen to avoid the loved-up picture of me and Liam, I tapped on Mum's text.

Just saw the pic on Instagram, you FINALLY got to see the Eiffel Tower, more pics please!! Xx.

I stared at Mum's message, confused. I didn't post any –

I froze, a sudden horror looming over me. 'Oh no, he didn't.'

I swiped and tapped the screen urgently, a part of me fearing that it could be true, and just as I tried to tell myself it wasn't, there it was. Loud and proud on Liam's

Instagram profile, a picture of the Eiffel Tower – a few, actually, from different angles, different filters.

'You've got to be kidding me!'

He was so distraught at breaking my heart, he'd gone on to take photos, whack a filter on them, even fucking hashtag them: *#Eiffeltower #parislove #wonderwhatthepoorpeoplearedoing*

And he didn't stop there: seemed like Liam had a busy afternoon being quite the tourist, while I sat here in my undies, cold, battered and bruised. I glowered at the screen, tears clouding my vision, barely believing how incredibly selfish he could be.

I threw my phone down and buried my head in my hands. It was over, I knew it was, and more than anything I wished I could bring the numbness back.

I wished I was a fucking robot!

Chapter Three

I woke the next morning on top of the covers, still in only my underwear. There had been no more knocks on my door. No messages, no phone calls, no pleas from Liam for forgiveness or to be taken back. When I dressed, packed and headed downstairs to check out, Cecile at reception told me awkwardly, and with a sad smile, that Monsieur Jackson had booked into another room late last night.

'Thank you,' I said, putting the room key on the counter. 'Has he checked out yet?' I hated to ask but I had to know; I had our tickets for the painful trip back to London, something I could barely think about.

'No, mademoiselle.'

'Okay, well, um . . .' *Leave the ticket at reception and just go.* 'When he comes down, can you please tell him I am in the restaurant?'

Cecile nodded. 'Of course, I am very sorry to see you go. I hope you have enjoyed your stay here in Paris.' Her eyes were kind, and I could tell it pained her to do her usual checkout spiel, knowing full well that Paris was not going to be the city of love for me – far from it. I had hoped to take to the city like a true natural and that maybe Liam and I could return here every year for the anniversary of our engagement. But now I thought if I never saw that tower again, it would be too soon.

'I did,' I lied. 'Thank you for everything. You have been very kind.'

Cecile's beaming smile was back once more, her eyes alight as she stood tall with pride.

'*De rien, merci beaucoup.*'

I smiled. 'Am I okay to leave my bags here?'

'Oui, I'll have Gaston take them for you.'

'Merci,' I said, quietly. I felt like I was annihilating such beautiful words with my accent.

In the restaurant I was greeted by the familiar sight of Simone, a bored waitress from Tottenham who wore her hair in an impossibly high topknot bun. From the intel I had gathered over the weekend, she had been working at Hotel Trocadéro near on three months, didn't speak French but made it work, seeing as a lot of tourists stayed here. Cathy, the other breakfast girl, was a local.

'Fake it till you make it,' Simone said with a wink. 'Where's your man?'

'Oh, um, he's in the shower,' I said, masking my lying mouth by sipping my coffee.

'So you heading back then, to London?' she asked.

'Yeah, and you?'

'Oh, don't even, I'm trying to stick it out just to prove to my ex that I can live without him.'

That got my attention. 'And how is that working for you?'

'He's here every bloody weekend.' She laughed, rolling her eyes.

'Oh.' My shoulders sagged. I had hoped she was about to tell me a heroic tale of girl power and self-discovery, not weekend booty calls, mid-week mind games and text arguments. I zoned out after a while, a glazed look in my eyes, until they refocused on a figure standing at reception, talking to Cecile.

Liam smiled at Cecile, thanking her for what could only be assumed was the message she had passed on for me, then he tentatively turned to the restaurant and approached me. Simone had mercifully moved onto the next table to address a dirty spoon crisis, as Liam arrived before me. His dark eyes glanced at the empty chair, silently asking permission to sit.

When I didn't respond he took it as a yes and pulled out the chair. I looked straight into his eyes with a deadpan expression; I wanted him to feel my pain, my disappointment, my heartbreak.

'I've ordered a taxi for ten fifteen,' he said.

I lifted my chin, giving nothing away.

'Do you have everything?' he asked, like he always did. Always the control freak.

'Of course,' I snapped.

'Well, I think the trip home will give us the chance to . . . talk.'

I shrugged. 'Why wait?'

Liam sighed. 'Claire, please don't be—'

'What? Difficult? Sorry, but you don't get to call the shots, not on this.'

Liam shifted in his seat, smiling painfully at the couple at the next table, before he turned back to me, leaning forward. 'The taxi will be here soon.'

'Okay, well, until then we have some time to kill.' I wasn't backing down on this, no way, no how. I crossed my arms and sat back in my chair, staring him down, much like the suited Frenchman had done to me yesterday. Who'd have thought I would actually be grateful to him for showing me how it's really done? Liam swallowed, shifting once more in his seat.

Ha! What do you know? It really does work!

Truth be known, I didn't really want to talk, not here or on the train. I had nothing in my head, no begging requests for him to take me back, no heartfelt speech to give; nothing. But seeing as the ball was in my court, a situation that was so rare in our relationship, I wanted to at least say something, and the only thing that had sprung to mind was the very same question I had asked myself on the long, rainy walk back to the hotel.

I looked at Liam, my hard stare finally faltering. 'Why?'

It was the simplest of words but held the most meaning, and I knew it was the very question that Liam had been dreading, if the look on his face was anything to go by.

He closed his eyes as if summoning the strength to reply. It made me feel worse that he had to psych himself up to answer me. Surely he would already know why – he was the one breaking up with me. Did he have a gambling problem? A secret wife and kids back in Australia? Did he love listening to Nickelback? How bad could it be?

'I, um – Christ, why is this so bloody hard?'

His big brown eyes looked so pitiful, for a second I actually felt sorry for him; I was ready to say, 'Never mind,' and give him a hug. Until his shifting stopped and he looked into my eyes and I saw it: for some inexplicable reason I knew the answer, I just knew, and all of a sudden I didn't feel sorry any more. I slowly let my arms unfold as the realisation washed over me like a tidal wave. I took a deep, steadying breath.

'Who? Who is she?' I scrunched the serviette in my fist with white-knuckled intensity. 'The girl who's watering our fucking plants?' I said way too loudly – even Gaston from the hotel door turned.

'It's not what you think,' he said. 'Nothing has happened.'

'No, but you want it to.'

He fell silent, unable to even look me in the eyes.

I had been hard-pressed to think of one question, but now it seemed I had a million of them tumbling in my head. *How long? Why her? Why Veronica from upstairs?*

But as the painful silence drew out between us, there was only one question that I really wanted him to answer.

'Do you love her?'

Only then did his eyes look up to my face and in a moment where I felt I didn't know him at all, I found I could read Liam better than anyone, and I could see the answer in his eyes. It was a crushing blow.

'It's hard to explain. It's different with her. She just . . . gets me.'

I could feel my stomach churning. I seriously didn't want to know the details. I had heard enough.

'Claire.' He took my hand. 'You will always be very special to me.' His face was creased in sincerity, and it took everything in my willpower not to punch him. I might have done exactly that if Gaston hadn't intervened.

'Pardon, your taxi is here.'

Snapping out of my violent thoughts, I pulled my hand away and grabbed my bag. Like a zombie, I weaved around the breakfast tables, following Liam out. It was almost like I was underwater, struggling for breath, disoriented. The smiles and goodbyes from Simone and Cecile all seemed as if they were playing out in slow motion, the sound muted as my foggy mind ran over every horrid moment from the second Liam had dropped a bombshell on me yesterday. Flashing images of our seventy-two hours in Paris pinpointed every time he had rolled his eyes, or argued that I was wrong, or told me not to be stupid; it was a montage of putdowns, something I hadn't even thought about before. His contempt for me hit me like the fresh air hitting my face as we left the hotel.

As the taxi driver loaded our bags into the car, I felt Liam beside me, touching me on the shoulder. 'Claire?'

I blinked, turning to see his concerned eyes, before my gaze dropped to my hand, holding the crinkled train ticket.

'Claire, come on, the taxi's waiting.'

I looked at him, examining his face silently before I smiled slowly and I shook my head. I shoved the ticket into his chest.

'I'm not going anywhere.'

Liam's mouth gaped as he clutched the train ticket. 'W-what?'

'I'm staying in Paris,' I said, lifting my chin. Spinning on my heel, nodding to Gaston, who was already retrieving my bags from the taxi with a big grin, I said, 'Goodbye, Liam. I never did like those fucking pot plants.'

READ ON FOR A PREVIEW

NEW YORK
NIGHTS

A HEART OF THE CITY NOVEL

C.J. DUGGAN

INTERNATIONALLY BESTSELLING AUSTRALIAN AUTHOR

Chapter One

Let's get one thing clear. Being an au pair is nothing like in *The Sound of Music*. To start with, I'm certainly not a nun, I have zero musical abilities, and I failed sewing in high school. There's no handsome Captain von Trapp and there's definitely no choreographed frolicking.

All that aside, it had sounded appealing. The plan was I would sacrifice x amount of hours caring for someone else's children, then stroll through a foreign city during my downtime, immerse myself in some culture, learn another language, study maybe, truly find myself, all before falling in love with a wealthy fisherman called Pascal who enjoyed crafting small objects out of wood with his bare hands. Come nightfall, we'd make an incredible paella with the freshest seafood while we sipped wine, arms interlinked as we toasted to us. I mean, we all have to have goals, right?

The reality was somewhat different. For one, I landed a job in my painfully small hometown in Australia, so the chances of meeting a handsome fisherman called Pascal were pretty slim. Instead, my days consisted of shampooing a toddler's hair or wiping the bottom of a five-year-old, and defrosting meat for an early dinner. It was hard to feel like an adult when sitting at a tiny table with my knees around my ears, trying to convince the children how delicious each mouthful was. 'Look, they're little trees, eat your little trees,' I'd say, coaxing them to eat broccoli.

And as much as my employers made me a part of their family, there was never that feeling of freedom, the kind that let me wander into the lounge to flake out on the sofa and idly channel surf, or to fling open the fridge for an impromptu snack. There was no inviting friends over for dinner and definitely no bringing guys around. It wasn't all bad, but it had been my whole life for the past three years, and I had needed a change.

Now, seemingly a million miles from home, I sat on a plush white sofa, shoulders squared, surrounded by white walls and fresh white flowers. Everything was white, save the glass-and-gold coffee table dividing me from them: Penny Worthington and her equally cold daughter, Emily Mayfair. Like her mother, Emily's smile didn't reach her eyes; there was no warmth there. She swept her blonde bob from her face and looked down at the paper she was holding, no doubt a background check they'd organised through a private detective. I wouldn't have put it past them.

'Won't be long now, we're just waiting on one other,' said Emily. Even her name sounded like she had married into money: Lord Mayfair or something equally distinguished. So distinguished I had been rather taken aback. The Worthington's driver – yes, they had a driver – had picked me up from the Park Central Hotel and driven me to a beautiful brownstone in Turtle Bay Gardens. I'm not sure what I had expected; I'd always thought of New York as cramped apartments with fire escapes and air-conditioner boxes hanging out of the windows. Instead I saw an enclave of row houses, gardens arranged to form a common space with a stone path down the centre and a fountain modelled after the Villa Medici in Tuscany, or so Dave the driver informed me.

'Oh, Emily, I think we'll just begin. You know what Dominique is like.'

Dominique? Who was she? Was Emily the mother of the children I was meant to be caring for, or the less-punctual Dominique? And more importantly, why was I about to be interviewed by three women? I took a sip of the water I was holding, kindly provided by the maid. A driver and a maid; they made my previous employers, the rather self-sufficient Liebenbergs, look middle-class. I chose to hold onto my glass of water for fear of leaving a condensation ring on the coffee table. I was certain that act alone would mean instant dismissal.

'So, Miss Williams, tell us a bit about yourself,' Emily said, skimming the pages before looking at me expectantly.

Oh God, how had I not prepared for perhaps the most obvious question of all? Somehow I'd thought I could simply wing it, turn on a bright and cheerful – not ditsy – façade and fake some confidence. I started by making eye contact with the maid, who promptly came forward and took away my empty glass. But before I could begin the Sarah Williams story there was a distant commotion; doors were slamming and a voice spoke loudly out in the entrance.

Penny Worthington closed her eyes, apparently silently summoning the strength to remain calm. Emily sighed deeply. The maid prepared to throw herself into the path of the impending cyclone.

'Hello Frieda, my love, how's that gorgeous man of yours?' A loud and heavily pregnant blonde woman burst into the room. She shimmied out of her jacket and handed it, and her purse, to a mortified-looking Frieda.

'He is well, thank you, Miss Dominique.'

'Frieda, how many times do I have to tell you? Call me Nikki; every time you say Dominique it's like you're running fingers down a blackboard.' Dominique, or rather Nikki, brushed wisps of hair out of her face. She had none of Penny and Emily's poise or elegance but as soon as Nikki turned I saw the same perfect nose and blue-grey eyes. There was no mistaking that she was Penny's daughter.

'Hello, Mother.' She pecked Penny on the top of the head. 'Sorry I'm late.' She waddled around the couch and sat beside Emily.

'You're always late,' said Emily through pursed lips.

'Well, you're always in a bad mood, so neither one of us can win. Ugh, Frieda, my love, can you please get me a water? I am so fat.' She sighed, turning to look at me with a big smile. 'And you must be Sarah?'

I knew within an instant of her turning that smile on me that I loved her. Warmth and authenticity just radiated from her.

I stood, leaning over to shake her hand so she didn't have to bend over her belly. 'And you must be Nikki?'

Her smile broadened as she looked at her sister and then at me. 'Oh, I like you, you don't miss a beat.'

I was flooded with relief, inwardly saying a prayer that it was Nikki's children I would be caring for and not Emily's. My eyes skimmed her belly, thinking maybe this was the reason I had been called here so quickly; maybe Nikki, clearly the black sheep of the family, needed help with her soon-to-be-here baby.

'We haven't begun as yet, Dominique. We had just asked Sarah to tell us about herself.'

Something told me that there would be no way in hell Penny would resort to calling Dominique 'Nikki'.

'Oh, come on,' Nikki said, rolling her eyes, 'don't you know enough about the poor girl? How many more hurdles must she jump before you give her the job?'

Penny and Emily had matching glares, and it wasn't just because they had the same eyes, although that probably helped.

'Let me ask a question,' Nikki said, propping herself on a cushion that looked like it was more for show than actual use. 'What brought you here, Sarah?'

It was a question that was not easy to answer. Being dumped from the Liebenbergs' employment had not exactly been part of the plan, but neither had following them to Slovenia where they were opening a remote medical practice. Admitting as much, however, might make me seem unreliable, and an au pair is nothing if not reliable; I would have to think of something better.

Nikki looked at me as if trying to tell me that she wanted my answer to be perfect, so I responded honestly.

'I've dreamed of New York City all my life. I am so grateful to Dr Liebenberg for setting up this interview for me, I know he is a very good friend of your family.'

Penny stared at me; there was a long, uncomfortable silence as I waited for her to say something, but she was giving me nothing. I cleared my throat and glanced at Nikki, who smiled and nodded, encouraging me to continue.

'The moment I stepped off the plane I knew I'd made the right move. I feel I'm more than ready for this new chapter of my life.'

'And you believe you can handle a challenge?' Emily asked, her perfectly sculpted eyebrows raised in interest.

'I'm the eldest of four from a working-class family so I've been surrounded by children all my life, in times when it wasn't easy. But my family worked hard, banded together and pulled through. I don't shy away from anything – my stomach doesn't turn, and the tears don't flow. I mean, I'm not a robot or anything, but I come from tough stock. I will love the children and I will care for them, something that was never more apparent to me than when working for the Liebenbergs. I cared for their boys, Alex and Oscar, since they were babies, which was a challenge, but I loved my time there.'

'Dennis did provide a rather impressive recommendation for you,' Penny said finally. 'And I am going to be completely honest with you: if it wasn't for that recommendation, I seriously doubt I would have let you through that door.'

Okay, ouch.

'You see, I don't much care how many brothers and sisters you have or how hard it was for your father to put food on the table – that doesn't affect me one way or the other. Nor do I care for any girlish fantasies you have about traipsing around New York City. What I care about is you being fully present; in your mind, in your heart. That your dedication is solely to my grandchild.

'You are to ask no questions, you are to simply do what is required and nothing more. If you are successful, you will be given a full induction on what is expected of you. You will sign a non-disclosure form.'

'And how am I to know if I am successful?' I asked, perhaps not as confidently as I would have liked.

'Well, we have a fair few questions to go through first,' said Emily in a no-nonsense tone.

'And another interview,' said Penny.

'Another?' Nikki and Emily both looked at Penny, confusion creasing their foreheads. Well, creasing Nikki's anyway; something told me Botox was keeping the wrinkles at bay for Emily.

Penny gave her daughters a pointed look. 'Yes, another.'

'You don't mean—'

'Are you sure that's a good idea?' said Nikki, cutting off Emily's question.

Penny sighed, the first proof of her having any human emotion. 'We can't hold off any longer, we have to get him involved.'

The three women looked grim, like they were about to encounter the bogeyman. Their dread was palpable, and although I had just banged on about being able to handle anything, now I wasn't so sure.

'Get who involved?' I asked tentatively.

Penny's eyes cut sharply to mine, and I regretted my words immediately.

'First lesson, Miss Williams: ask no questions.'

I glanced at Nikki, hoping to find some comfort in an eye roll or a wink, but I saw nothing more than her sad, worried expression.

I swallowed, nodding my understanding even as I thought, *What the hell have I gotten myself into?*

Chapter Two

I knew I'd screwed up the interview. I would be hearing 'if you are successful' for the rest of my days. I went down the steps of the brownstone and made my way back to the car, feeling deflated despite the VIP experience. The driver was holding the car door open. Such a different world, I thought, as I smiled my thanks to him. Not really knowing the rules, I had tipped him on the way here, and I supposed I had to tip him again. I was seriously going to run out of money at this rate. Maybe there was something in my NYC guide about tipping etiquette for private chauffeurs. I flipped through the pocket guide, wondering how this could be my biggest drama right now.

Then the door opened. 'Slide over, sweetie.'

Juggling my book, I did as the voice said, too shocked to think. Then I recognised the body of Dominique as she got in beside me.

'Where are you staying?' she asked, holding her belly and catching her breath.

'Park Central Hotel,' I said, looking at her, slightly worried we might be taking a detour to the hospital.

'Oh, nice. Hey, Dave, drop Sarah off first then drag me home. I know how much you love going to Brooklyn.'

A smiling pair of brown eyes flicked up in the rear-view mirror. 'I would drive to the ends of the earth for you, Nikki Fitzgerald.'

'Aw,' she said, tilting her head and offering a high-wattage smile.

'You live in Brooklyn?' I asked.

'Much to my mother's disgust.' She laughed.

Silence fell as Dave indicated to pull out into the street.

'Hey, don't worry about that interview, it's just a process my mother and sister like to go through to ensure they are in control, when they're actually not. The job is yours.'

'You really think so?'

'They haven't even interviewed anyone else, and if the recommendation came from Dennis Liebenberg, you could be an axe murderer and they would be hard-pressed to go against it.'

'Well, I'm not an axe murderer, so hopefully that would go in my favour, too.'

'I should think so,' she said, examining me. 'I would pack my bags if I were you, I don't think you'll be staying at Park Central too much longer.' She turned away to look out her tinted window.

I was afraid to hope, but then I thought, if I was going to be the au pair to her baby, shouldn't she have a say?

'When are you due?'

Nikki sighed, her hand going to her belly. 'Never. I am never, ever having this baby. I feel like I've been pregnant for twelve months already.'

'Your first?'

Nikki burst out laughing. 'Oh no, but definitely my last; I have four more rugrats waiting for me back in Brooklyn. As much as my mother complains about my location, I am sure a big part of her is relieved that I don't visit with the grubby-fingered little munchkins often. I mean, you've seen how white that place is, that couch would be smashed within seconds.'

If not for the physical resemblance, I'd have sworn Nikki was adopted. She had a warm, genuine aura about her; she had alleviated the thick tension when she entered the room. I liked her, but I couldn't help but swallow at the thought of five children. Was I destined to become the au pair for them? Was this what the cryptic interview was about? Capture my interest and then hit me with the big reveal?

I cleared my throat. I knew I wasn't meant to ask questions but I wouldn't sleep tonight unless I had some more clarity. 'So have you had au pairs before or is this your first time?'

Nikki looked at me and frowned. Now she resembled her mother. Then her face lightened as she broke into laughter. 'Oh God, no, I'm not hiring an au pair. No, no, no, I would never subject any poor soul to my brood. Oh, you poor thing, is that what you thought? No wonder you've gone white.' She continued to laugh, which didn't make me feel any better because that left a far worse alternative: I was going to be an au pair for Emily Mayfair, ice queen. I felt sick.

'Oh, okay, so how many children does Mrs Mayfair have?' I asked gingerly.

'Emily?'

I nodded.

'Emily has a boy and a girl, precious little poppets who have been sent away to the best boarding school that money can buy. Don't stress, my sister's au pair days are well and truly over.'

Now I was confused. Why was I even here? Who could I possibly be employed by? I knew they were being cryptic but this was just getting ridiculous. The no-questions rule be damned, I had to know.

'So, why are you here?'

'Exactly.'

Nikki smiled. 'Well, you're about to find out. Dave, can we take a detour to Lafayette, please?'

'Are you sure?' Dave asked.

'Oh, it's okay, he's not there today,' Nikki said, waving dismissively as she tapped away on her phone.

'And Mrs Worthington—'

'It will be our little secret.'

Dave mumbled under his breath.

'Don't worry, Dave, she hasn't put a tracking device on your car . . . yet.'

As much as I was looking forward to the mystery being solved, I didn't want to get Dave fired. I leant across the leather seat. 'You know, I think I'll just wait until tomorrow's interview. I mean, what's one more day anyway?'

'Absolutely not, I don't want anyone else for the job, and I certainly don't want you having a night to think about it and change your mind.'

'Why would I change my mind?'

Dave's eyes flicked up again, meeting Nikki's briefly before she looked out to the streetscape again. 'Oh, no reason,' she said unconvincingly.

Now I was worried. From the moment Dr Liebenberg had spoken of helping with a 'situation' it was obvious that I was signing up for something strange. What was this place on Lafayette? If I woke in a bathtub of ice without my kidneys, I was going to be seriously pissed.

Chapter Three

I wish I could say the beauty of the rustic building made me feel more optimistic about things, but I was tired, hungry and over it as we rode the elevator to the ninth floor. It opened directly opposite a set of rich mahogany doors with a gold 9A in the centre. Nikki walked toward the doors while I stood in place, widened eyes taking in the luxurious space. The white and grey marble floors gleamed, reflecting my totally inappropriate outfit choice back to me. The click of Nikki's low heels bounced off the ornate high ceilings. I tried not to let my mouth gape, because, well, that would just be embarrassing.

Then I remembered, whatever the feeling churning inside me, I was in New York fucking City!

Nikki had already announced herself via the video intercom and now she confidently pushed the unlocked door and made her way through, leaving it open for me. She grinned as I followed her, sensing that I was rather taken aback by the scale of the apartment.

'Three-and-a-half-thousand square feet, Brazilian hardwood flooring, twenty-six-foot-high ceilings, roof garden.'

'Wow!' I said.

'If you think this is impressive, wait until you see the star attraction,' she said, gesturing for me to climb the sweeping stairs that wrapped around the wall. As I ascended, my attention was diverted to the massive windows with their sweeping city views. I misstepped a few times and made sure to grip the balustrade to make the climb without serious injury. With a view like that I didn't begrudge the detour anymore, I could sightsee from the apartment. The whole day had been a bit of a magical mystery tour; from Seventh Avenue Park Central Hotel, to a Turtle Bay Gardens brownstone to a Manhattan penthouse. Yeah, just another Monday.

On the landing of the second floor we were greeted by an older lady, the penthouse equivalent of the brownstone's Frieda, except this woman seemed a little more guarded as her eyes swept me over.

Nikki slid off her scarf and handed it to the woman. 'How is she?' Nikki whispered, not an easy feat when she was trying her best to recover her breath from the ascent.

'You shouldn't be climbing those stairs, Miss Nikki, I will not be mopping up if your waters break. I could have come down to you.'

'No, don't wake her.'

'She's awake.' The woman waved her words away as she went to the closest door.

Nikki's eyes were alight when she looked at me. 'Come,' she said, and stepped into a nursery bigger than my parents' lounge, dining, kitchen and bathroom combined. A light grey shaded the walls and was highlighted by white furniture and pink fabrics, and another giant window that overlooked the city. A rocking chair next to the window made for the most out-of-this-world nursing corner. I stood in the middle of the room, taking it all in, hardly believing that people could be born into such places. It was such a far cry from my world.

Nikki crept forward, peering into the white cot that had pride of place in the centre of the room. As she tucked her hair behind her ears, a beaming smile spread across her face. 'Hello, beautiful,' she crooned. 'Look who's awake.'

I walked closer, but before I could cover much distance, Nikki reached in and carefully lifted the baby from the cot. Bigger than a newborn and far more alert, at a guess the baby was three or four months old.

Nikki shifted her into her arms with well-practised ease. 'Did you have a good sleep, Gracie girl?'

And almost as if on cue, the crinkled little pink face yawned. We all smiled, even the cranky maid, who watched from over Nikki's shoulder.

Nikki looked at me, as if seeing me for the first time. 'Now, Grace, I want you to meet someone very special.'

She came over to me, rocking the baby ever so gently.

'This is Sarah. Don't tell anyone, but she's going to be your new au pair. You are going to be hanging out with her a lot, and she's new to New York, so you're going to have to take care of her, okay?'

Grace's wild, roaming gaze shifted around the room, flitting from Nikki to the ceiling, and then my way – I could almost feel my heart tighten. A jet-black mop of hair and those blue-grey eyes I had seen before; the worldly, distinctive gaze of a Worthington.

I held out my hand, placing it in the little curve of her soft, wrinkled fingers. 'Nice to meet you, Grace, I hope you can keep a secret.' I smiled, admiring the perfect bow of her lips, and her button nose.

Nikki laughed. 'Don't worry, she won't tell anyone.'

'What? Not even me?'

A deep voice pulled our attention to the nursery door, where a man watched with interest. It wasn't the shock of his voice or that he'd appeared out of nowhere that caused my breath to hitch in my throat. It was that his unnerving blue-grey eyes were looking right at me.

'Hello, Ben,' Nikki said, turning her attention back to Grace. 'I thought you weren't going to be in today.'

'No such luck,' the man said as he walked to the other side of the cot. His demeanour made Penny Worthington seem like Mary Poppins. He scooped a soft teddy from the mattress and looked at it thoughtfully.

'You say that like you don't want to see me,' Nikki teased.

'Just how often do you use this place as a drop-in centre?'

'Can't an aunty come see her favorite niece?'

My eyes shifted to Ben with a new interest as the penny finally dropped: this was Nikki's brother, Ben Worthington. I quickly turned away when he looked at me, focusing on Grace, now fully awake and squirming in Nikki's arms.

'Don't let Emily hear you say that,' he said, his hardened eyes changing as he regarded his daughter. Love softened his face, transforming him, making him more human and no less handsome. His hair was dark, as were the circles under his eyes, and there was stubble along his jawline. His tall, lean frame was encased in an immaculate business suit, but his look was tempered by something unkempt. I tried to stop them, but my eyes kept straying back to him. I had never felt more awkward, but then it suddenly hit me: Grace was the 'situation', and I was to be the au pair for this little baby. Ben Worthington was my potential, rather intimidating, new boss; the one I was meant to meet tomorrow. He probably had no idea.

Until Nikki let the cat out of the bag.

'Ben, this is Sarah, the one Mother has been grilling about the au pair position for Gracie.'

Ben's eyes went from soft and lovely to harsh, flicking to me then to his sister.

Nikki read the change, and handed Grace over to the maid. 'Ruth, can you take Gracie, please?'

Perhaps I should have been grateful that Nikki was on the receiving end of those eyes, but I felt even more uncomfortable when the siblings continued to speak as if I wasn't there.

'A little young, don't you think?' he said.

'Don't start, she is more than qualified. You read the profile.'

'It's just paper.'

'Well, what are you going to do then, Ben, because you can't keep up what you're doing; it's ridiculous. Ruth may be a wonderful housekeeper but she can't be your nanny, too. Have you even held your daughter today?'

His rage was palpable. If looks could kill I would have been seriously concerned for Nikki's safety. But she refused to back down, ignoring the vein that bulged in his neck.

'Go home, Nikki, and worry about your own brood.'

Nikki breathed out a laugh. 'You are just as selfish as Dad. Come on, Sarah, I'm sorry you had to witness this.'

I was more than happy to follow her out and get away from him. At least I had clarity once and for all: come Thursday, I would fly home and write this off as an experience.

We had barely made it to the stairs when Ben's voice stilled us.

'I didn't ask Sarah to go, just you.'

Nikki looked at me from the step below; she appeared as shocked as I was. 'What?' she asked.

Ben leant casually on the doorframe, sighing wearily and rubbing the stubble on his jawline. 'Might as well get this over with, saves having Mother and Emily on my doorstep tomorrow.'

'Yeah, well, nobody wants that,' agreed Nikki. She stepped up to be level with my terrified expression. 'I'll wait for you downstairs, and then Dave can drive you back to the hotel,' she told me.

'I'll make sure she gets home.'

'It's no trouble, I'll wait,' Nikki said adamantly.

'I don't know how long this will take.'

How long could it take for him to say I wasn't suitable for the position? I could tell Nikki was thinking the same.

'I'll wait,' she said pointedly.

Ben shook his head. 'You're stubborn as a mule.'

'I could think of worse traits.' Nikki turned to me. 'Go on, I'll be downstairs.' She spoke like I was about to go off to war. Maybe I was.

As she started to descend the stairs, leaving me alone with Ben Worthington on the landing of his penthouse suite, I switched into another mode. Adopting a new bravery, I turned and met his expectant stare, ready to hold out my hand and properly introduce myself, but I was curtly cut off.

'This way,' he said, pushing off the doorframe and stalking down the hall.

All I had to do was follow.

I really didn't want to.

C.J. Duggan is the internationally bestselling author of the Summer, Paradise and Heart of the City series who lives with her husband in a rural border town of New South Wales. When she isn't writing books about swoon-worthy men, you'll find her renovating her hundred-year-old Victorian homestead or annoying her local travel agent for a quote to escape the chaos.

CJDugganbooks.com
twitter.com/CJ_Duggan
facebook.com/CJDugganAuthor

ALSO BY C.J. DUGGAN:

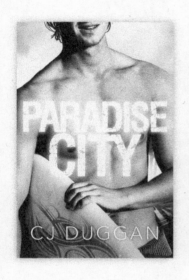 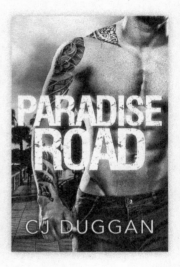

THE PARADISE SERIES – SEXY AUSTRALIAN
NEW-ADULT ROMANCE FULL OF SUN, SURF
AND STEAMY SUMMER NIGHTS.

**THERE'S BOUND TO BE
TROUBLE IN PARADISE . . .**

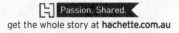

hachette
AUSTRALIA

If you would like to find out more about Hachette Australia, our authors, upcoming events and new releases you can visit our website or our social media channels:

hachette.com.au

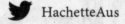 HachetteAustralia

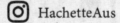 HachetteAus

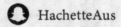 HachetteAus

HachetteAus